Twilight of Memory

Julia Faye Smith

Twilight of Memory by Julia Faye Smith
Copyright 2014 by Julia Faye Smith

ISBN: 13: 978-1495420207
ISBN: 10: 149-5420205

Cataloging Data:
Smith, Julia Faye, Julia Smith, Faye Smith, Faye Dockery, Faye Dockery Smith, 10th Mountain Division, 10th Alpine Division, Camp Hale, CO, Leadville, CO, WWII, Italy, Val D"Orcia, Tuscany, Riva Ridge, Mt. Belvedere, Colorado, Grand Junction, CO, Historical Fiction, Historical Romance,

Author contact: twilightofmemory@gmail.com
Author websites: http://fayeswordbasket.blogspot.com/
http://www.fayeswordbasket.com/

This is a novel. Its characters and scenes are imaginary. There is no Henry, Lilly, Daisy or Ginny Townsend forming a core family in Grand Junction, Co. The established Japanese community of Grand Junction, well known for its fruits and vegetables, did not disappear. There is no Townsend Farm and Ranch as presented in this story in Grand Junction.

To my knowledge, there is no Esther, Isabella, Antonio, or Luciano Coppo making up a core Tuscan family. There is no Villa Coppo as presented in this story in this part of Tuscany.

There was a great world war that we now know as World War II, and there was horrendous fighting throughout Europe, including Italy. There was and still is a U.S. Army Division originally called the 10th Infantry Division, Light Alpine, later Mountain, Division. During WWII this Division trained at Camp Hale, Colorado to be American's Alpine fighters, and they did fight up the spine of the Apennines Mountain Range in Italy. Their time in Italy was short; their victories important, and their losses many.

Henry Townsend is completely fictitious, and any resemblance to any soldier living or dead, is accidental. His letters home are however, based upon the memory and memoirs of men who trained at Camp Hale and who served with the 10th Division in Italy.

I chose not to create fictitious battles for the 10th Mountain Division in Italy so the battles mentioned are part of their history. I have, however, placed fictional characters in the battles. I tried to remain true to the men, their courage, and the outcomes of the battles. Any mistakes are my own, and I take full responsibility for them.

<u>Twilight of Memory</u> is dedicated with great admiration to the men of America's 10th Infantry Division, Light Alpine (10th Mountain Division) WWII, and to the men and women of today's 10th Mountain Division with a prayer for their safety.

Twilight of Memory

Preface

On September 16, 1940, U.S. newspaper headlines across the United States carried the story.

Selective Training and Service Act of 1940 becomes law.

"All men between the ages of 21 and 45 are required to register for the draft. This is the first peacetime draft in United States' history. Those called will be required to serve at least one year in the armed forces."

Once the U.S. entered WWII, draft terms extended through the duration of the fighting. By the end of the war in 1945, 50 million men between eighteen and forty-five had registered for the draft, and 10 million had been inducted in the military.

Henry and Lilly

Chapter 1

Grand Junction, Colorado
1941

With the late September sun gently warming her face and a light breeze softly flirting with her long dark curls, she was the vision of Henry's happiness. He watched her as she passed from guest to guest receiving and giving hugs, kisses, and love. He smiled. *My love, my life, my Lilly.*

Today was her 19th birthday and in the tradition of her Japanese American family, Lilly Yamamoto was now a woman. Because of an early childhood illness, she was still in high school, her senior year, but that did not make her a school kid. In her eyes and in Henry's eyes, she was a woman. Finally. They felt that they had waited their entire lives for this day.

To celebrate the occasion her parents were hosting a celebratory picnic rather than a formal occasion for Lilly's favorite type of gathering was a picnic. So much fun. So much freedom and not much trouble.

No sense of apprehension touched the scene. No threat of horror. Henry and Lilly were adept at keeping thoughts of war at bay. Today it seemed as if her guests were also practiced in that area, for all were laughing, smiling, and playing. The young beauty and her handsome guy saw nothing but sunshine and happiness ahead. War, after all was not here. It was across an ocean on another continent.

As Henry watched her glide, making her way to him, there was only one thought racing through his mind. *She's mine.* The thought, like a crazy whirling dervish, continuously danced in Henry's head. *All mine. How can I be so lucky? How can I wait another day before possessing her?* She glanced across the picnic tables to him and gave him one of her mischievous smiles.

As she approached Henry, she stopped at the nearby table and picked up a pitcher of lemonade "Henry," she asked with a knowing look in her eyes, "do you want more lemonade? More birthday cake?"

"You know what I want, Birthday Girl," he whispered.

In keeping with her grandparents' old world ways, this was her first birthday party with boys invited, not that Lilly cared. Not that anything even slightly romantic was going to happen for every guest, as expected, brought at least one parent so there were as many grown-ups as young people. Her family considered themselves so modern, so American, but this gathering proved that the conservative ways of the old country sometimes came through. Still, even with so many family and friends surrounding them, she felt the force of Henry's love. It was their shared secret, and it made everything beautiful.

Lilly heard someone clear his throat. She looked around to see that it was her father, standing just a few feet from her. Standing next to him, her mother had a knowing smile on her face. Of course they knew, her parents, Toru and Mariko, or Tom and Mary as they were known in the valley for they, like so many of their generation had adopted what they felt to be Americanized versions of their name. They were so in tune with their children's feelings that Lilly saw immediately that they intuitively knew the secret that really was no secret.

She looked around for her brothers, Frank and Ned who were always overprotective of her except when they were torturing her with their jests. Much to her relief, she saw that they were busy trying to impress some of her female friends with their imitations of Hollywood stars.

Happily looking further she saw that all of her cousins were there. Cami with Aunt Kiri and Uncle Sado. Cousins Leni and Kim with Aunt Coria and Uncle Akira. Only Uncle Nago could not make the party because the last of the peach crop had to be taken to market.

School friends were there. Eva Wilson was busy flirting with Rick Hygard, Joanie Sal sat with Walt Brennerman, Henry's best friend. Joanie and Walt were talking quietly, a change for Walt who was the most athletic of the group. Annie Markland, Polly Simmons, and Patsy Prescott were lounging under the tallest cottonwood tree watching Joe, Phillip, and William Banks casually toss around a football while surreptitiously keeping their eyes trained on the girls.

Most importantly, the Townsends, all of them were there. There was old Mr. and Mrs. Townsend, Henry's Grandparents, Young Mr. and Mrs. Townsend, Henry's parents, along with dear Virginia, Ginny to all, Henry's sister and Lilly's best friend. And of course, there was Henry.

At 22, Henry was tall, bronzed from the sun, with thick black hair that casually fell over the right side of his forehead with a rather sensual quality, at least in Lilly's mind. This muscular young neighbor who for as long as either could remember had secretly linked pinkie fingers with Lilly as a means of conveying what he, even as a very young man, could not yet articulate, was, in Lilly's eyes, the most handsome man in the world.

Lilly sighed with the perfection of the day. It was a wonderful late September afternoon just made for this picnic birthday party in Robin Hood Park here in the center of Grand Junction. The Aspens on the distant Grand Mesa were glorious in their shimmering shades of gold. Against a cloudless blue curtain of sky, these tall slender ballerinas danced in their white leotards and gold tutus. The afternoon sun warmed the skin and the air smelled just faintly of the coming Colorado autumn.

When Henry noticed Lilly looking intently at the Mesa, he turned his eyes there also. As he glanced at the mountains, he dreamed of snow. Cold snowy weather and Henry were meant for each other. He was slowly convincing Lilly of the joys of frozen cheeks, parched lips, and stinging lungs if one breathed in too sharply and deeply.

When Lilly glanced at the dancing mountains she dreamed of lying on a bed of fallen leaves, looking out over a clear lake and writing her poetry. Henry, of course, would be right by her side slowly trying to seduce her away from her poetry.

Her birthday afternoon was a perfect afternoon for sharing love and family and dreams of the future. No one noticed, or if they did, no one commented on the wonderful blending and acceptance each felt for the other on that golden day. Everyone belonged. Everyone was a member of the Valley community. It was never a question. You don't question what is natural. It was only later, looking back on that day that one might wonder about origins and ancestry.

Answering her almost forgotten question, Henry smiled and held out his glass to Lilly. "Yes, more lemonade, please and Happy Birthday, Birthday Girl." As she passed the glass back to him, he leaned closer to her, handed her two small packages and whispered, "Happy Birthday, Sweetheart. I love you."

With eyes dancing with delight, Lilly unwrapped the smaller of the two packages. "Oh, Henry, a book of poetry. You know how I've wanted this book. It's the same one we saw in the Book Nook window downtown. Thank you." With that she placed a quick kiss on his cheek, just as she had to everyone after she opened their gift.

Still holding the larger of the two packages, she teased him "Two presents, Henry? Are you trying to spoil me?"

She then quickly opened the second gift, stopped suddenly and gasped. She tried to say something, but instead a tear slid down her cheek. Working hard to control the urge to cry, she quietly hugged Henry again and whispered, "Thank you for understanding."

In her hands she held another book, this one homemade. On the cover was the title. POETRY. Further down the cover were the words, 'By Lillian Osada Yamamoto'. Inside, the pages were blank, waiting to be filled by her.

As they looked into each other's eyes, neither Henry nor Lilly could have imagined that in the not too distant future, they would remember this day as one in which everyone had been happy and relaxed. Everyone in his or her own way had put away the news that the local radio station kept reporting. For that afternoon, at least, the world started and ended in their peaceful valley.

Deep within, however, they all knew differently for it seemed that by the afternoon of Lilly's 19th birthday the entire world was on the brink of war. For years the news had been of Japanese aggression in Asia, German aggression in Europe, and Italian aggression in Africa. Through it all, the Americans had remained neutral.

Lately, the news was worse. Hitler and his German forces were sweeping through Europe. After France was conquered, only England was left and now that nation, while being attacked daily, was trying to stop the Little Dictator.

America's stance of neutrality seemed to be disappearing and just last month the American Congress had taken a step closer to war. They began to strengthen the military forces of the United States. A measure was approved that allowed young American men to be drafted into the armed services.

Who would be called? How soon? Where would they go? What would they do? What would this move mean to Henry, to them? Henry and his friends discussed this new development daily.

On this special day, however, Henry did not have to work hard at putting aside these troubling thoughts because he knew that he was in love with Lilly and that love made his world warm and safe. He had loved her for as long as he could remember, but today, on her 19th birthday, she was a young woman, and in his truck on the way to the picnic, he had told her of his deep love. She loved him too. That was her gift to him on her birthday.

"I love you, too, Henry. More than you will ever know. Forever."

That day, Henry could look ahead, not toward war, but toward love for he knew they would have a life together. A life that would have to wait at least another year because Lilly was an honor student and wanted to be a teacher, the first in her family. The entire family took pride in her accomplishments and looked forward to the day she would walk into the classroom as the teacher rather than the student. Henry would not interfere with those plans. He would simply give her the gift of his love to help her along the way.

As family and friends observed them, their love was apparent. No one seemed surprised. No one questioned it.

Life in the valley continued to be all that he could wish. Even with war clouds on the horizon, life looked good. Besides, those war clouds had still not hit America. Maybe they would never cover this secluded little valley they called home.

A few days later, Henry and Walt headed up to the Mesa for a day of hiking. They had chosen the perfect day to complete their first long hike of the fall. The air was invigorating, the colors surrounding them were warm and welcoming, and the chance to be out in one of their favorite escape areas too great to pass up. They were hiking east of Grand Junction out Land's End Road, a gravel road heading away from the main highway into the Grand Mesa Reservoir area. The road followed the north rim of Deep Creek Canyon for several miles and arrived at Land's End Observatory, a spot well known to the area hikers for invigorating day hikes and to the area lovers for breathtaking vistas for a little romance.

The lush, tree-filled landscape surrounded the best friends as they made their way past the remains of an old cow camp, a remnant of the cattle ranches established in this area after the Ute Indians were forced out.

"Are you going to be able to leave her?" Walt asked as they leaned into the steep pathway while making their way upward.

Neither of them had spoken for several minutes, but Henry knew immediately what Walt was referring to, but he answered his friend with a question.

"Leave her?" he asked without taking his eyes off the climb ahead.

"Leave Lilly. Are you going to be able to leave Lilly?"

"Why would I do that?" Henry replied although his sinking heart knew what Walt meant.

"Come, on, Henry. You're not dumb. You know the world is at war and that in all likelihood we will be in it soon. Actually, in the fighting, on the front lines probably. Don't tell me you haven't thought about it."

Henry kept climbing the mountainside, but Walt stopped walking and gazed first at the hillside ahead and then turned and looked down into the valley below---their valley.

Not taking his eyes off the valley, Walt continued. "Now that President Roosevelt has signed the induction law, don't you think there is a great possibility that we will be drafted? You're not fooling me. I know you've thought about it. Hell, Hen, we all have thought about it, but all of us don't have a lovely Lilly to leave behind."

Henry finally stopped walking, turned and walked back a few yards. "Do you want me to knock you off this mountain? I hear it's a long way down, especially for hard-hearted friends."

With that he turned back to the trail and continued upward. For the rest of the upward hike neither spoke. Finally they reached the observatory. Although a picturesque structure for artists, today neither noticed the walls and terrace that were built of basalt stones selected from the mesa and carefully fitted together. Today all the beauty of the summit went unnoticed as each man stood lost in his own thoughts as they looked out from their lofty perch.

On a clear day one can see westward across the valley beyond the Yamamoto and Townsend farms to the Colorado National Monument, north to the Bookcliffs and Fruita, and south to Montrose some 60 miles away. When viewed from the valley below, Land's End, standing majestically above them, always signified home to the young people of the valley.

Today, none of that mattered.

"No," Henry said without taking his eyes off the distant side of the valley. "No, I cannot imagine leaving Lilly."

Chapter 2

The following Saturday was a brilliant October day. A cerulean blue sky stretched for miles without a cloud in sight. The air was crisp but warm enough that a coat wasn't necessary. The smell of applewood from distant fireplaces wafted in and out with the slight breeze. Lilly had been able to persuade her parents that she should have the entire day for hiking and picnicking with Henry.

They drove up to Mesa Lakes for a picnic lunch at their favorite lakeside spot. At the altitude of this hideaway, the air had what they thought must be an Alpine quality. They talked about one day building a cabin overlooking this part of the lake.

"An A-frame cabin," said Lilly looking around. "Right here!" She reached a spot and with outstretched arms twirled in a little dance move.

Henry grabbed her and after a few minutes of nuzzling asked, "Why an A-frame?"

"All the travel photos I see from the colder European countries seem to have A-frame cabins snuggled against the mountains and covered with snow. We have the mountains and the winter snow. All we need is the cabin."

She paused, then continued. "Just think, Henry, when we own an A-frame cabin, we can ski all morning and come back in for lunch, ski up to the spread legs of the cabin, and rush upstairs to the warmth. It will be our own European A-frame. Our own paradise, right here at home."

She looked at him and asked, "Yes?"

"Yes," he replied pressing close to her. "Tell me, where will the bed be?"

Later that afternoon they drove as far up Land's End as

possible, then climbed to the top. Henry could not forget his earlier conversation with Walt. Upon reaching the top, Lilly quickly sat near the ledge against one of the ballerina Aspens and sighed contentedly.

"It's a good thing we tramp around outdoors a lot," she said. "We have been very active today and I am not even tired."

Henry knew she was flirting and inviting him to come sit beside her for more nuzzling. Instead, he walked the few steps to the peak and without turning to look back at her he began the conversation he had been rehearsing in his head.

"Lilly, if I ever have to leave you, know that it will be the hardest thing I ever do. It will be so against my will. But know that I will return to you."

Suddenly afraid to her core, Lilly asked in a trembling voice, "Henry, have you been drafted."

"No.

"Have you volunteered?"

"No."

"Then, what?"

Henry finally turned to look at her. "Then nothing, Lilly, but I know that possibility is something we must think about because it is something that I am afraid we might be forced to face."

Slowly Lilly stood and walked to him. She put her arms around him and cried softly into his chest. Finally, Henry held her at arm's length and said, "I never want to leave you, to lose you."

As they walked back to the truck at the base of the climb, both were quiet. Upon reaching the truck Henry said, "It's been such a wonderful day. I'm sorry I spoiled it."

"No, no you didn't, but Henry do we have to go home just yet?"

"Maybe not just yet. No one will worry if we are a bit late. Why?"

"Please take me back to our cabin. I need the warmth it gives me."

Over the next two weeks, as autumn continued to dazzle them, Henry and Lilly visited their Alpine dream as often as possible. They reveled in each other's company, sometimes wondering if other lovers in other parts of the country were storing up dreams that might be called upon to take them through the future. Surely so, but none loved as they did.

Then one Friday night while the valley slept, winter arrived and blanketed everything with the first downy white snow of the season. Outdoor enthusiasts, and that included Henry and Lilly, met the beautiful snowfall and the brisk morning air with joy. They grabbed their recently winter-prepared skis and poles, snowshoes and sleds, ski books and coats and joined the joyous exodus from the valley to the Mesa.

Days later, on their first trip up the mountain alone after several more snowfalls, Lilly snuggled close to Henry. "Let's park back a ways and ski in to the cabin, " she suggested.

For an imaginary cabin, their A-frame saw a lot of them during that fall and early winter of 1941. Life, in fact, seemed to be progressing beautifully for the two of them. While ever mindful of the war news, they went on with their lives. Lilly was enjoying her final year at Grand Junction High School, and Henry was almost finished with his agriculture classes at Grand Junction Junior College across town. They had more free time and they spent it together.

They both were accomplished horsemen, Henry more so than Lilly, but she could keep up with him on the many quiet rides they enjoyed throughout the fall and even after the early snows. They rode the many trails they had blazed years ago on the Colorado National Monument that formed the back border of their adjoining properties.

They hiked not only the Grand Mesa across the valley from their farms, but also the lower canyons of the National Monument. They hiked in both glorious autumn sunshine and in the early days of winter's white magic.

And they skied. Oh, how they skied. They skied downhill when the snow was plentiful, and when after a few days of cloudless sunshine and warmth, the snow was not as heavy, they skied a modified version of cross country. With a passion and a vengeance they skied. Always with the same destination, their cabin.

Thus they passed October and November of 1941. Falling more deeply in love, loving the closeness and the oneness they were creating.

Chapter 3

December 7, 1941

After church services on December 7th, Henry and his family returned home from Sunday School, had an early mid-day meal, and were enjoying a quiet afternoon. Ginny was in her room writing to a friend in Denver; Mom and Dad were in the living room listening to the weekly broadcast of Sammy Kaye's Sunday Serenade from the University of Chicago, and Henry was in his room listening to the static-filled broadcast of the football game between the Giants and the Dodgers in New York. He would see Lilly later when they went for a late afternoon horseback ride in the foothills of the National Monument.

Henry was leaning in to hear the description of the 'hard hit' by Bruiser Kinard on the 27th yard line. Suddenly, came a new voice through the static.

"We interrupt to bring you this important bulletin from United Press. FLASH, Washington: The White House announces Japanese attack on Pearl Harbor."

While Henry's mind tried to convince him that he had heard incorrectly, the game returned to the airwaves and the play continued. Henry stood and walked into the living room.

"Mom, Dad…," he began.

"Shh," both parents said as they too leaned closer to their radio. Henry could hear what they were trying so hard to hear.

"…from the air. I'll repeat that. President Roosevelt says that the Japanese have attacked Pearl Harbor in Hawaii from the air. This bulletin came to you from the NBS news room in New York."

As the music started once again, Henry's Dad flipped off the radio and looked at his wife and son. For what seemed to Henry a very long time, no one said anything.

Finally, his father spoke. "God help us. We're in it now."

Upon hearing the news, Henry ran to Lilly's home. The curtains were closed. No lights were on. He could hear crying. They would not let him in.

The following day the United States' Congress declared war on Japan. Again Henry ran to Lilly's home. The curtains were closed. No lights were on. He could hear crying. Again, they would not let him in.

Suddenly America was grieving and vowing justice.

Japanese Americans were grieving and becoming fearful.

Three days later, Germany and Italy declared war on the United States. The United States, in turn, immediately declared war on them. The entire world seemed to be at war.

Soon, the Grand Junction community would learn that two of the casualties at Pearl Harbor were from their own peaceful world. The serene valley slumbered no longer. Japan had declared war on America. In so doing, they had declared war on the valley. The dark clouds of war hovered overhead.

Across America the attack on Pearl Harbor created bitter feelings towards Japanese immigrants and Americans of Japanese descent. Even in the valley, where the Japanese community was well-liked and accepted, there were some people who questioned the loyalty of the Japanese Americans.

"It's not your fault," Henry tried to reassure Lilly. "Don't listen to anyone who questions your loyalty."

It was a week after the attack on Pearl. Initial anger was giving way to mistrust. Lilly and her family could feel this mistrust.

"That's easy for you to say, Henry. Your skin is not 'yellow' and your eyes are round. Your family has lived here forever."

"Your family has lived here for two generations," Henry responded. "Your grandparents were willing to renounce their country and become American citizens. I know how much your Grand Pops wanted to do that, but because he is Issei, foreign- born Japanese, they could not become American citizens.

"I remember the pride in the old man's eyes when he told us of arriving in America, how he considered living on the west coast but instead ventured further East, settling in our valley, and learning to speak English. I know how he loves being an American, even if he is barred from citizenship because of his place of birth."

"You cannot understand, Henry." Lilly sighed. "You simply cannot."

Henry continued with his own train of thought. "Your grandparents were only twenty years old when they came to this country. They have lived here over 40 years, twice as long as they lived in Japan. How can anyone question their loyalties?" he demanded.

"It does not matter. They are suddenly considered to be JAPANESE." Lilly whispered through her tears. "They are Japanese. They are American. They hurt. They hurt."

"But your parents," Henry said, hoping to touch on some ray of hope for Lilly, "Your parents are American citizens. They have never even been to Japan. Why, they were both born here in this valley. Surely they don't feel any prejudice or distrust toward them."

"Yes, it has happened." Lilly remarked quietly.

"Well, you and your brothers were born in America of American citizens. Surely, no one will think you are disloyal to our country, my country and your country. Lilly, how can anyone question you?"

Lilly looked at Henry and knew that he did not understand.

Christmas that year was strained. On Christmas Eve Henry's mother and father persuaded Lilly's family that they had no reason to be fearful or ashamed. They were not to blame for Japan's attack on America, and they would feel no retribution from their friends and neighbors in the valley.

The Yamamoto's finally accepted an invitation to Christmas dinner with the Townsends. They needed to again feel part of the community. Generally, they were still keeping to themselves and staying close to home, but they did feel comfortable in accepting an invitation to the home of their nearest neighbors and their children's closest friends, the Townsends.

It was a very unusual day. Everyone wanted to be happy, but that was difficult. Mr. and Mrs. Yamamoto were nervous. Mr. and Mrs. Townsend were trying too hard to pretend nothing was wrong.

Henry and Lilly were glad to be together. They smiled and held hands throughout the day, but even they could feel the difference. Still, it was Christmas.

Ginny had received a camera, one of the new Kodaks everyone was raving about. She took lots of pictures. She kept sneaking up on Henry and Lilly and snapping away.

After Christmas, life in the valley seemed to return to normal, as normal as possible when one's country was at war. Because the fighting was on other continents, not here at home, no one need be afraid. Here everyone was safe, weren't they?

Shortly after New Year's Day 1942, a beautiful snowfall lightened the mood for all. The crops were in, the temperatures did not remain below freezing long enough to be a problem, and students still had a few days of vacation time.

Once again, Henry and Lilly broke away to be alone and quickly packed the truck for a winter picnic on the Mesa. As they approached their cabin, Lilly again suggested that they park back a ways and ski in.

"No," Henry answered surprising her for he usually gave her anything she wanted. Then he continued, "I think more snow is on its way, so let's drive to our parking spot, leave the car and ski away and then back in. That way we can still get the Alpine feeling of skiing in that you seem to crave, but we will still have the truck handy if needed."

Nodding her agreement, Lilly slid across the seat snuggling closer to him as he drove to their cabin. Upon arrival, they changed into their ski boots, buckled on their skis, and skied away from the site. A couple hours later they returned, removed their skis and turned to walk the last few feet to what they thought of as the entrance to their cabin.

A fine mist surrounded them. Lilly stopped and held out her hand, palm side up as if she wanted to catch the floating mist. As Henry watched her, mist became frozen air crystals. The crystals danced around them and Lilly danced around in them. She danced over to Henry, reached out and pulled him close. She opened his jacket and slid her arms around him, holding him tightly. After a few minute her hands began an exploration of his body. Henry groaned but stood still, enjoying her dancing hands in this wonderland that they had to themselves.

Finally he whispered, "Come, let's go in and build a fire."

She stopped her movements and leaned back in his arms, keeping only their lower bodies tightly touching. "Oh, Henry, that would be a wonderful idea, but you know open fires are not permitted here on the Mesa"

He bent his head and nuzzled as much of her neck as he could find which was very little considering how swathed she was in her ski clothing. Even this lack of access to that soft white neck that he knew was under all that clothing excited him.

Looking down into her eyes, he managed to mutter, "Not an open fire, my Lilly, a fire within."

Smiling a wicked smile of comprehension, she pulled away, grabbed his hand and led them to their spot.

Chapter 4

By the spring of 1942 America's recent entrance into the world war and the newly expanded draft law was on every young man's mind. Henry Townsend was no different. He was athletic, strong, healthy and of draft age. Like so many men his age, he wanted to serve his country, but he wanted other things also. There was often a battle raging within Henry.

His registration card for military service was in his wallet. Always with him. Always a reminder. Earlier that card was just a formality, but with the United States now a major combatant in the war that was raging in Europe and the Pacific, it was more. It was a weight, a promise. It was a was a call that Henry Townsend knew he must answer, either waiting to be drafted or volunteering for the draft.

Some of his friends were already in the military, having volunteered early after their country's entrance into the war. As Lilly heard of each of the enlistments she cried and begged Henry not to enlist but to wait. Her tears were powerful, but Henry knew that soon a decision would be needed. Just a few months short of completing his final semester of agricultural studies, he was hoping to wait that long before making any decisions.

Today, returning home after a short trip to Colorado A & M on the other side of the Rocky Mountains, he felt only slightly guilty that he was on top of the world. He was twenty-two, madly in love with a woman who returned his love, and he had just learned that there was a possibility that he could serve his country as they fought the enemy without having to leave home or more importantly, without having to leave his Lilly.

Henry did not shrink from the possibility of serving his country. He knew that somehow, somewhere, he would serve. He wanted to do his part to save the world from Germany, Japan, and their allies, but not at the expense of being away from Lilly. Just the thought of life without her turned his heart upside down with fear. Now, possibly, there was an honorable way to keep her at his side.

As an outstanding senior in the college of agricultural science, he had been selected by the department's professors as their nominee to take part in the farm deferment program. The program, emphasizing the importance of agriculture to a nation at war, exempted farmers from the imposed draft if they met stringent requirements. Their farms had to have a certain number of animals, grow certain crops, and benefit the war effort. Henry's family's farm met these requirements, and Henry was knowledgeable enough to help the other local farmers who had been forced to replace their lost hands with wives and children and unskilled laborers. Men like Henry were viewed as a valuable part of the military machine.

Henry had spent the last four days, long, lonely days at Colorado's major agricultural college learning more about the program and meeting with agricultural leaders from around the country. It had been an enriching experience filling him with hope.

Now he was home and full of plans that he needed to share with Lilly. She would embrace his ideas; he had no doubt of that. Even though she was just completing her senior year of high school, she wanted their married life together as much as he did. A way to happiness and service had been given to them. They could begin their life together sooner rather than later.

As soon as he dropped his luggage in his room, he gave his mother a quick hug, bounded out the door and quickly made his way from his family's farm and orchards to her family's farm. His arms ached to hold her. He wanted time alone with her. They had plans to make. She knew when to expect him. She would be waiting.

Throughout his life Henry had made this short trip

hundreds of times. He knew the Yamamoto's home as a warm cluttered place. Everyone and everything was welcome. He had been in and out of the house as a child. He was a little more restrained but equally as welcome as a teenager and then as Lilly's 'young man caller' and since her nineteenth birthday celebration, as her 'intended'. The house and the people inside were always welcoming.

Until that spring day.

Slushing through the early spring snowfall Henry had no premonition of impending doom. Perhaps his mind was so crowded with his news and plans that unwelcome thoughts were kept at bay. Even the misery of this quick spring snow escaped him. This was unusual for he normally would have noticed this unexpected snowfall which he hated. Unlike the heavy winter falls which were dry and long-lasting, these spring storms were wet and miserable. At least they came and went quickly. Today, though, with the sun now peeking through the fleeing snow clouds, no amount of wet and miserable could dampen his enthusiasm.

He quickly arrived at the Yamamoto's home and happily tapped out a signal on their front door. Soon, Lilly would answer.

She did not. No one answered. Henry waited impatiently for someone to answer his knock.

"Let me in or I'll huff and puff and blow the house down," he growled.

No answer.

"Hey, anybody? It's cold and wet out here. Let me in!"

Still no answer.

He tried to open the door; it was locked. The window shades were pulled down. *Maybe they didn't want anyone tracking slush into the living room. I'll go around back.*

"I'm going to the back door," he yelled to anyone who might hear.

Passing the garage he noticed that both of Mr. Yamamoto's trucks were gone. He thought nothing of it. Mr. Yamamoto was probably out in the orchards checking the buds and branches. This weather could hurt this year's crop. Frank and Ned might be with him picking up fallen limbs in the older truck. Ned would have wanted to drive. He was allowed to drive around the orchards on the property even though he was a year shy of the legal driving age. He would have volunteered to help his father and brother if it meant he could drive the truck.

Stomping up the back steps, Henry noticed that the porch was unusually clean. The assorted clutter common to most Colorado back porches in winter and early spring was missing.

"Hey, let me in. I'm really cold." Henry yelled once more. No one answered his call.

Suddenly a strange feeling came over him. His stomach seemed to tighten; his head started to hurt; he felt even colder. Something was wrong. Someone should be here; someone should have let him in by now.

On wooden legs he walked across the porch to the kitchen window.

Nothing! Absolutely nothing was in the kitchen. The table and chairs were missing. The assorted pots and Japanese crockery that Mrs. Yamamoto used were missing. The counter space was absolutely clean.

Robbed! They've been robbed! The thought sped to Henry's brain. They're not home and someone took everything from the kitchen. He started back down the back steps ready to run home and call for help, but the unusual appearance of the back porch checked his departure. I'd better get inside and see if anything else is missing.

But where was everyone? Someone should be here. Henry's mind suddenly painted pictures of the Yamamoto's tied up inside, or worse, hurt and even now on the way to St. Mary's, the nearest hospital.

He rushed to the back door, turned the knob and prepared to heave his body against the door as he and Lilly had seen Errol Flynn do at the movies last week. There was no need for him to heave. The door was unlocked. Henry almost fell into the kitchen. It was empty. Totally bare. Not even a crumb from some delicious pastry baked by Mrs. Yamamoto was to be seen.

Henry bounded through the empty kitchen to the dining room. It was empty. Bare.

He ran to the living room. Bare.

Everything, even the pictures on the wall were gone. A horrible thought was beginning to form in his mind. No it was unthinkable.

He ran across the hallway to Mr. and Mrs. Yamamoto's bedroom. Empty. He ran to the Grandparents' room. Empty. Then to the Frank and Ned's room. Empty.

Finally, slowly now he turned again into the hallway and forced himself to Lilly's room.

The climbing wisteria blossoms on the wallpaper seemed to dance in the glow of the late afternoon sunlight flowing through the window.

"She's not here, she's not here," the dancing blossoms whispered to his jumbled mind. Other than dust bunnies floating in the shafts of sunlight, that room, too, was empty. There was no trace of Lilly.

A deadly calm engulfed Henry. He slowly retraced his steps. He revisited each room. Then, like a magnet, Lilly's room drew him back. Dazed, he leaned against the wisteria vines for support. They offered none. He slid down the vines, onto the floor, and did something he had not done for years. He cried.

Chapter 5

It was here, in Lilly's room, that his father found him. Henry looked at his father from unseeing eyes. He made no move to stand, so his father sat on the floor and held his son.

Later, how much later Henry neither knew nor cared, he opened his eyes, took a deep breath and asked himself dozens of questions. Slowly he turned to his father with some of those same questions.

Where were they? Why had they left? Had they left voluntarily or were they forced to leave? Could he have stopped them? How could she have left him?

For weeks he was numb as he and his family, along with other members of the community tried to piece together the reasons behind the disappearance of the valley's Japanese community. The Yamamotos were not alone in their disappearance; all the Japanese families were gone. Overnight, they had all disappeared from the valley, and no one knew why.

On the west coast of the United States, in California in particular, bitterness towards Japanese Americans was intense. This bitterness turned to distrust. Many were accused of helping Japan. Many western politicians and military leaders insisted that "something be done about the Japanese living in our own front yard."

Here in the valley, feelings were not that intense. There was no anti-Japanese hysteria. After the first few weeks when some had questioned the loyalties of the local Japanese Americans, the community had settled down.

And why not? The Japanese Americans here were all hard working, respected citizens. They were mostly farmers; farmers who grew some of the largest, sweetest tomatoes around. Their zucchinis and squash were sought after by valley housewives, and their peaches large and juicy enough to tempt many a school boy to climb the low fences and try one. They paid their bills, supported their churches, and could always be counted on to help at any school function.

They were accepted. Just last year Timmy Tamayaka had joined the softball team. Sure, he stood out in his uniform, but after the first few games it was only the visitors who noticed. If anyone from another team said anything about the 'slant-eyed kid', the entire team came to his defense.

Slowly, as the weeks passed, a possible reason for their leaving became more apparent. From Washington came word that President Roosevelt had issued an order that called for all Japanese aliens and Japanese Americans to be removed from their homes and interred, held captive, in '"relocation centers"' established for that purpose.

These camps were usually farther west than Grand Junction but they seemed to be getting closer to the valley. In Utah, just miles away, there was Camp Topaz. In Wyoming there was Heart Mountain, and in Arizona, Gila River and Poston.

The valley had known of the discontent across the country and on the west coast. Situated as they were in`their western Colorado valley, had the Japanese American community felt the cold wind of fear mingling with the harsh winds of war throughout that winter of 1941-42?

Perhaps they felt themselves being surrounded. Were they rounded up, clandestinely? Or did they really think it so unsafe for them to remain that they fled on their own? Either way, overnight they were gone.

Overnight Lilly was gone.

Henry believed that somehow they must have known, or at least suspected, that something was about to happen to them. They simply chose to take matters in their own hands. They simply removed themselves before the government could do it for, or to, them.

But where did they go. Why didn't they tell anyone? Heartbroken, Henry searched the hills and the valleys, looking in the many desolate canyons and auroras that dotted the landscape. For weeks, nothing occupied his mind but finding Lilly. At first he insisted on going alone; after a few weeks, he willingly accepted Walt's help.

He found nothing.

"What will you do now, Henry" Ginny asked for the thousandth time. "They are not here and not nearby; no one can find a trace of them. Will you give up?"

"Never," Henry answered tersely, which was his new fashion. "Never."

The Japanese American families had been gone for two months. The entire community had searched for them. First as friends searching for friends, then the law enforcement became involved as legal questions began to arise. Through it all, nothing.

For weeks Henry had daily returned to the empty house next to his own. He had wandered the rooms, searched for clues, and silently talked to each family member. He always ended up in Lilly's room, sometimes searching for something, a clue, a message, something. Sometimes he just sat there, hoping. There was never anything there but Henry, his memories, and the dust bunnies still dancing in the sunlight.

He often thought back to that day on Land's End when he told her that someday he may be forced to leave her, but that he would never want to do so. Instead, she left him. Had she known that she would? During those last few wonderful weeks together, those moments in their cabin, had she known? He could not and would not believe it, but still the question nagged at his heart.

At the same time, something else was nagging at him. Once he had accepted, to the best of his ability, that she was gone, at least for now, life was nagging him. What was he going to do now? His agriculture classes seemed senseless. His interest in them disappeared even as Lilly had disappeared. So what was left for him? Would he enlist? Could one enlist and not fight against the Japanese? What should he do?

His family was trying hard to give him time and space, but daily their concern for him grew. All the other young men in the valley were making decisions, choices for their immediate futures. Henry needed to do the same, but inertia engulfed him except when he was searching for Lilly.

Then one day his father and mother asked him to stay at the dinner table after the meal was finished. He looked at them, then at Ginny. Ginny gave a resigned sigh as she stood to clear the dishes and get out of hearing range. Her posture said that she was not happy about being excluded.

Once she was in the kitchen, noisily washing the dishes, his parents gave Henry some choices. He could apply for exemption to the draft as an agricultural student whose knowledge would become valuable at home. He could join the draft and see what he could get. Or, he could cross the Rocky Mountains to Eagle Valley and look for work as a civilian helping to build the new U.S. Army camp being constructed there.

For some reason, his parents seemed excited about this last option over the other two. His mom's eyes shone and his father sat up a little straighter and leaned toward him.

"This is made for you, Henry. You will be helping our war effort without actually serving, and it is far removed from anything to do with the Japanese. I assume you do not wish to fight the Japanese even though you have not said so."

"Of course I don't. Would you?"

His father did not answer but continued. "From what I hear this new camp is being built to train men in mountain warfare, or Alpine warfare as it is referred to in the army."

Henry sat up straighter at their use of the term "Alpine." For reasons they would not understand, it hit home with him.

His father noticed the change and, encouraged, continued. "Mountain or Alpine warfare refers to warfare in the mountains or similarly rough terrain. It is called Alpine warfare because it is used in the Alps Mountains of Europe. This type of warfare is one of the most dangerous types of combat as it involves surviving not only combat with the enemy but also the extreme weather, dangerous terrain, and altitude."

"The US Army has a small mountain unit," his mother interjected, "but that unit needs to expand. At the moment, the mountain camp is in Ft. Lewis, Washington, but the army needs a camp that more closely fits what they expect the Alpine unit to run into in this current war. The army has been searching for a site on which to build a new base."

At this point Henry's father became even more animated. "They have settled on a site on the Pando Plateau over on Eagle River. You know, north of Leadville, between here and Denver. The Army has explained that the location provides natural features necessary for training for the type of fighting these men may encounter if they are asked to go to the mountainous areas of Europe."

"Of course, we all hope they will never have to go, but nothing is certain these days. We all know that only too well," said his mother.

His father again took up the conversation, obviously planned by his parents before they approached him. Henry thought that was an interesting observation.

"The site," his father continued, "sits at nearly 10,000 feet in altitude. Able-bodied men, accustomed to the altitude and other conditions will be very helpful in the construction of the camp. We, your mother and I, are in agreement on this. We think you should drive over to the construction site and see if there is anything you can do in this construction effort."

"Just think, Henry," his mother said in a voice that was almost pleading, "You will be helping our country, our military, but you will not be in the service. I prefer that for you for as long as possible. I don't want you to go to war." By the end of her plea, her voice was quavering with emotion.

Henry looked at his parents, aware for the first time that they had been hurt by their neighbors' disappearance, but that they also had been worried about him and his reaction to the disappearance.

Although he didn't say anything Henry actually knew more about the subject than he let on, giving them time to talk and explain seemed to make them feel useful. It also gave him time to think.

"I'll consider it," he finally responded, kissing his mother on the cheek as he left the room.

Chapter 6

Camp Hale, Leadville, Colorado

He left early the next morning; he had known he would. Halfway through his parents' explanation and pleas the previous evening, he had known, so before going to bed he slipped into their bedroom and told them that he would check it out and decide if the construction project was for him.

"I know," he confessed as he started out of the room, "that at the moment I am doing nothing constructive around here."

By 8:00 he was on his way. His truck was packed with clothing for a few days. He had his camping equipment and a picnic lunch. At the last minute he threw in his skis, grinning a sheepish grin. "You know," he said, "we always have a late spring snow close to Mother's Day. Perhaps it will come in the next couple of days. I'll be ready if it does."

With that, he hugged and kissed his family and jumped into the truck. Half an hour later he was headed eastward, passing through Clifton and Palisade and into a long stretch looking into the rising sun on that Federal Highway the Army planners seemed to think was important to their current project. Henry knew that he had about 175 miles to travel and not all of it would be on this nice Federal Highway.

As he drove, he flipped on the morning radio and finding nothing but farm reports, flipped it off again. He passed the turn-off to the Grand Mesa and instinctively went a little faster. He passed the turn off for the communities of Parachute, and Rifle. Along this stretch he stopped to stretch his legs and eat the morning snack Ginny had slipped in, a fried egg sandwich with mustard. Her favorite, not his, but he ate it gratefully. On his way again he tried the radio. Hearing nothing but love songs, he flipped it off and tried to concentrate on the driving and not the reason for his trip.

At Glenwood he stopped for a long lunch under a tall tree. He stretched his legs, tried to nap but couldn't, and walked around the small town for a while. Soon, as he knew he must, he returned to the truck and continued eastward for a few more miles. Finally, he spotted a sign for US 24. Here Henry turned south and knew that he would soon be in Leadville.

As Henry approached Leadville he remembered all the jokes and elbows in the ribs that just the mention of Leadville always brought to him and his buddies. It was a wild town, a town of women who wanted to please men. At least, that was the youthful perception. The fertile adolescent minds of the local boys always pictured beautiful women, only half clad, walking up and down the wooden sidewalks smoking cigarettes. The adolescent minds of the local boys knew, of course, these women all wanted the boys. Jokes, more rib punches, and pretended exhaustion would follow any boyish discussion of Leadville.

What Henry found as he approached was a town of fast walking, business-on-their-minds men. They had papers in hand, cigarettes dangling from mouths, and scruffy boots. Henry looked around for the infamous women.

Suddenly a door opened and a sweet looking lady appeared. "Hi, Hon," she said.

Oh, boy, here it comes. A Lady of Leadville. My chance.

"Are you looking for someone, and if so, can I help you find them?"

What? No 'you wanna come up to my place'? Henry felt a little cheated.

"Ah, no thank you, ma'am." Henry managed to mutter. "I'm

here to see about work."

"In construction?" she asked knowingly.

"Yes, ma'am."

"Well, you just go to the top of the hill, to the green building with the faded yellow door, and go on in. They should be able to help you or steer you in the right direction."

"Oh, okay."

"Just tell them Nellie said to help you out."

"Oh, I will." Henry started off, then turned back and smiled as he said, "Thanks, Miss Nellie."

"Oh, Lord, honey. It's just Nellie," she said laughing as she went back inside.

So that was a famous Lady of Leadville. She seemed harmless enough to Henry.

Upon finding the green building with the faded yellow door, Henry ran his fingers through his hair, and went in. A gruff older man sitting at an improvised desk looked up.

"Yeah," he asked with a question mark clearly punctuating his one word. Nothing more. He seemed to be waiting for an answer.

"I'm Henry Townsend, from Grand Junction, and I came over to see if there was any construction work I might do." Clearly Henry should have thought about how to approach these people.

"Hey, Donny, we got any construction jobs?" Mr. Gruff turned and shouted to someone somewhere in the room. Laughter followed from most of the men. One, however, approached Henry and stuck out his hand.

"Name's Donny Donalson. Don't let Mr. Sweetheart here bother you. He's just upset that he drew desk duty today." He turned and gave the man at the desk an exasperating look.

"So you looking for construction work?" Before Henry could answer he went on. "Ever done any construction? Got any references? When can you start?" He stopped to light a cigarette.

Henry jumped in, trying to think and answer at the same time. "Well, no, not construction exactly. Just helping to keep the buildings in good repair on our farm. I can swing a hammer and hit the nail as well as most, I guess."

"Drafting? Engineering?" Donny asked.

"No."

"Okay, kid, what do you do in your spare time? We need hands here, but you gotta help me out."

"Well, I work the orchards, ride the trails on the western slope, ski, hike, backpack, camp out, fish, white water rafting," he paused to think and Donny jumped in.

"Okay, okay, I got it." He turned to a man at a table in the back. "Say, Sam, don't you still need some help laying out trails?"

"Always," said Sam. "If the fellow can stay on his feet while walking up and down the mountainside."

"I can," said Henry a little louder so that this Sam might hear him above the din. "I've been climbing and hiking since I first learned to walk. On Colorado mountainsides, I might add."

"Go see Sam," said Donny nodding in that direction. "If he can't use you, come back and we can probably find something for you to do."

As Donny turned to leave, Henry said, "Oh by the way, Nellie said to tell you she sent me." With that the entire room erupted in hearty laughter. Henry didn't see the humor.

Henry walked to Sam and soon learned that he was a man of few words. This suited Henry who was tired of the constant talk and questions surrounding Lilly and her family. How could he move on if no one would ever leave the subject, so he was delighted with the prospect that no one here knew of his 'abandonment'

"We are about to start laying out ski runs and trails. Are you familiar with those?" Sam asked by way of introduction.

"I am," responded Henry.

"How long you been skiing?"

"Since I was five."

"How old are you now?"

"Twenty-two."

"High school graduate?"

"Yes."

"Good at math?"

"Yes." Henry said getting into the spirit of the conversation.

"What else?"

"Sir?"

"What else you good at, kid?"

"Whatever you need."

"Fine, fine. Can you start today?"

"Now? It's after 4:00 and the sun won't last forever."

"Do you watch the clock, son?"

"No, but, I, well, yes, I can start today, but soon I'll have to go home for more clothing and stuff."

"Good, give me two days and then go home this weekend."

"Yes, sir."

"Now sit down back at our drafting table and I'll tell you what we have to do in a very short time. Game?

"Game."

On Saturday, Henry drove home with his great news. On Sunday he drove back to the Pando Plateau as the locals called the area where the camp was to be built. He had with him everything he thought he would need for weeks of work and everything his mother could squeeze into his truck. There would not be many trips back and forth for in addition to the hard work he was to begin, there soon came tire rationing as the rubber was necessary for the war effort.

He also had with him Ginny's promise to write him every week, "with news." The news, of course, was to be about Lilly and her family.

Lilly

Chapter 7

"Mom, where are all the kitchen decorations? Why is it bare in here?" Lilly asked.

It was a brilliant sunlit April day and Lilly had just returned from school. She was full of news about the plans her committee was making for their graduation next month. She was anxious to complete this last semester of high school and move on with the rest of her life.

She was eager to be with Henry, not as his high school girlfriend, but as his sweetheart, his love. Somehow, she thought that was much more grown up and was much more appropriate for them. No more playing at going together, they were sweethearts and lovers, bound together forever.

On this early Spring afternoon, full of plans, hopes and dreams, she had eagerly rushed up the back steps and into the kitchen to share the plans with her mother, at least the final graduation plans and to await Henry's return from Fort Collins.

She found the kitchen bare and her mother scrubbing down the cabinets.

"Mom," she asked again, "Where is everything?"

"Oh, did I forget to tell you?" her mother asked a little too brightly. "We're going to paint the entire house tomorrow, top to bottom, so we've moved everything out to the barn."

"Everything?"

"Well, everything but the things I sent out earlier this week to be reupholstered. I certainly didn't go out and bring those back just to store overnight in the dusty barn."

Lilly walked through the house. She had never seen it like this; Empty. It was creepy to see it stripped. For several days they had been living with an almost bare living room and with every upholstered chair from the bedrooms missing. She didn't think they needed reupholstering, but she didn't care one way or the other if that would please her Mom.

Lilly returned to the kitchen. "Where are we going to eat? Where are we going to sleep?"

"We're going over to Cousin Cami's for dinner and to stay the night," Mom answered with a smile. "But first, let's share one last pot of tea. You can fill me in on the graduation plans while we drink it. I kept out a pot and two cups, so we can have an afternoon treat."

"One last pot of tea?" asked Lilly becoming a little frightened by this unusual afternoon.

"One last pot before the house gets a complete makeover,"

"Where?"

"I have everything we need waiting for us on the back porch. Come now."

As Lilly stepped out onto the back porch she was shocked again. It was bare. All of the clutter that lived there was gone. How had she missed that?

"Mom?" Lilly asked looking at her Mom with a questioning look.

Smiling brightly, as if it were the most important part of the news yet, her Mom replied to Lilly's unvoiced question.

"Oh, yes. The porch will be scrubbed and painted, too. Won't that be wonderful? Now let's sit here on the top step and have some good hot tea. It's a good day for a relaxing cup, don't you think? I know I could use a cup myself. I'll pour and you tell me all about the meeting. Was Ginny there?"

Hours later, Lilly awoke with a groggy feeling. It was dark, and she was moving. Stirring slightly, she realized that she was leaning against someone and they were in a car, driving through the darkness of the night.

Forcing herself awake, she sat up. Looking to see who she was leaning against, she saw her cousin Cami. Looking up to the front seat she saw Aunt Kiri sitting beside Uncle Sado as he drove.

"Where are we? What's happening? I have to go see Ginny and discuss some final details. I want to see Henry," she slurred through her dry mouth.

"What's wrong?" She almost shouted.

"Shhh, dear, it's okay," whispered her Mom from her shadowy spot on the other side of Lilly.

"Mom, what's happening? Where are we? What time is it? Why are we driving at night with Uncle Sado and Aunt Kiri?"

The questions tumbled out of her. Her mother licked her lips, breathed in deeply and looked straight ahead. No answer came.

Finally, Uncle Sado said quietly," You are a young lady now, Lilly, so listen carefully and I will explain. You need to fully understand and accept what I am going to say."

Lilly looked at her Mom who was now staring out the side window into the vast darkness. There was still no response from her.

"What? Uncle Sado. Tell me," she demanded turning back to her uncle.

"We had to leave home."

"Leave home?"

"Run…, escape…, save ourselves."

He briefly looked at her in the review mirror. His eyes showed compassion, making her more afraid. She shook her head to get rid of the sight.

"Lilly, you know that things have not been the same for us since December 7th. You know we have been 'suspect' in the eyes of many."

"Not in the eyes of those who count," she responded loudly.

"Shh, don't wake Cami. I can only explain this to one of you at a time. I can't handle questions from both of you at the same time."

"Where's Dad. Why isn't he explaining 'this' to me?" She looked around at her Mom who, still staring into black nothingness, again did not respond.

"He's on his way."

"On his way where?"

"Okay, Lil, let's start over, shall we?"

Aunt Kiri reached across the front seat and gently placed her hand on her husband's arm. "Can you pull over, Sado, and Lilly and I will trade places. This will give us a few seconds to stretch our legs, and then you two can talk more quietly. I don't want to wake Cami."

"I don't think she will wake up. She's out, Aunt Kiri. Like she's been drugged or something," said Lilly.

Then recognition dawned. Lilly turned quickly and looked at her Mom. "The tea. Mom, you drugged me!"

Her mother said nothing, just pulled her lips tighter into her mouth and continued to stare out the window.

Uncle Sado pulled over and the switch was made with no one speaking until they were back in the car. Aunt Kiri said gently, "Now speak softly, please, and maybe I can join Cami in her sleep."

Lilly said nothing, just looked out into the inky black night. Finally her Uncle began again. "As I was saying, we are often treated differently these days. With suspicion by some and the number seems to be growing."

"Not by Henry or Ginny or their family. Not by my friends."

"You're right. The Townsends have been very supportive. Others in the valley have also. Some know that we are 100 percent American. Others who still accept us see us as 'good' Japanese Americans. But others only see the Japanese part and they see us as the enemy.

"I still don't know where we're going? I still don't know where Dad and the boys are. I still don't know what's happening , Uncle Sado." Lilly started softly crying. "Please, tell me everything."

"Are you sure you're ready?"

Lilly nodded her head and moved closer to her Uncle. "Please," she whispered.

"We are leaving in the middle of the night because we knew that some of our friends like the Townsends and Henry, especially, would try to stop us. My parents, your grandparents, and the elders of the other families left last night. They truly feel that we have to leave. They think that while we may be safe for the moment, we will not be safe forever. Did you hear the latest news from Washington?"

Lilly looked at him and shook her head. She was afraid to think about what news could send her family running in the dead of night.

"You know about the plans the federal government has made to gather Japanese aliens and Japanese-Americans together in camps. A letter from California brought us more news. They are terrified out there. The movement has started and, they warn, the movement is moving toward us.

"My parents, your parents, and our entire community have been secretly preparing for such an emergency for months. We have slowly drawn most of our money from the bank. New cash that Pops, your Father and I earned was not deposited, but hoarded or spent stocking up on supplies we thought we would need."

He slowed the car as a deer sprinted across the roadway. "Groups of scouts have spent days looking for places of refuge for small groups of us. It is not just our family, Lilly. This is a community wide decision," he said as he slowly accelerated.

"Not my community," Lilly asserted stubbornly.

"Yes, YOUR community, Lilly. Your ancestral community and

you are very much a part of it. Again, it is not just our family, but every Japanese American family in the valley."

"All?"

"Yes, all. It would not have worked for families to do this on their own. We needed a full community."

"Why?"

"It just seems prudent," replied Uncle Sado. "As time passes, we may need others not just our own family members," he paused. A deep sigh escaped from his lips, and he resolutely continued. "Honey, we don't know how long we will be away. For a short time I hope, but wars can go on for years. Mixing of families may be the only way for us to continue to exist as a community."

After giving her time to think about this, he began again. "If only families leave together we might not be able to withstand the hardships. If we leave in small family groups, perhaps we will find it necessary to take the chance and return to civilization much earlier. At any rate, the elders of the community made this decision."

"I won't abide by it," responded Lilly fiercely.

"Yes you will. It might be against your will, but you will. Let me continue, will you?"

Lilly said nothing, just looked at her Uncle with accusing eyes.

"I didn't make these decisions, Sweetheart, but I, like all the community will respect and abide by them. Do I make myself clear? I am speaking to you in place of your father right now."

"Why, what's wrong with Dad? Tell me!"

"Nothing. He just needs your support when we get there. He will not need a rebellious daughter. None of us will need rebellion of any kind."

He drove without speaking for a few minutes, and then continued. "Your father's new truck was loaded with your family's supplies as was mine and your Uncle Kimo's. Your Dad and Frank came out in that about midday. Ned was even allowed to drive your dad's old truck even though he is only 15, but he and Pops Yamamoto rode out together.

"We expect to pass only one community after leaving the valley. We won't be able to see it, of course, because of the darkness. It really is not a community. There is only a small dilapidated general store and filling station combined. Miners, ranchers, and farmers go there for groceries and news a couple of times a year." He said no more.

Finally, Lilly said. "I can take it. Go on. Why did you stop? Have you come to the 'bad part' now? Uncle Sado, it is all bad. I hope I'm dreaming and that I wake up soon in my old, unpainted, fully furnished room." She sobbed softly for a while.

"Go on," she said.

"I know it's a lot to take in, but you need to know that this was not a quick decision. This move has been well thought out and prepared for since December."

He looked at her, but she didn't respond, so he continued. "Our families have tried to prepare for a long stay. We hope it will not be too long, but if we are doing this, we have to be prepared to stay for a long while, maybe several years."

"Years?" She was almost shouting now. He gave her time to absorb that devastating information and then continued.

"Yes, I hate to say it, but I think we could survive for several years if necessary. We have been planning and preparing, each family separately and together. We have food staples, medical supplies, clothing, and anything else that a community needs. We are surprisingly well prepared."

"Oh, good," said Lilly under her breath but still heard by her Uncle. "Must be well prepared."

"Yes we must."

"Okay, where, exactly are we going?"

"A deserted mining town has been found for us. It is very isolated. I drove out here last week to bring some of the supplies; otherwise I may not have been able to find it in the darkness."

He looked at her and gave her a self-deprecating grin. She knew he was trying to bring levity to the situation, but she didn't want levity. There was nothing funny here. She glared at him and said nothing.

"It was once a fairly large mining town. It must have been prosperous because the abandoned buildings, homes, shops, a saloon and dance hall, and even a church, were well built. Good lumber had been used."

When again there was no response from Lilly, Uncle Sado continued. "This is one of the reasons we think we can survive for a while. Most of the buildings still stand because someone took very good care of them until abandoning them. We feel we have been given a precious gift, a real chance to survive, and we will. Have no fear on that part."

"That's not the part I fear, and you know it, Uncle Sado."

"I know, Honey, I know."

The transplanted community was many miles from Grand Junction, at least in Lilly's estimation. She spent the last part of her journey trying to mentally reconstruct the route they had taken. Of course, she had been asleep, or knocked out, during the first few hours, and then it was dark and she was too upset to think about roads and directions.

She had just fallen asleep again when the sun came up and awakened her. Looking around, she began to pay more attention to the countryside. It was about that time that they turned off the paved road onto a dirt road heading west. She knew they were going west for when they turned off, the morning sun was coming into the car through the back window.

She guessed that they had been traveling south from Junction. She looked for landmarks and sites that could help her when she made her getaway. Already she was planning to run.

After a couple of hours they turned left onto a much smaller road and traveled south toward mountains. Lilly decided that these were the La Sal Mountains of extreme southwest Colorado and eastern Utah. Soon they turned west again onto a small rutted trail, certainly not a road built for cars or trucks she decided.

Later, they were arrived at the base of towering mountains. Uncle Sado pulled off next to a stream, and they all got out to stretch their legs, drink from the clear mountain stream rushing past them, and eat some of the food Mom and Aunt Kiri had prepared. Cami still slept and Lilly was grateful that her mom had not drugged her so heavily. She knew that if she closed her eyes, she could sleep again, but she fought it.

Back in the car, they slowly made their way to the top of the mountain. Traveling on the switchback trails going up the mountain, clear evidence of an abandoned mine could be seen. A forlorn looking sluice, broken, fragmented and looking like a snake skin abandoned by its owner, slithered down the mountainside. Although great rivers of water must have once roared down the mountainside in that sluice, even the water was gone now.

The desolation of the mountainside gave Lilly hope for there was no sign of life or the possibility of life here. Surely no one would choose this place. Lilly was silently grateful for she hated the look of it.

As they crested, Uncle Sado slowed the car and said, "We're here." Lilly looked around carefully and at first saw nothing, and then in the trees gracing the downslope side of the mountain buildings came into sight, leaning, dilapidated, long ago abandoned buildings.

"This is it?" Lilly cried in disbelief. "It looks abandoned and totally unusable. How can anyone live here?"

"It is abandoned," replied her uncle, "but it has many buildings and most of them can be made livable and serviceable for other purposes. This has been chosen as our new home for a while."

Soon he brought the car to a stop. As he climbed out and stretched, Lilly could see her father and brothers coming from a large building that looked unsafe. Looking toward them through the car window, the anguish Lilly had been trying to control broke through her reserve. She no longer wanted to try to understand, or to be that perfect Lilly she always felt she had to be.

"I'll wait in the car," she said stubbornly.

"Fine," replied her uncle.

"I'm not staying," she said forcefully. "You'll see."

"Fine," Uncle Sado said again.

"Stop that!" She realized she was yelling at her uncle. She had never yelled at her uncle. She had rarely yelled at anyone, and then it was usually at her brothers.

Uncle Sado opened the back door and helped her Mother, Aunt Kiri, and Cousin Cami out. Cami was still too asleep to comprehend where they were or why, so Uncle Sado carried her.

The family headed toward a large building. Her Dad and brothers met them half way and exchanged a few words. Dad looked toward the car with anguish written deeply on his face. Her brothers also looked like they wanted to jump in the car and head back home, but they did not. Everyone turned and continued the walk to the big building.

Lilly remained in the car, alone and confused. She threw herself across the front seat and sobbed. She cried until her throat was raw.

She cried until the lost sleep of the previous night overtook her.

When she awoke she was on a bed in a small room with sunlight streaming through the one miniscule window. She didn't wake with a start, wondering where she was. She knew.

"Oh, good. You're awake. We need to talk," her mother said with a steeliness in her voice that Lilly had never heard. "You don't like what has happened. I don't like what has happened. Your Dad doesn't like what has happened. Do I need to name everyone here?"

Lilly didn't reply. She thought it was a rhetorical question. Obviously it wasn't.

"Well, Lilly. Do I need to name everyone here who doesn't like what has happened?"

"No," Lilly said quietly.

"Good. Now listen to me carefully. This was not done suddenly or carelessly. It was done with careful consideration for each and every person here, especially for our children. We want you to have a future. It may not be the future you had hoped for. It may someday be that future, but for the moment, we had to take matters into our own hands before the government did it for us." She paused, giving Lilly time to digest these bare but salient facts.

"Many of our countrymen, our Japanese American cousins, our Sansei and Nisei, have been threatened and some arrested. They are expecting orders any day now for the imprisonment of them all.

"Yes," interrupted Lilly. "In California. Not here. Not in Colorado."

"Not yet," her Mom admitted. "But camps are being built closer to us. There is now one in eastern Utah, just next door and one has been authorized for Colorado."

Startled, Lilly asked "For Colorado?"

"Yes."

"Near us?"

"Near enough."

"Where?"

"Near Colorado Springs."

"But, Mom. That is eastern Colorado. Across the mountains from us."

"Yes, dear, I know. But you do see the trend, don't you? We easily could be rounded up and convoys could take us across the mountains to the new camp. Or even into Utah to a camp. We had to protect our families and our community." She ended with a heavy sigh and remained silent for a while. She finally broke the silence with a sharp demand.

"Now, get up and start helping us. You are, you will be, a part of this community."

"How long are we staying?"

"Until it's safe."

Henry

Chapter 8

June 1942

Dear Henry,

Have you fallen down the mountain yet? You know I'm just kidding. If anyone can conquer a mountain, it's you.

Are your construction duties what you expected? Mom and Dad are so proud of you, but still they worry. Especially Mom, but doesn't she always?

Walt stopped by yesterday to get your address, so you should be hearing from him one day soon. I heard him tell Dad that he is trying to make up his mind about what service he wants to join. I think he said he was leaning to becoming a pilot. Walt, in the air? I can see him skiing with you, but not flying above. Can you?

The official announcement came today that the July 4th Land's End Road Race will not be held this year. The war, you know.

Well, no more news about Lilly. I'm really sorry. I miss her too.

Take care of yourself and remember your promise to write once a week. We'll see how long that lasts, won't we.

Love,
Ginny

June 1942

Dear Ginny,

It was good to get your letter. I had a note from Mom, also, but yours was newsier. Is that a word? Don't tell her I said that.

The construction is in high gear. Throughout every hour of daylight, you can hardly hear yourself think. I'm glad I spend a lot of time laying out trails in the mountains because the valley floor never seems to have a quiet moment. The hammering and nailing and sawing and shouting are constant.

I've heard that these guys must build barracks to house over 15,000 men! Just imagine 15,000 men in one small place at the same time. Well the place isn't too small, somewhere around 300 square miles, I would guess. Within those miles are not just eating and sleeping space, but marching, training, skiing and mountaineering spaces.

What a place it is going to be. Don't mean to brag, but I am proud to be a small part of this building effort.

Well, gotta run. More later. Hello to Mom and Dad and all my friends. Although I am often tired, I am never too tired to think of Lilly. Have you heard anything? Please keep me informed as only you can.

Your loving brother,
Henry

August 1942

Dear Henry,

Another letter, just like I promised. Your last one wasn't real newsy, more like a report, but I loved it anyway. Keep writing and pay no attention to me.

Life here goes on, but most definitely not the same. Some of us girls who just graduated get together and wrap bandages for our boys. We tried working with our mothers' group on this project, but their conversations were pretty lifeless and depressing so Joanie offered her back porch, you know, out 26 Road.

Well, the first afternoon out there we were just getting the back porch ready, cleaning and moving furniture and plants around when her mother came out and offered us that little building they have near the house. Her mom said that her brother and his family sleep out there when they come, so it is almost like a little house. We jumped at the chance, especially when Mrs. Sal said we would not have to put the supplies away each time. We can just come, roll, and leave stuff out ready for the next time. How great is that. So, I am helping some and will look for other ways to help our boys.

Walt stopped by to ask about you and then we went to a movie together. It was nice having your best friend around. He makes me feel safe, and he makes me laugh. The movie trip was fun. Do you have a movie theater nearby?

By the way, Grand Junction High School won the state wrestling title. Did you hear about that? Now the seniors on the team are talking about what branch of the service they want to join.

I hope this war is over soon.

No new news from Lilly.

> *Love,*
> *Ginny*

October 1942

Dear Ginny,

This camp is almost complete. You should see it—we built a city, complete with a ski area, and yes, to answer your question from this summer, we do have a movie theater.

The barracks are complete, standing like soldiers at attention in the straightest lines you ever saw. They are so white I think they will likely disappear when the snow flies. I wonder if anyone gave any thought to that.

The Eagle River, which once flowed through the area that is now the camp, has been redirected by the Army Corp of Engineers, and it now flows around the camp. Imagine that. I think if we can change nature, we should be able to win this war.

Over this past frantic summer, we, my construction fellows and myself, have built a T-Bar, four ski trails, storage sheds and warehouses of all types, communication facilities, barracks, administration buildings, a bakery, 4 mess halls, a movie and recreation theaters, a newspaper office, a dental clinic, an infirmary, a post office, and fire stations. Of course, for military purposes, we have marching grounds, mountain training terrain, and pistol ranges. It is, I tell you, a little city, and I am proud to have been a part of the building of it.

Soon the troops will begin arriving, but before they do, I will join them if they will have me.

Your loving brother,
Henry

October 1942

Dear Henry,

What kind of letter was that last one? In the final sentence you announce your plans to 'join them'. Mom, Dad and I need details.

Ginny

October 1942

Dear Mom and Dad, and Ginny, too,

I hope you can understand and support my decision. We all knew, even if we never talked about it, that sooner or later I would either have to volunteer or be drafted. I would rather volunteer and be where I want to be, doing the kind of training for the kind of fighting that I know will become important to our eventual victory.

As the months have passed and as I saw Camp Hale take shape, I have been proud of my involvement. In fact, I think I knew early on that I wanted to be involved with the military training that would take place here, not just the construction of the camp. I think my outdoor knowledge, both in skiing and in other outdoor activities have proven valuable to the construction of the camp.

Now, I want to be useful as a soldier. Again, we all knew that I would be expected to be part of our military after this crucial construction venture was completed, and what better place than right here with the troops?

So, I have volunteered for the Army Ski Troops, which is a part of the United States Army. We will train here at Camp Hale, receiving training in mountain and winter warfare. Contrary to what some would have you believe, it is not all skiing, although that is important.

I hope you can support my decision, but since I'm getting older and have seen my country go to war, I wanted to make this decision on my own. Please support me.

Your loving son and brother,
Henry, U.S. Army

Early November 1942

Dear Son,

Of course you have our love and support for your courageous decision. Yes, we all knew it had to come sooner or later. We think this is the right decision for you. You cannot know how proud we are of you.

Do you know when you will officially become a soldier? How long will your training be and will it all or most of it be at Camp Hale? Even though we have not been able to see you often, it has been such a comfort to us having you nearby. Please give us the particulars as soon as you learn anything.

We do what little we can collecting scrap metal, pennies, and anything anyone thinks might help the cause. The ladies and young girls are always wrapping bandages and all the while praying that they are making too many, that their bandages will not be necessary. We listen to the news and it is awful, but we don't want you to worry about that.

We hear news about your friends and classmates as they join various branches of the service. Walt has joined the Army Air Corp. We pray for your safety and their safety nightly.

Along those lines, Ginny has some news of her own, but we will let her tell you in her enclosed letter.

Take care, son, and know that we are proud of you, as always.

With our love,
Dad

Late November 1942

Dear Henry,

I hope you are well, blah,blah....I have great news and can't wait to tell you. I hope you will be as happy for me as I am for myself. So, you think your life is changing? Well, brother, so is mine. In only the best way possible.

I am getting married!!! Wait....wait....wait...have they picked you up off the floor yet? Ha Ha.

I know you are surprised. I am, we all are, but I am also so happy. It is so right and so natural. We want to get married sometime during the Christmas season for he has to report for duty early in January. Can you make it home during December? Anytime. You pick the date. We want you here for the wedding and he says you have to be his best man.

At first Mom and Dad were reluctant to 'give us their blessing', not because of who I'm marrying but because of my age and the suddenness of our decision. They wanted to be sure we were not just jumping on the bandwagon and doing what many other young couples across the country are doing. This is for real, Henry. Our love is real. I know I'm only 19 and he is 22, but we know. We just KNOW. So don't try to be the protective big brother and question us, or question him.

One day we were just laughing at some silliness together and our eyes met---I know, corny, huh? But when it happened it was like it was for the first time. We were both blown away by the wonder of it all. I love him, and he loves me. Nothing else is important.

Am I babbling? Well, you know how I get when I'm excited. So please, please, ask for time off close to Christmas. You simply must be here.

I love you forever,
Ginny

PS. Nothing new regarding Lilly
PPS. Walt says to get your b--- home for his/our wedding!
PS from Walt. Hey big brother. Yes, I do love her. I always have, just in a

different way. Now, I love the woman that Ginny has become. I want to spend the rest of my life with her. And yes, I will be good to her and take care of her. I know you will watch me like a hawk, but really, brother, I don't need that. You'll see, I love her. Come home soon.

Chapter 9

A few days into December, Henry went to the Army recruiter and asked how he could join the Ski Troops. Again he was asked questions about his outdoor activities and qualifications.

"Can you get three letters of recommendation attesting to your skiing and winter outdoor ability?" he was asked.

"Of course," replied Henry wondering at this. Several of his friends had already joined various branches of the service and none of them had mentioned letters of recommendation, but he could, and he did.

"Fill out these papers, go to the base infirmary as soon as the doctor reports, which I have heard will be within days, and then get back with me."

"Will do, Sir," Henry responded in his best military style.

"Oh, and have those letters sent to me promptly."

Henry made it home for Christmas and for Ginny's wedding to his best friend. He was still shocked and unsure of the whole thing until he saw them together. He recognized the look.

He drove to Grand Junction on Friday, Christmas Day, 1942. On Saturday they all settled in and spent time together making last minute arrangements, and then on Sunday, December 27, 1942, his little sister Ginny became Mrs. Walt Brennerman.

Watching the two of them made his heart ache for what he now believed he would never have. The dream of Lilly. He knew he had to let it go, no matter the pain. When he had a moment alone with Ginny he told her she could stop giving him reports that showed no activity concerning the Japanese community.

"Only tell me," he said, "if there is news. Good or bad, I want to hear it."

The following day, a cold but sunny Rocky Mountain winter day, Henry returned to Camp Hale, immensely pleased that he had put in motion his entry into the 10th before he left camp for Jenny's wedding. By doing so he was able to be a full-fledged new member of the Division before the new year of 1943 dawned cold and clear over the Rockies.

Across the country, the need for boot camps increased and some basic training had to take place at the site of many divisions' training facilities. Henry felt lucky to be able to begin and continue his training on site at Camp Hale. Now, he was at the camp, as a member of the 10th Division he had heard so much about. After a few days, the camp was home to the soldier in him, and the construction worker was forgotten.

Henry was soon immersed in the life of the 10th Infantry Division, Light Alpine, as the ski troops were officially called. The Division had three regiments, the 85th, 86th, and 87th Regiments. Henry was assigned to the 86th Regiment. This turned out to be a fortuitous assignment for the 87th Regiment was soon shipped out to Kiaska, Alaska, to fight the Japanese. Henry still had no taste for that type assignment although as he had explained to his new brother-in-law Walt, he should feel like taking on the whole damn Japanese Army because they were the reason Lilly was lost to him.

It seems that both the 85th and 86th Regiments were undermanned and thus new recruits were being assigned to them through transfers from other divisions. Based upon his skiing ability and mountaineering knowledge, Henry was selected to help train these recruits.

As it turned out, his knowledge and patience, and even his sense of humor, were necessary for many of these new members were flatlanders and had very little useful skiing and mountaineering experience. This was a tough assignment for them.

While Henry and the other men selected to train these recruits were very enthusiastic about this assignment, enjoying the outdoor activities of downhill and cross-country skiing, camping, and mountain climbing, that soon merged into the training many of the new men did not share their enthusiasm for all these things 'outdoors'. In fact they found their leaders' enthusiasm irritating. The large majority of them could not ski and considered even trying to stand up and move around on those small boards absurd. They didn't like the cold, the snow, the walking sideways on a mountain and the thin air.

They despised the inversion that covered the camp and the surrounding valley with coal-laden smoke from the camp's five hundred coal stoves and from the nearby Denver & Rio Grande locomotives. The recruits felt that the army had sent them to hell and soon they began calling Camp Hale, Camp Hell.

Many of these newcomers were arriving from bases or homes close to various entertainments. They had loved their ability to enjoy the entertainments offered to them. There was no such opportunity at Camp Hale. The closest town was Leadville and it was off limits to the Ski Troops because of the "Ladies of the Night" who were numerous in Leadville.

These were the men Henry and the others were to train, and train quickly. They began each day with early morning runs up and down the flat streets of Camp Hale. This simple exercise, however, because of the altitude of Camp Hale, was taxing for many of the recruits. They then had to learn the life-saving skills they would need when they reached mountains of the war zone. They practiced walking in soft snow and hard snow. Walking up the mountain and then back down. Waxing their skis. Building a campfire on the snow, and entrenching themselves in the snow as a means of keeping warm.

It was arduous and should have been a long slow training, but by February of 1943, with just a couple of months training behind them, the Army decided to test their abilities. Large scale maneuvers were called for, in the highest range, in the dead of winter. After the maneuvers were over, Henry took time out to write a letter to Walt.

March 1943

Dear Walt,

Should be writing to Ginny and the folks, but just wanted to talk to you tonight. Hope your training is going well and you still feel that you made the right choice. I think of you whenever a plane goes over. Are you a pilot yet?

The name of this camp has been changed....by the new recruits. They now call it Camp Hell. The recruits' name was not far off during our recent maneuvers. I won't say the timing was wrong, the men not ready, the results disastrous, I'll just describe it to you in its icy details.

Orders came for a full battalion and a pack artillery to march five miles from Tennessee Pass (about 10,400 feet, you remember?) up another 1000 feet to the top of Homestake Lake. We were to make camp on top and take part in various exercises designed to mimic life at the front. Well, if the enemy had been waiting for us, they could have picked us off quite easily. Thank goodness it was just inexperience by our newbies and Mother Nature waiting for us; otherwise we would have been sitting ducks.

Although a few of the brass expressed the belief that our recruits were still two green for such an exercise, the higher-ups had their say and demanded that the exercise take place. They wanted a 'starting point' for future reference. Well, they got it.

I'm sure you fly-boys would have had a good laugh at our expense, at least until you saw how dangerous the whole thing became. Our recruits were already at the camp altitude and now they were expected to march even higher. They were carrying their rucksacks on their backs, 90 pounds at least. The guys carrying the guns and ammunition had additional weight. As you can imagine, for anyone not acclimated to this altitude, breathing problems started immediately.

Some of the men began to look like a newsreel cartoon show. They had not learned how to wax their skis or how to climb the mountain. Up they went, down they came. Back up, back down. It would have been funny if not so sad.

The pack mules didn't fare any better. Mules, hundreds of them, were used to pull Howitzers up the mountain. Howitzers in the Rockies! Just think of it. The mules sunk so far into the snow that their legs no longer showed. Supplies and guns were transferred to sleds and the men required to haul them up.

Once we finally reached the top, we were to remain for eight days!!! The first day saw the men's sweat turn into ice, frozen quickly by the zero temperatures. One morning, we heard that the temperature was -28 degrees. Some of these boys had never been north of Memphis. They could not believe they were to 'do' things in that kind of weather.

I'm just sure that the grumbling and cursing echoing off the canyon walls could be heard over the mountain and into Aspen. Curse words, even when spoken in a soft southern drawl, are still curse words. Some of those Southern boys could take the word damn, which they did often, and turn it in to a three syllable word.

Now as I said, all of this would have been funny except that serious health problems were everywhere. Frostbite, oh my goodness, the number of cases, but frostbite did get you sent back down the mountain to the warmth of Camp Hell! There was a suggestion that some of the men tried to get frostbite just to get sent down. Can't say as I blame them. If the situation was reversed and we found ourselves so far outside our own element, who knows how far we would go to get back to relative safety?

There was an 'enemy' detail of some of our men already in place. We were to engage in combat with them. That engagement could not take place because our numbers were so decimated by the experience. Hundreds of our men suffered. Still, the experience was helpful to hear the brass tell it. At least, anyone with any rational thought could see that there was still a lot to do with our new recruits.

There were times, though, when we had a good laugh and even felt a little successful while we were up there. Those of us who skied taught the newer recruits who were still able to function to wax their skis with tacky klister wax when climbing. This lesson seemed simple enough to all.

Then we decided the new boys needed to learn to stay warm. That's when the howling began. 'Better late than never, ski boys,' one newbie yelled. We just ignored them and got on with the lesson of tummy warming to keep your feet warm. When we told them to partner up and explained how to use your buddy's tummy to warm your feet howls of indignation and disbelief filled the air. Still, they learned.

We moved on to fire building on snow, which they thought to be impossible, but soon they caught on to that. One of our experienced skiers brought out a large can of bacon grease and told the men to cover their exposed skin with it. It took a little convincing, but they all learned to do it. Several, however, still don't believe it will ever be useful as a way to protect their skin. They accused us of using them for bear baiting.

Finally, we introduced the idea of building snow caves for warmth. This last lesson brought even more hoots of disbelief from the non-wintery guys. They did learn to make them and we even used them.

So you see, despite all the setbacks and failures in the beginning, some good came from the almost total fiasco. I just hope it is not repeated anytime soon.

Now we're busy really getting them into shape. If the next mountain excursion is in France, Germany, Italy, or anywhere the enemy is located in Europe, we have to be better prepared. Last week our entire unit could have been wiped out by the enemy.

Of course, a jolly thought occurs. If you and your group have such problems, they would probably be in those new training mock up planes or in the air in real planes. All that vomit and misery would have nowhere to go except to float around the cabin. That gives me delight, to think of you dodging vomit.

Take care, 'brother,' we all love you,
Henry

Chapter 10

March 1943

Dear Mom, Dad, and Ginny,

One letter for all of you this time. We have been quite busy lately. I hope all is well with the farm and everyone. Is someone riding or at least walking Steki for me? She needs to keep in shape and I hope she misses me for I sure miss riding her.

Dad, I've thought it over and I want you to take some money from my bank account and pay the taxes on the Yamamoto's property. If they do come back, they will need their home. You might occasionally ride over and make sure all is in order over there. Since it's been a year, I am beginning the think they will not return, at least not for a while, but I think we owe it to them to keep their home in tact and in their name. I will continue to have my check sent home. You and Mom should use what you need, send me a little, and put the rest into the bank account you and I set up while I was there. Thanks, Dad.

A couple of weeks ago we had a two week training campout at Homestake Lake. It was quite an excursion. The recruits, imagine recruits from the deep south, from southern California, and even Hawaii learning to make snow caves. It took a bit of coaxing, but they finally got the hang of it and then became proud as peacocks that they could actually make a cup of hot chocolate in there!

One exercise involved mountain-warfare with artillery target practice. On one such occasion the commander decided to see if he could actually cause a snow slide by firing at the peak of a mountain. This would give us the advantage, should we ever need it, of using the snow as an additional weapon against the enemy. Well, it worked. After guns were fired at the top of Homestake Lake, snow thundered down the mountain in a wondrous avalanche. Anyone caught below would have been in great trouble.

After the snow disappeared from that side of the lake, the lake's water and ice poured over the lake's edge. The frozen wetness stopped just short of our brass.

We thought this was a great sight, a needed chance to belly laugh at the brass. The men renamed the lake Slide Lake. I think I like it better.

Now with training back down at our normal level, the commanders are assessing the two weeks of training, and our men are getting better. Camaraderie is building among the new recruits and the 'old hands.' When the time comes, we will be a cohesive unit. It is just taking more time than I imagined it would. Still, the more time it takes, the longer I am near home.

Ginny, what do you hear from Walt? I can't wait to talk with him in person and compare notes since we are both in newly developing units. Take care of yourself.

Love,
Henry

July 1943

Dear Ginny,

We are surrounded by blooming wildflowers., It makes me think of home and all of you. Our commanders don't give us a free moment to 'stop and smell the roses,' or the Columbine.

With the snow all melted except for in the higher crevices, we have forsaken our skis and poles for ropes and pitons. Again, we are a mixture of experienced and novice. I place myself at the level of 'some experience' for the knowledge and skill I have because Walt, Joe, and I spent our summers scaling whatever vertical surface we could find when we were not jumping into the irrigation canals, But, that was for our own amusement and this is serious business.

I will say, only to you, that I am glad I am better prepared for this Alpine training than our flatlanders , and those Florida boys who have rarely seen a foothill much less a mountain. Since I have chosen this service, I am glad that I grew up living at 5,000 feet and playing at elevations up to 12,000 feet.

One recruit in particular, Johnny K. fresh from Florida, keeps breathing in deeply, exhaling fully, and rolling his eyes. We tell him it will get better, but we do have fun at his expense.

He keeps saying, "Well, come on down and let's train in the deep water of the Gulf. We'll order up some high temperatures and humidity for you. Then we'll see who is huffing and puffing and rolling their eyes." At least he says this with something like a smile on his face.

Most of the men are good as gold and good natured about all this training. They do, however, still miss their fun times with the ladies.

Anyway, we are training amid the granite outcroppings on the Eagle and Homestake Rivers. One bad part is that we sometimes have to dodge live rounds of machine gun fire—practice for the real thing we're told. Only problem is that we know these rounds are aimed over and behind our locations. Don't think the enemy will be so kind.

One obvious benefit of the rock climbing instruction is the growth of our company's solidarity. You know yourself that even when skiing with someone, it is *still essentially an individual activity. Rock climbing, real rock climbing, involves a partnership. Sharing a rope while hanging vertically high above the ground below makes people work together. In our case, this seems to be building a stronger, more cohesive unit.*

How are the orchards this year? How do the crops look? I hope it is a good season for everyone. Just picturing the fruit, melons and vegetables makes my mouth water. The eating back home should be getting pretty good about now. Eat a few peaches for me, will you?

You realize she's been gone over a year now.

Miss you,
Henry

February 1944

Dear Mom, Dad, and Ginny,

Hope you don't mind sharing a letter again, but I would tell you all the same thing, so here it is.

We have just returned from a great adventure. I know that we are training for war, but still, it was an adventure. We are reminded daily of the seriousness of our training, and I think those of us who are true skiers and mountaineers count our blessings, that when the time comes we will be able to serve while still 'in our element' so to speak. When we have news from places like Corregidor, Guam, or any place in the tropics, I shudder. I don't think I'm tough enough for that kind of fighting. I know I made the right choice when I joined this group.

Anyway, back to our recent adventure. It was a training exercise with Aspen and its glorious ski trails waiting for us at the end of the line. What a trip. You know it's about a four hour drive from here to Aspen. Sure, anyone just looking at a map wouldn't think it would take so long, but what with the winding drive down one mountain and up another just to get from here to there it does. Still, many of the camp's soldiers make the trip when they have a weekend pass, so the business owners around Aspen know us.

Well, our commanders decided we should make the trip on foot, forgetting the roadways, and cutting through the winter landscape on our skis. This allowed us to practice our downhill, cross-country, and survival skills as we made the trip. It was expected to take days not hours! The reward? Time off in Aspen. Who could resist?

Each man packed ten days' food supply, tents, and other needed items. It was not a lightweight walk in the woods by any means. We had fresh snow and had to break trails as we went. We climbed 13,000 feet and skied down to begin the climb again on the next mountain. We melted snow at mealtime and boiled rice stew and Nescafe cocoa. When not cooking up rice stew we had meatloaf, ration-style. Believe me, Mom, ration-meatloaf bears no resemblance to yours. Or even to Gin's. Ha Ha

But we did have chocolate for dessert. Just one very big problem, though. The chocolate had been reformulated by the army or the manufacturers or both so that it would not melt in the tropics. Well, guess what. Not only would it not melt in the tropics, it wouldn't melt in our hot pans! It was harder than hardtack!

We finally arrived in Aspen, after several hard days and we skied right into town to the welcoming arms of the Jerome Hotel. (No Mom, not those kind of welcoming arms!)

Mr. Elisha, the proprietor, is always welcoming to the soldiers. On this day he greeted us with some bottles of spirits open on the bar, hot showers, and beds for the night. Just what we needed, I must say.

Mr. Elisha is a mountain man himself and he knew the task we had just completed. He always seems concerned about us. I think he knows, as we all know, that in the end there will not always be happiness and comfort waiting for us.

Anyway, Mom and Dad, things are fine. We are still here, still stateside, still training. I know our unit is a new experimental unit for the US of A, but sooner or later they have to turn us loose and we should be well prepared by then. That is, we will be if practice makes perfect.

One final thought. A question for Dad. A really serious question. Dad, have you ever had an Aspen Curd? Maybe after a day of skiing in your youth? No? Yes? Well, I will admit that I've had one or two during my times in Aspen.

Gotta run. Don't worry about me. I am fine. Hope you are also. Ginny, tell Walt to write. Send him my news if you think he is interested in it. Wish he was here rather than wherever he is now.

Love to you all,
Henry

PS: An Aspen Curd is a milk shake made by Mr. Elisha at the Jerome. After a day of skiing it is just the thing to have in front of the roaring fireplace. It is a milk shake spiked with good whiskey! (I can see Mom and Ginny making faces right now.)

April 1944

Dear folks,

I am exhausted. We have just returned from a three week set of maneuvers.. We were again in mock-training at Homestake Lake.

You know how April weather in Colorado is a roller coaster ride. Good one day, lousy the next. Apparently our commanders did not know this, or on second thought, maybe they were hoping for what we got. The first few days we had fine weather, then came Easter Sunday a couple of weeks back. I'm sure you got the same snow storm that we did.

We were in our maneuvers when it blew in. Man was it cold! Still there was patrolling, digging, and moving about to endure. The maneuvers were meant to be as real as possible. We were in enemy territory so to speak, so there were no fires or cigarettes allowed.

"Enemy" forces overcame some of us and took prisoners, and thoroughly interrogated those prisoners. It wasn't fun and games. The army seemed to be very serious about this exercise. Perhaps they know something we don't.

Anyway, after three weeks of frozen toes, fingers, lips, and even eyelashes, and 21 nights buried in our sleeping bags in the snow, the army decided we were fit enough and ended the exercise. I think we gained more than expected from the exercise. We are no longer strangers passing through this together. We are a unified front. Johnny K, and so many others are no longer flatlanders. They are bona fide members, as we all are, of the real Alpine ski troopers.

I think we are ready if we are ever called.

Love,

Henry

Chapter 11
Texas,

Late June 1944

Dear Mom, Dad, and Gin,

I know it's been a while since I put pen to paper, but life has become a hectic confusion, at least from my part and I think most of the men agree with me, but nevertheless, here we are, wherever here is! I know that on a map we can be pinpointed as 30 miles east of Austin, but in reality, where are we?

In limbo is the generally accepted answer among the men—in limbo. We don't think the Army knows what to do with us. We've trained, tested new equipment, and developed as a cohesive unit for almost 2 years. So why are we in east Texas? We feel torn, tried, and tossed into chaos.

I know you have heard about the movements in Europe and the landing by the Allies at Normandy. The men in Europe seem to have started a mighty push. A push intended to remove Hitler from Europe. Pray for the strength and perseverance of our troops over there.

When we first heard the news of the landing, we thought that maybe now we would be needed. Maybe now our time had come to do what we have been so fully trained to do. Perhaps you even thought the same thing and even worried about it.

Well, worry no more—yes we were called upon to move out. In fact since we got word of impending movement the day after the landing, I think it was a well-founded assumption by us that we would be headed to Europe, or even the dreaded Pacific, but instead we headed to Texas. Camp Swift, Texas for God's sake! (Sorry, Mom, but I even cleaned that up for you.)

That's all I know at the moment, but will be in touch with news if things change as we all hope they will. You might even know more about what is going on with the Army than we do. For us, though, we are, or so it seems, simply pawns in someone's chess game. That is not a good feeling.

I've got to run. The humidity, flies, fleas, and snakes are calling me. Hate to sound this way, but you must know how I hate this. Is this how Johnny

K. felt when he first arrived at Hale? I hope not. He is a good kid. They're all good kids. Listen to me; I sound like an old man don't I?

Just wanted to let you know that, in spite of the tone of this letter, I am okay. Hope Walt is faring better.

Love you all,
Henry

July 4, 1944

Happy Fourth Mom, Dad, and Gin,

I hope that you have a fun filled day. Junction always knows how to celebrate the 4th, but I guess during these war years the celebrations have been a bit different. I know they must not even be thinking about another Land's End road race what with gasoline rationing still in high gear. Those were marvelous races to watch, but we may have seen the end of them.

There's not much to tell from here, at least not much that will make for pleasant reading. This is a miserable place. Sorry to be so down about it, but truth is truth.

I think many of us in the 10th, especially those of us who were skiers and mountain people before joining are having an especially hard time of it here in this hot, flat, creature-infested place. I think many of us are finding that we don't have the temperament or constitution for life here. I know that describes me!

Most of us, especially those who have been together since the beginning, felt comfortable in the Alpine training grounds. Even on the worst of days, the mountains were comforting. I know now how privileged I was to be serving my country and training in the comfort of my mountains. I look back on them as something like a mother's welcoming and comforting arms. Some had a hard time becoming accustomed to the harsh winters, but this harsh and hellish summer is much worse.

Even the flatlanders, beach-dwellers, and pure Southern boys agree that this place is a scene from Hell. We have poisonous snakes that are not as afraid of us as we are of them, and every insect known to man and some, I think, that are not. Flies, mosquitos, scorpions, and some nasty little thing called gnats by some and no-see-ums by others.

Anyway, these little creatures fly into your eyes, nose, ears, and mouth. They fly continuously. One new recruit from Georgia has been trying to teach us to 'talk around them" which you have to do if you are going to have a conversation. This involves screwing your mouth to one side, blowing out a stream of air, saying a couple of words, and then repeating the process over and over until you have said what you want to say. Some of the guys have mastered the technique to such a degree that they look like a comedy routine. But that's the only thing funny around here.

Pray that the Army is not training us here for Pacific duty. I wouldn't survive.

Sorry to be so negative.

Love to all,
Henry

November 1944

Dear Mom and Dad,

I know that I have not written much lately, but I realized I was beginning to sound like a whiney school boy. The weeks still crawl, the bugs still crawl and fly, and the snakes still slither, just not as much anymore.

Have you had a good snow yet? I would love to rub my parched, yes still at this late date, skin in some pure white snow. Ah, such memories, but enough of that. We don't want to call to mind too many memories for some are still painful. Not as much as before, but still memories can bring a fresh quick pain.

We have been receiving new recruits weekly. Seems our 10th was short, but now, I hear, we are considered 'full and complete.' Of course, these new men are not receiving all the training that our earlier troops did for we are not at Hale with the conditions for winter training. Strange mixture, I think.

Maybe these new troops mean that we will soon move out. I can't stand the thought of being here as long as we were at Hale. And to think that some people thought it was hell, no, it was heaven.

Even those of us from Hale who in great numbers suffered from heat exhaustion when we got here, myself included, have adjusted somewhat. Heat exhaustion is no longer the problem. What a relief that is.

We are training with heavier weapons. Some men grouse that we are the 10th Light Infantry, so the training and the name don't fit. I think, hey, we are training for war. Period. Our Alpine division has been completely reorganized, and we even have a new name, the 10th Mountain Division. But we are still in the dark about if, when, and where we might be needed.

My greatest fear, enhanced by all this recent training, by our new name, and of course, by the ever present army rumor mill, is that we will be sent somewhere tropical but mountainous. To add to my anxiety, a large map of Burma, with its many mountains standing grandly above the lower terrain, has suddenly appeared near one company's headquarters. You can imagine the rumors that prompted.

Well, that's life here at Camp Swift-Kick-In-The-Pants! Pass this letter on to Ginny. Tell her I send her my love and would love to hear from that flyboy husband of hers.

Love,
Henry

November 26, 1944

Happy Thanksgiving Mom, Dad, and Ginny,

I know I'm late with the greeting, but we have been very busy and I had duty around Thanksgiving for several full days. I am glad I waited to write, though, for I have news!

Our division has a new Commander. A real, honest to God soldier and war hero, General George Hays. Have you ever heard of him? What a needed shot in the arm he is for us. This is his second war and he really is an acknowledged hero in both of them. Maybe you have even seen him in the newsreels before the movies down at the Realto. Look for him. Look for us, for he expects great things from us and he believes in us so he makes us want to deliver for him. What a great turnaround for the Camp. It feels good.

He keeps telling us to have fun. Now, doesn't that sound silly under the circumstances? But we love it. He also tells us that if a German ever sends a bullet our way, we should return ten to him.

We still don't know where or if we are going out soon, and if Gen. Hays knows, he's not saying.

Hope all is well. Miss you. Must run.

Love,

H

December 3, 1944

Dear Mom, Dad, Ginny,

It was good to talk to all of you two days ago. I know it was a short call, but I just wanted to let you know of our orders. We had very little time to execute them, and no time for even thinking about them. While we talked there was a line of fellas all waiting to call home, and waiting not too patiently.

Nothing like connecting through Ma Bell. Wish we could do it more often. Anyway, we are now on the train moving eastward so I have some time to write.

As I said, we still don't know our final destination but we have left Texas for Camp Patrick Henry, which is in the Chesapeake Bay area of Virginia. I understand there is a military port nearby. I think that is significant as that should tell us that we will be on the high seas soon. I'm hoping and praying that we are headed somewhere in Europe and not to the tropics. Don't you think if we were headed to Guam or Burma or anywhere in the Pacific the Army would have sent us to the west coast to depart? That's what I'm counting on.

We are all reinvigorated—looking forward to doing our job and pleasing our new commander. What a refreshing atmosphere that is. Some thought we would go down in history as the division that trained and was never called. What an insult that would have been!

I am personally looking upon this next leg as a new beginning for me. Old hurts, old memories, and old plans will be left behind. Amazingly, I am looking forward to the future at last. Quite an unexpected insight isn't it?

More later.

Love to all,
Henry

Chapter 12

December, 1944

Dear family,

> *Wow! Air mail out of Junction? How did you manage to get a package to me just before we departed? The package arrived just minutes after my last short call to you. Why didn't you mention it? Thanks so much for the good things you sent. Of course, I had to share everything.*

> *As I tried to say during my last call, we were told to keep out calls short for our entire regiment needed to call someone. So for most of us I think the gist of calls was 'Hi, I'm fine. We're about to embark. Miss you. Don't worry about me.' Now that we are on the open sea we have more time to write.*

> *Dad, are you all right? You sounded a little tired when we talked. Don't overwork yourself. Let Luke take care of everything. He has been our manager for as long as I can remember and he thinks of the farm and the orchards as his own, so let him shoulder the load. Any demanding or heavy work that you would give me, give to Luke. Use him! He will love it.*

> *After the hurry-up- and- wait time following the phone call, we finally started the loading process. You should have seen it. What a zoo, but a rather organized zoo. Some of the guys were wolfing down last minute coffee and donuts the Red Cross ladies were serving. You'd think they don't think there will be coffee and sweets on board. I don't know, but I hope so. Coffee anyway.*

> *We formed a long line for boarding. All of us in Army green shouldering duffle bags and gear. We must have looked like a sluggish millipede snaking our way to the gangplank.*

> *We all made it on board and have been at sea for two days. We are on the U.S.S. Argentina. She was formerly a luxury cruise liner, but She is now a troop carrier. Still, She is a luxury compared to Camp Swift.*

> *Ginny, you should see the size of this vessel. She is so large that we have USO shows on board. Now, that is a treat. Still the real luxury has been stripped away like a spring blizzard will strip away the beautiful blossoms of the fruit trees.*

The basic form is there but most of the beauty is gone.

The once luxurious and spacious individual cabins now hold dozens of men, stacked on top of each other, literally. The Army has outfitted all sleeping quarters, except those of the officers, of course, with bunk beds stacked over six bunks high. I am not kidding. Luckily, I am on a third tier bunk, not a top tier. Hope none of those guys take up sleepwalking.

There has been some vigorous complaining but most of the men have adjusted. Many of the men plan to sleep on deck after they get their sea legs and when the weather is fine. We are all making a gallant effort to catch up on our sleep. I think most of us will succeed.

Outside of quarters there is still some evidence of the faded glory of this old girl and much to occupy our time. The first few days there was the thrill of doing something, going somewhere and for most of us the uniqueness of ocean travel. The flatlanders handled the transition without much difficulty, but for some who had never been in a boat or on open water there was a period of seasickness.

Thank goodness I wasn't affected, but, Ginny, I kept thinking of Mrs. Fine making us learn the Latin for seasickness, 'mal de mer', so that we could be prepared to use the proper Latin phrase should the opportunity ever come up. I remember that my class laughed heartily and someone asked if getting sick at Mesa Lakes qualified as 'mal de mer.' If you run into her, tell her.

There are different recreational programs going on all day. There are movies on deck along with boxing on promenade deck aft. (See, I'm trying to impress you with my nautical terminology. Is it working? Ha Ha). We even have our own radio station, WARG, which provides music, news and variety programs.

Sometimes, we just like quiet time, and there is plenty of space for finding a spot to read or watch the waves Mother Nature or the other ships in the convoy kick up. We have an escort of destroyers and sub-spotting aircraft. They aim to keep us safe.

There are some serious moments on board. Most importantly, I guess, are the lifeboat drills. After an alarm thunders across the ship, everyone grabs a life jacket, putting it on while rushing madly on deck.

Mom, I hope I have put your mind at ease and erased some of the fear I heard in your voice when I called before embarkation. We are safe and enjoying a cruise. I still don't know how long we will be on the ocean for we still don't know our final destination. We all theorize about that. We seem to be sailing East, more or less. If I ever learn where we're headed, I'll let you know if I can.

Take care of each other, and Mom and Dad, take it easy. You are precious to me. You, too, Gin.

Love,
Hen

December 27, 1944
Dear Ginny,

Happy Anniversary! See what a good big brother I am. I remembered your big day. I wish I could be there to help you celebrate. More importantly, I wish Walt could be home with you, but I know he's busy over here being a flyboy. You can be proud of what our boys in the sky do. I sent him a post card from the ship. Anniversary hugs to you.

Love,
Henry

Dear Mom and Dad,

How's this for a two-in-one letter. Hope you are well. Dad did you think about my advice in my last letter. Take care of yourself, please. And don't let any worry about me ever cloud your day.

Finally, we made port, disembarked, learned our destination, saw one of the wonders of the world, and also one of the once wondrous cities of the world. How's that for a lot in a short time?

First of all…our destination! Italy! Wow! I am so pleased. I hope the censor doesn't cut too much of what I am about to tell you, but I know they have a job to do. Still I hope they leave enough in that I can share this with you.

On our way here, we passed through the Straits of Gibraltar, and many of us recognized the Rock from our high school or college geography and Latin books. I felt such a sense of relief when we saw it for it meant Europe and not the tropical islands.

We passed surprisingly close to the Isle of Capri, and an impromptu chorus of "Isle of Capri" broke out among the guys. Some tried to reach the soprano high notes and sound like Gracie Fields, but no one made it.

As you can see, we were in good spirits on December 23rd when we made harbor in the Bay of Naples where, at first glance, the water surrounding the ship was green and clear. Soon though, we had a better view of two things that sobered us immediately.

The first was Mount Vesuvius. Even though it is miles away it was impressive but ominous. There was a snake trail of grey-brown smoke still rising from it even though it has been nine months since its last eruption. Just think of that—a woman could make a baby in that length of time and yet it was still showing its power.

The second sight was even more sobering and much more personal—the destruction of war. Up close and quite clear for all to see. The Bay of Naples waterfront had been bombed by both the Germans and the Allies, and the resulting twisted, burned, and half sunken ships were everywhere.

Upon debarkation on the 24th we were driven through the streets of this fine old city to a former orphanage. It is no longer fine or beautiful but a shelled out ruin of itself. Again I thought of my many hours spent with Mrs. Fine in Latin class and of beautiful Miss Swanson trying to get us into the humanities. They would be in tears if they saw this.

We know now, beyond any doubt, that we are at war and it is very close and very real.

We soon left Naples because the main fighting had moved northward through Italy, and our job is to follow the enemy, the Germans, and end this reign of terror. We think we will be engaged with their troops soon, but I will try to get another letter off to you before then.

Love to all of you. Hope you had a Merry Christmas and New Year and hope your world lies under a blanket of peaceful white snow. Ginny, make a snow angel for me. Remember how you and Lilly would cover a field with them? Some sort of contest I think. See, I can talk about her now and it doesn't hurt, well not nearly as much.

Take care. Dad, slow down!

Happy New Year. Say a midnight prayer that 1945 brings peace and healing to the world.

Love to you both,
Henry

Chapter 13

Before Henry's letter arrived in Grand Junction, he had a telegram from Ginny. It was delivered to him at their staging area south of Pisa.

<u>Western Union</u>

To: Pfc. Henry Townsend
01/01/45
10th Mountain Division, 86th Rgt APO 345

DAD DIED PEACEFULLY 12/28. HE DID NOT WANT YOU TO WORRY OR TRY TO COME HOME. NO TIME. WE ARE OKAY. MOM IS STRONGER THAN YOU THINK. WALT IS HERE. PRAYING YOU REMAIN SAFE. SENDING OUT LOVE. LETTER TO FOLLOW.

GINNY

After a few hours of processing this, Henry sent a quick response.

<u>Western Union</u>

Mrs. Irene Townsend
01/02/45
Townsend Farms
Grand Junction, Colorado
MESSAGE RECEIVED. UNDERSTOOD. ARE YOU OK? WE ARE IN **XXXXXXX**. THIS IS OUR STAGING AREA. NOT IN BATTLE. DO NOT WORRY. I   AM FINE. MY HEART IS SHATTERED. I WISH I COULD BE WITH YOU. LETTER FOLLOWING.
HENRY

January 5, 1945

Dear Mom,

My heart is breaking for you, for Ginny, and for me. How can we (you) go on? But we must. That is a hard lesson that I have learned from life. We must go on. We may hurt and cry and even scream a bit, but in the end all we can do is go on.

I know the community was there for you with hugs and tears and food. Some probably didn't know what to say. Some probably said too much, but they were there showing their love for Dad and you and Ginny. Please accept their help if you need it for I know it was offered many times over.

Now we must keep our memories of Dad alive. We must hold on to pictures, keepsakes, stories, and love. When we are all together again, we will repeat stories about him many times over. Occasionally one of us will tell a story, recalling something long forgotten, and it will be a new story for the others listening. Won't that be a wonderful gift from Dad? There will be times of great sorrow, but let's also have times of celebration for the man he was and the life he lived. I loved him dearly.

I am, and always will be, proud to be his son.

All my love is with you,

Henry

January 10, 1945

Dear Mom and Ginny,

I think of you constantly and wish I were there with you. I know that Walt has probably returned to duty by now, but I am so glad he was there for you. Ginny, please tell him that he is truly my brother.

Mom, if you have not done so, go see Mr. Griff. All the official business that Dad and I had together is in his law office. He will see to it that everything continues as before. Mom, he can help you make sure that my monthly checks come directly to you, in your name. Even the Red Cross in town might be able to help in this regard, or the Army recruiter. Let Mr. Griff be your guide.

Also, this may sound cold, but if you have not mailed a copy of the obituary, please do not do so. I don't think I can read it right now. I hope you understand.

Even though we are in a staging area, death has found us. In the form of a leftover reminder from our enemy. Our Chaplain, the one who brought me the telegram and counseled me after Dad's death, and several medics along with another soldier, have been killed. A soldier walking alongside the railroad track bordering the training area stepped on a 'bouncing Betty' mine, one that jumps up at you and explodes. This brought the Chaplain and medics rushing in to help him and they were also killed. We are devastated at the way it happened, but we have no time to stop and mourn.

All of our Regiments are now here, and plans are being made. What they are I don't know and certainly couldn't say if I did know. We are warned constantly about the enemy gaining intelligence from our correspondence. So, mum's the word from now on about our actions or even whereabouts.

I will stop for now. Take care of yourselves. Rely on others as needed, and know my love surrounds you as someday my arms will do again.

Hugs,

Henry

January 31, 1945

Dear Henry,

Mom wants me to tell you that she is taking care of everything that needs to be done. And she is too. It's amazing how much 'work' goes into the aftermath of a death, even a peaceful death such as Dad had. `

Yes, Henry, it was peaceful and Mom, Walt, and I were with him. We told him you were there in spirit. He smiled and said, 'Leave the boy alone. Don't distract him with tales of me.' So you see he was thinking about you right up to the very end. He was an amazing Dad wasn't he?

Mom is being amazing now. I think all this 'business' that comes with a person's death helps the loved ones left behind heal gently. Mom has no time for weeping and being a grieving widow all day. She has things that must be taken care of. I'm sure that when all this stuff that comes with death slows down, she will fall fully into her grieving, but not yet. She is being strong.

We understand about the muzzle on news. Just let us hear from you to know that you are safe. Long intervals without news will frighten us.

Walt has returned to duty but he sends his love. You know Mom and I do the same.

Hugs right back to you,
Ginny

Chapter 14

Somewhere in Italy
February 1945

Henry and his fellow soldiers were rushing ahead, rushing into battle. He felt it. He heard it. The earth shaking, the grenades popping, the artillery screaming, and the men shouting. Anguished shouts by anguished men. Was he shouting?

Yes, he was rushing ahead, shouting, not in anguish but in determination and anger. Suddenly he was not rushing. He was in the air as the ground exploded beneath him. Sometime later someone, more than one someone, grabbed his arms and legs and lifted him. This was the final pain needed to again render him unconscious, at least momentarily.

"No, not in the corner," someone said. Henry tried to think. Did he recognize that voice? "They might not spot him. Let's leave him out in plain sight. We want the medics to find him quickly."

No one else spoke but his limbs were again lifted and his consciousness again disappeared. Sometime later the stomping of heavy boots brought him back to awareness long enough to realize that he was lying on a stone floor unable to move. He could open his eyes just enough to see the boots stomping toward him.

"Schau, ein Amerikaner." " Look, an American."

"Kill him."

"No, no. We take him."

"But, the Americans are still out there, still firing."

"Sounds like they are getting closer. Let's go."

"What about him?"

"Ok, we leave him."

"He is a prisoner. We can't leave him alive."

"Don't be stupid. We kill him and leave him. It is the way."

"Yes."

The two German soldiers proceeded to take his boots, jacket, and gloves. They stripped away any insignia that could be ripped from his remaining clothing.

As one soldier pointed his rifle at Henry's head the other demanded, "Warte, warte," "Wait, wait."

Then bending down he grabbed Henry's dog tags and forcefully jerked them off his neck.

"Jetzt schießen." "Now Shoot."

The second German again pointed his rifle at Henry's head and fired.

Thus, Henry was rendered unconscious once again. This state kept him from knowing that again his limbs were seized by mighty hands that took his unconscious form into a nearby wooded area. This time the hands swung his body back and forth gaining momentum. When satisfied with the amount of force they had, they slung Henry's lifeless form down a ravine.

He felt nothing of the winter briars and brambles that grabbed at him. He did not feel the numerous tree stumps, made short and sharp by yesterday's bombing, that punctured his body. And he did not feel or hear the soft thud his head made as he hit a tree that stopped his descent just feet from the frozen stream below.

<u>Western Union</u>

hs   44   govt   wux   Washington D.C.
February 25, 1945
To: Mrs. Irene Townsend
Townsend Farms, Grand Junction, CO

WHILE ADVANCING ON GERMAN LINES MORNING OF FEB 19, PFC. HENRY TOWNSEND STRUCK BY ENEMY ARTILLERY IN HEAD AND CHEST. GRAVELY INJURED. UNCONSCIOUS BODY RECOVERED AND PLACED IN VACANT STRUCTURE TO BE RETRIEVED BY MEDICS. UPON ARRIVAL AT SAID LOCATION, MEDICS UNABLE TO LOCATE PFC. TOWNSEND. AFTER SEARCH, IT WAS DETERMINED PFC. TOWNSEND RETRIEVED BY OTHERS, IDENTITY UNKNOWN.

THE SEC. OF WAR DESIRES ME TO EXPRESS HIS DEEPEST REGRETS THAT PFC. TOWNSEND HAS BEEN LISTED AS WHEREABOUTS UNKNOWN/MISSING IN ACTION. IF FURTHER DETAILS OR INFORMATION IS FORTHCOMING, YOU WILL BE PROMPTLY NOTIFIED.
H.A. HOKE
ADJ. GEN.

Lilly

Chapter 15

The New Community
Somewhere in Colorado
1945

Lilly woke slowly. Knowing instinctively that it was still early, she didn't open her eyes. Still, something was nagging her into wakefulness. Slowly, she turned onto her right side and opened one eye just enough to peer through the early light at ever faithful wind up clock.

Her eyes popped open, her mind awake, her heart skipping. She saw not the clock, but the dress.

"Oh no," she groaned aloud, "My wedding day."

Sheer distress forced her to close her eyes again, turn back to the other side of the bed and try, try to go back to sleep and forget what surely she must do today. Or must she?

It had been over three years since she had last seen him, the man she loved. Three long, lonely, frustrating years. The fear, the flight, the forcefulness of that time often came back to her rocking her world once again, but today, she was about to rock it herself.

I have no choice she repeated to herself as she slowly walked through the new community or This Place as she thought of it. This abandoned mining town that was now her home. There was evidence that the original town did not last long, but it must have been prosperous for a while. Over the general store one could still read the faint words, Doc's General Store and Post Office. Est. 1885. On the walls inside were notes, drawings, and even a calendar for 1895. The elders assumed that the little town died about that time as did dozens of other mining towns in Colorado. Left behind were the long counters and the massive pot-bellied stove. Out back was a two-hole outhouse.

Walking toward the community church, putting off her wedding as long as possible, Lilly paused to look at the few buildings as if she had never seen them before. There was an assay office for filing claims by the original miners, a bank, and a jail. On this, her wedding day, they all seemed endlessly fascinating to Lilly.

Running in front of this 'business district' was a wooden sidewalk. Although when they had arrived it was in total disrepair. It lent credence to the thought that this must have been an upscale community with ladies present.

Out of some inbred feminine trait, Lilly held her long dress up to keep the skirt off the newly repaired sidewalk. When she realized what she was doing, she scoffed at herself, nevertheless, she held the skirt tightly in her hands.

As she walked past cabins, Lilly slowed her steps even more. She thought of each family living within those walls. She knew the families and she knew the cabins themselves. They were now her world. Again she slowed her steps as if seeking a refuge somewhere within those cabins. Some were very small and dark. Others were two-story, usually with the second floor still not looking safe, but offering promise of more room. Some were large and spread out. The largest even had a bay window extension, suggesting former affluence. Remnants of curtains, disintegrating with age, had originally hung from several windows.

When the community first arrived some of the cabins contained a book or two, some calendars, again with time standing still in 1895. There were bits of pottery and cookware found in a few of the cabins. Others were bare, giving no hint of a former life. Today, they held Lilly's family and friends. Today, however, they were empty again as the community was gathered in the church waiting for the bride.

Still, the bride, hesitated. As she approached Uncle Sado's house, she took a deep breath, and looked toward the sun wondering if she could spend just a few moments on this porch where she spent so much of her time. Sinking into Uncle Sado's chair, she wondered why the past was crashing in on her today.

She looked back past the business district and into the mountains, reliving all those early anguished days here. Slowly, she looked in the other direction, toward the church, and knew that everyone was waiting. Her mother did not like the idea that she insisted on dressing herself and walking to the church alone. Soon, Mama would send someone out to find her. Still, she lingered.

Thinking back to those first few weeks here, she remembered that the elders rather quickly had the community getting down to the business of living. They made sure everyone had a home, some in better condition than others, but all with a roof and doors and window openings if not actual windows.

After a few weeks, the women had their cabins looking and feeling as much like home as possible. This was made easier by the fact that most of the families, like Lilly's family, had brought everything with them. Lilly had soon seen the upholstered furniture which had not been sent out for upholstering at all. It had been sent to this place before their arrival.

A central storehouse had been quickly established in the old general store and post office. This was a large open building and would be used for many different events. The local Japanese American grocer from Junction was the logical selection for the storekeeper. The many extra supplies and any household goods that could not be used by any family, and even any relics found that were salvageable, were immediately taken to the store for free distribution to anyone who needed them.

Early on, Lilly recalled, a garden was started. The men and boys, and some of the women and girls, tilled the ground, preparing to plant crops.

The community shared a couple of horses and cows. They established a communal kitchen in what must have been the saloon. Most of their meals during those early weeks were taken together in the shared space

The elders, to the dismay of the younger generation, established a school using the old school house once again for its original purpose. Here, too, the massive pot-bellied stove remained. Most of the desks were broken beyond repair, but one, sitting off to the side, was in pristine condition, save for years of dust and bird or rodent droppings.

Lilly remembered that in the early days everyone had been kept busy. This helped get the community established and kept minds occupied with many daily tasks. An idle mind tended to wander back to Junction, or to the future. Both were unsafe topics in the beginning.

Slowly Lilly turned and again looked toward the far end of the main street where the church stood, and where her future waited.

A lofty bell tower sat front and center on the roof. The community never heard a bell toll from the tower because the clapper was missing. This suited them for they wanted nothing to declare their presence in the area. Inside, most of the pews and the small pulpit were intact. It had originally had glass windows, but most of them were broken by the time the Japanese American community arrived. Still, the church was serviceable and a welcome sight to most of the community.

This was the community Lilly awoke to on her wedding day. This was the community she knew she could not escape. This was the community she must support. Her heart was breaking, but she would marry Jock. He was a good man. He would not demand that she love him, just honor him and work with him to make life better. So, she rose and went to meet her fate.

Henry

Chapter 16

Tuscany, Italy
May 1945

Henry slowly awakened to a semi-state of awareness. He could hear birds singing lustily. He could smell flowers, food, and something antiseptic. It was not a strong smell, but without opening his eyes, his muddled brain decided that he must be in a hospital or an evac tent.

He took a deep breath and tried to open his eyes. He decided he didn't have the strength to do so, so he lay quietly listening and smelling this world.

"Wake up, my love. Wake up. I see your eyelids moving and your face muscles twitching, so go ahead and wake up," said the softest voice Henry had ever heard. He could feel her, hear her, and smell her. She was with him, calling to him, pleading with him, to wake up.

Suddenly a cool cloth was placed gently on his forehead. With a start he finally opened his eyes. There, just inches from his own were two of the biggest blue, or maybe green, eyes he had ever seen. And they were smiling at him.

The vision leaned forward and gently kissed him on the lips. "Ti amo," he heard just as he drifted back into his own world.

Sometime later, he again tried to awaken. Slowly he was able to focus his brain and open his eyes. His vision was fuzzy, his thoughts were foggy, but he kept trying to join the living world.

Again, the vision was there. Again she leaned forward and kissed him on the lips and whispered her 'Ti amo.'

Then, oh blessed relief, she pressed a cool, wet cloth to his lips. The moisture was like nectar to Henry. He pushed his tongue between his lips, trying to capture more of the nectar.

"Slowly, slowly," admonished the vision as she removed the cloth.

Henry felt his lips purse and open. He felt them become little bird lips as he silently begged for the wonderful liquid.

"One teaspoon," the vision said. "One teaspoon now and more next time you let me see your beautiful brown eyes." With that she placed a cool silver teaspoon against his lips and slowly, oh so slowly, let the moisture drip into Henry's mouth.

When she had finished, the bird lips reappeared and Henry knew he was begging. She laughed a lovely laugh and said, "That's enough for now. Go back to sleep."

With a sigh, Henry obeyed.

The next time Henry awakened it was late afternoon. He could feel soft sun-fed warmth on his body. Opening his eyes, he saw not the lovely angel, but another.

"Ah, there you are," said a kind, motherly face. "I have been waiting to meet you and welcome you to Villa Coppo. I am Isabella Coppo, but you must call me Zia. That is Italian for aunt, and that is what Daisy calls me."

When she said Daisy, Henry opened his eyes wider and looked around.

"Oh, you didn't know her name did you? She is Daisy, daughter of my dearest friend who was killed in the bombing. No, no, don't look upset. It was several years ago, in London, and Daisy has adjusted."

Henry, again, looked around the room.

Seeing this, Zia Isabella said, "She has gone to check on your dinner."

Henry's eyes lit up. The lovely lady laughed and continued.

"Not much, mind you, just two, really only two, teaspoons of broth. I told Daisy that anything would taste good to you, but she wants to make sure it is perfect. If your body tolerates this liquid as well as it did the water, you may have more, but we must progress slowly."

Daisy entered the room and rushed to his bedside, handing Zia the tray she was carrying. She bent low and whispered, "Ti amo."

As Zia Isabella left the room, Henry's eyes sought the bowl holding the liquid.

"It is only clear broth, but soon, I promise you will have the best food you ever ate. Soon, I promise."

The Henry bird appeared again and with a big smile on her face, Daisy slowly dripped the broth into the bird's mouth. When she finished and set the tray aside, she leaned forward and again kissed Henry on the lips.

She could taste the broth, but what she really tasted was her love for this unknown man who had landed in her life.

"Ti amo," she said softly to the man quickly falling asleep. "Ti amo, mi amore."

Chapter 17

Life at Villa Coppo progressed in this fashion for several days, days that passed in long periods of sleep and soft wakefulness and various temptations upon his lips.

Finally, Henry found his voice strong enough to carry on a conversation. It was again late afternoon and he was awaiting what his vision said would be a wonderful dinner. His body and mind, and finally his voice seemed to be healing.

The vision was holding his hand and explaining that the flowers filling the room were from the people of the village. "You are a hero," she said.

"Why?" croaked Henry.

"We found your dog tags yesterday and the news spread like wildfire. It seems you are American. I always suspected that. You don't look Aussie or South American and I think that somehow I would have known if you were a Brit like me. Yes, you are an American and the Americans who came through here last liberated the many small towns and villages as they chased the German troops north through the Apennines and around Lake Gardo and finally out of Italy. The villagers see you as one of those who saved them and defeated the enemy. So, you are a hero."

Henry shook his head as if trying to comprehend. "How far away are the troops? And the Germans?"

"Henry," she said softly, then paused and looked at him. "That is your name, do you remember it? You never said it."

"You never asked. I never thought about it, but yes, I am Henry Townsend. Have I had amnesia?"

"No, you were just unconscious, but many things have happened while you were recovering in that state."

She leaned in and kissed him, and whispered, "Henry, the war is over. Your troops helped put an end to Hitler and his madness."

Henry was astounded. "No," he said, forcing strength into his voice. "How can that be? How long have I been here? Where are the troops? Surely, I didn't sleep through the rest of the war. That is absurd. Shame on me." He looked directly into those big eyes and demanded, "Daisy, how long have I been here?

"Oh, Henry, don't get agitated," Daisy said softly. "You were not unconscious for too long, only about ten weeks."

Before she could continue with her thought, Henry tried to raise himself on his elbows, slumped back down and said with despair. "Ten weeks? Over two months? That is inexcusable."

"Okay, stay calm and while we wait for Esther to prepare your dinner, I will try to fill you in on the events since you were wounded. But you have to be calm and stay quiet."

"Who's Esther?" he asked, seizing on anything but the disturbing facts he was hearing.

"Later," said Daisy in answer to his question. "Later, you will meet Esther and become her dear friend, I know. But that is for later. I think you need to know what has happened to you and around you since you were wounded. At least what I know of it."

Henry just nodded his agreement.

"But first," said Daisy as if a thought had just occurred to her, "tell me what you last remember."

Henry took a deep breath, looked over toward his cup of water and raised his eyebrows in question.

"Okay, water first. Still not too much," she said holding the cup to his lips. He lifted his hands, softly surrounding her hands, thus capturing the water. When finally a large sigh escaped his lips, he began.

"It was late in January, I think. It was cold and misty, sort of miserable. Too cold, even for me," he said shivering at the memory.

"Our mission was a routine one, one we had trained for many times; a combat reconnaissance patrol. We were to determine if the Germans were still using an Observation Post that had previously been seen on Mt... Mt. La Serra. If they were, we were, of course, to destroy it. If the Observation Post was no longer being used, we were to return by a different route, through someplace…, something like Piano Camp."

Daisy laughed and said "You must mean Campetti-Pianosinatico."

"Isn't that what I said," asked Henry with a wry smile.

"Ah, a sense of humor. Another reason to love you."

Henry just raised an eyebrow and shook his head.

"Why were you going to Piano Camp?" Daisy asked with a smile.

"We were trying to locate the enemy's forward movements. To see where he was at that time. To do so, we climbed a couple of mountains for better vantage points. We found an empty Observation Post, but it was so well provisioned that we knew the Germans must be in the area. We waited around for a while, no one returned, so we headed toward Piano.

We went through a little place called Quercia and kept going. It was tough going. Some of the snow was very soft and a person could sink in up to his waist and like I said, it was foggy and wet; the sort of the day to stay in by the fire. As we neared Piano we encountered the enemy and exchanged fire. Hand grenades, carbines, and submachine gun fire was soon flying in both directions." Henry paused and took another deep breath.

Daisy jumped in with a question that seemed important to her. "Is this when you were wounded? You were found a good piece from Quercia or Campetti-Pianosinatico."

"No, not then. I'm just working up to it, I guess."

"Okay. Then what, love?"

He smiled at her endearment but said nothing about it and went on with his memory.

"We were soon relieved and sent back to rest and train again near Lucca. Do you know Lucca?" he asked Daisy.

"Everyone knows Lucca. It is full of history and art and of course, it has its famous wall around the town. Did you see it?"

"I did, but I couldn't be the tourist I would have liked to be. Maybe another time, another year."

Daisy smiled at him, gave him a small sip of water and waited for him to continue.

"Well, as you can expect, we now knew for certain that we were among the enemy. There was a somewhat grim suspense in the air. It was from Lucca that I wrote my last letter home." Henry stopped with a quick jerk of his head. "Home," he repeated. "Do they know what has happened to me? Do they know where I am?"

"We haven't told them anything, Henry. It was only yesterday that we learned your identity. We will be in touch with them and with the American authorities very soon, I promise. As for your army, I don't know what they might have told your family. When we write, who will we be writing to? A wife? Parents? Siblings?" she asked looking him directly in the eyes.

Henry gave her a big grin. "You are a sly one," he laughed. "Maybe you should have been an Army interrogator."

Then the reality returned and he said quietly. "My poor Mother. We just lost Dad. I know she and Ginny are worried to death."

When he did not continue, Daisy asked quietly, "Ginny?"

Grimly nodding his head he replied. "My poor Ginny. She has had to shoulder so much since I've been gone. When Dad died in December, so much was dumped on her beautiful young shoulders. I am thankful that she was there for Mom. If I had them with me, I would let you read her letters. You would learn to love her."

"I doubt it," came a muffled reply.

Henry reached up and cupped Daisy's chin in his hand. "Daisy," he said, "Ginny is the most wonderful sister in the world. Except when she is being a brat."

Daisy let out an undignified whoop, swooped down on him, and gave him one of her trademark kisses.

"Someday," he said, "you are going to have to tell me where you learned to deliver so much in a kiss."

"When we are old and gray," replied Daisy with satisfaction. "Yes, rest assured, we will get in touch with your family immediately. Now, can you continue telling me how you were wounded?"

After another deep breath and a moment of trying to organize his thought, Henry continued. "After a short while regrouping at Lucca, we were ordered into an official combat operation, not just reconnaissance as the last had been. We knew we were about to be tested by fire because the enemy had held on to Italy too long to go away without a fierce fight."

Shaking his head, Henry exhaled softly. "At last the order came. We were to attack and secure Riva Ridge leading to an attack on the Mt. Belvedere-Mt. della Torraccia Ridge. The men knew this was an important objective. We knew that this area must be secured for the Allies to move forward. As it turned out, our Division was on the front of this attack."

Looking at Daisy, he said, "You can imagine what that means."

"Yes," she replied. "I know full well what that means and I know Belvedere and della Torraccia Ridge. They are formidable mountains, but you did it, Henry. That is part of the reason you and your mates are heroes."

Henry just shook his head and continued. "We left Lucca and hiked the miles, about 15, I think, to the five villages at the base of the mountains eastern slope. Our objective was Belvedere, but we knew we would have to secure the entire ridgeline flanking it. This ridgeline had already been secured once, by the enemy, and it was still in their hands. We knew there would be fierce fighting. The fiercest we had seen to date."

Looking closely at Daisy, Henry continued. "Belvedere was important because one could see forever from the top. It offered the Germans who now held it a magnificent observation point. From it they could see every move we made and also that of the Brazilian forces, our Allies in the area. They were not going to give up without the fight of their lives, and as long as they held the ridge, the movements of the Allied troops would be known to them. The Germans probably knew where we were much better than I did. We moved when told to move, marched long night marches, and places were not always specifically identified."

Henry stopped and looked around. Daisy stood and walked across the room. When she returned she held a wine glass with a miniscule, in Henry's mind, amount of wine in it. "Sip," she said. "Do not gulp it down."

She sat again and Henry sipped just once and took up where he left off.

"We knew that other Allied attacks had been made on Belvedere and that Germany had fought like hell. Oops, sorry," he said smiling. "But we were prepared for this. This is what we had trained and suffered for, all those winter months in Colorado. This was our time."

He stopped speaking, gulped down the wine in spite of Daisy's warning, and spit out the words, "And I didn't even see it through. Me the mountain kid. Me, the skier. Me, the winter fanatic. I didn't even make it to the end."

At this point, Daisy did something she had never done before, but something she had wanted to do. She crawled up on the bed with him and held him in her arms.

Anguish, exhaustion, and wine combined to plunge Henry into a deep, long sleep.

Chapter 18

It was morning before Henry awoke. When he did Daisy was there with a portly gentlemen sitting beside her. Without embarrassment or hesitation, she leaned in and gave him one of her magical kisses and whispered "Ti amo."

"Buon giorno," said the portly face with a wide smile. "Welcome to Villa Coppo. I am Antonio Coppo, and I am pleased to have you with us."

Henry looked at Daisy who smiled at him then back to the smiling man. "Buon giorno," he replied. "I'm afraid that is about all the Italian I know, so I'm glad you speak English so well. Thank you."

"No problem, no problem," replied Antonio laughing. "We have a lot to talk about. Daisy shared your story, as far as she knew it, with us last night. I hope that is okay with you."

"Yes, of course," Henry replied.

"Bene, bene…, good, good. Do you think you can tell us more?"

"Yes, I think so. I need some water, first."

"You will have water and a light liquid breakfast and I will return in an hour if that is agreeable to you."

"With the little Daisy gives me to eat, 10 minutes will do. And I do tend to drift off to sleep after my visits with her." Henry said as he looked at Daisy with a smile.

"Si. Half an hour. I will return then. Now, I'll leave you in Daisy's care. She is a first rate nurse, I understand."

After Antonio left, Henry looked at Daisy and asked, "A nurse. A real nurse? Trained and everything?"

She laughed and began his quick morning bath. "Trained and everything," she replied.

Later, when Antonio returned, Daisy set the stage by moving closer to Henry and saying, "When you drifted off to sleep last night, you were upset that you were wounded on the Belvedere expedition. Please don't be upset, or we must stop. It is not good for you."

"I'm calm now. I've lived through other things that upset me when I first learned of them, but finally realized that when a thing is done, it is done. No amount of anger, or grief, or frustration can change a thing that has already happened. I know that our assault on Belvedere has happened, apparently been completed and is now history. What I don't know is the fate of my Division, the10th Mountain Division, trained specifically for Alpine warfare. Did our training pay off? Did we do our job?"

Antonio leaned forward in his chair and said, "Yes to both. They are heroes. You are a hero, but we will tell you that part of the story after we hear your personal account. I have been treating you. Don't look surprised. Did Daisy not tell you that I am a dottore? No? Shame on my Daisy. Yes, Henry, you have been in medical hands all around. Mine, Isabella's, she is a dottoressa, a female doctor, and of course, Esther and Daisy are both skilled nurses who have witnessed more than either ever should have. You landed in 'good company', as you Americans say. Now, can you continue?"

Without preamble Henry took up his story. "It was a Monday I think. about the middle of February, I believe. We grouped in preparation for the attack. It was awfully quiet. No talking. Maybe everyone was being reflective, thinking of home or love, or just surviving. Maybe some were praying. The moon had risen over Belvedere. Into the quiet the order came. Move out. It came not as a shout, not as a command, but as a whisper. We passed it around on whispered breath. We started moving forward. Again, the thought that we must surprise the Germans was paramount in our minds. The irony is that we entered that first battle with the enemy with our weapons unloaded."

Daisy broke her silence with a startled, "What?"

"We had been told not to fire until daylight." He smiled at her.

"An order would be given. The leaders wanted no one tripping and accidently firing or getting trigger happy before the time was right. No weapons would be loaded or fired until the order came. The going was tough. The tension great, but no one gave us away. I think we achieved our element of surprise.

"As the first day began, we were pumped up. As I remember the first cliffs were rugged, but we were ready. We progressed without any opposition from the enemy since they were not expecting us. Since that first day's movement was so easy, we felt that someone must be watching over us. Then came the next day. I'm not sure if this would be day two or day three. It is somewhere in the middle of February. I can't say exactly when. Do you know, sir?" Henry asked Antonio.

"I only know that the attacks on the cliffs and ridges leading to Belvedere, and on Belvedere itself, took place from February 17th through 24th, or in that range somewhere. We will find out for you."

"Well, during that time is when I was wounded." Henry said with a sigh.

"Do you actually remember that event?" asked Antonio. "That is what I really need to hear about, if you can."

"I remember, as if in a dream, so maybe it is a dream, sometime during the second or third day running toward the enemy. I could feel the energy generated by the battle. I could hear it, the artillery screeching, the bombs exploding, and the men shouting. The earth was shaking. I was rushing ahead, gun extended, shouting. Shells, bullets, screams, such noise after the quiet. All hell was breaking loose around me.

"Suddenly, I was thrown in the air as the ground exploded

beneath me. I remember nothing for a while. How long, I don't know. Then I remembered that General Hays had once said 'you must continue to move forward. Never stop. If your buddy is wounded, don't stop to help him. Continue to move forward, always forward.' So I tried to move forward, but I couldn't move in any direction.

"I think I fainted again. I believe it was later that someone, more than one person, grabbed my arms and legs and lifted me. I don't know how far they took me. Probably only a short distance for they were supposed to be moving forward and it must have been obvious that I wasn't."

Henry recounted hearing the voice of a fellow soldier. "Finally I heard a familiar voice, at least I think it was a familiar voice, saying to someone else, 'No, not in the corner. They might not spot him. Let's leave him out in plain sight so the medics can find him quickly.'"

Henry paused and looked at Daisy. "I think that was Johnny K, a flatlander from Florida. Oh, I hope he didn't bite it there in the cold and snow."

No one spoke for a moment. Antonio stood and walked across the room, returning with another miniscule glass of wine.

"For medicinal purposes," he said.

Henry took a couple of sips, smiled at him and returned the glass to the kindly dottore. Then he continued. He told Daisy and the dottore about the German soldiers and their treatment of him. He ended with, "And then they shot me. I think. I knew nothing until a few days ago when I woke to find Daisy sitting with me. Daisy told me that I was unconscious for ten weeks. Please tell me that isn't correct. That is inexcusable."

"That is correct and not only is it excusable, it was medically the best thing for you. I certainly did not try to force you to wake up until your own brain was ready."

Looking at Daisy, Henry tried to smile and said, "If you say so, dottore. That's it, all I remember. At least at the moment. Sorry." He reached for the wine glass and drained the remaining small amount.

Antonio rose, extended his hand, and gingerly so as not to reinjure his patient, said, "That is enough, son. I am proud to be able to help you recover. Now, I must go for Isabella and I must travel into Florence tomorrow and let the authorities and your family know where you are and what has happened.

"Even though the fighting has ceased and your troops have moved on, I am sure the authorities will want you returned to them. Personally, I think we can better care for you here. I will ask of your authorities whatever you wish. Do you know where you want to spend the next few weeks of your recuperative period? I will try to arrange whatever you want. Do you know what that is? Do you wish to remain here, or do you want to be transported, if possible, to an American hospital?"

Henry looked at Daisy, then looked around the room which was beginning to feel safe, like home, and then turned to Antonio. "Sir. I would like to complete my recovery here, if that is possible. Can you do what is needed for me? Am I a nuisance? Do you want me to go somewhere else?"

"I want you to do whatever your heart and mind desires and needs for a complete recovery. Frankly, I believe that can be accomplished here at our ambulatory and in our home. So, bene, I will ask permission to continue caring for you. Again, son, it is an honor to know you."

"Thank you, Sir," Henry replied quietly.

As the dottore left the room, he turned to Henry. "I will return after lunch, and then I will tell you what I know of the war effort and of your division. I should know more tomorrow evening when I return. You rest now, sleep a while, have your lunch, and then we will talk again."

Henry followed his dottore's orders and was feeling more alive than he had in a long time by the time of the dottore's returned. What Henry soon heard thrilled him, disturbed him, and made him proud to be a member of the 10th Division family. His tears were often near the surface. His pride in his fellow warriors always shinning in his eyes.

The dottore explained that fighting had continued on Riva Ridge and Belvedere until February 25. He said the inhabitants of the valley were aware of the Allies moving from Riva about the 20th of the month. The fighting then picked up on the neighboring ridges of Mt. Belvedere. He said the local population watched from below as attacks and counterattacks waged on the mountainside and ridges above them. Finally, it was clear to all that the Germans were fleeing.

"It is during this period, Henry, that you were wounded and unconscious. I have heard that the Germans did not allow the Allies to safely gather their dead and wounded. If they had, perhaps you would have been found earlier, or perhaps not. You were, in my opinion, discarded and left for dead by those Germans whose conversation you overheard. They thought they had killed one more American soldier."

Henry squirmed uncomfortably.

"We'll get back to that in a minute, but let me tell you what I know of your fellow soldiers."

"Yes, please, do. I don't suppose you were able to meet any of them?"

"No, we were at our secondary farm, further away from the villages along the foot of the two mountains. So, no, we actually saw no one until Nonno Luciano, Grandfather Luciano, as you would say, and I found you." When Antonio saw the look of disappointment that covered Henry's face, he added quickly, "But many of the locals in that area had the chance to meet your troops, share meals with them, and treat them as the heroes they, you, are before the men had to move on."

"Please, do not count me in that honored number," Henry said bitterly.

"Oh, I always will," Antonio replied smiling warmly.

Dismissing Antonio's answer, Henry said, "So they took both Riva and Belvedere. Were there many casualties?"

"Quite a few, I'm afraid. I do not know numbers, but the locals were humbled by the gallant effort your troops made. Of course, this was not the first fighting in the area. The German troops and a few of the left-over Italian Fascists, I spit on them, had been fighting across this area for months, and they had repelled all Allied advances. They thought Italy was theirs."

Antonio's 'I spit on them' brought a look of amusement to both Daisy and Henry's faces. It was just the right touch to keep Henry from sinking into despair.

Antonio continued, "I think the mountains were finally acknowledged to be in Allied hands and the enemy retreated quickly by the 26th of February. That is around the time we found you." Seeing Henry nod with a small look of satisfaction, Antonio expanded on his last thought. "From what I hear, your guys chased those fleeing Nazi's all the way to Lake Garda, and then out of Italy! Finally out of Italy," he finished closing his eyes and crossing himself reverently.

Henry closed his eyes and said quietly. "I think I'll rest awhile. Thank you Antonio."

Daisy leaned over, kissed the silent Henry and whispered, "Ti amo, cara."

Henry only nodded slightly in response.

Chapter 19

What Antonio couldn't tell Henry, because he didn't know the details, was that late in the day of February 21, after an all-day assault, four battalions of the Brazilian Expeditionary Force, a strong and faithful Ally serving alongside the 10th Division, captured Mt. Castello. This helped secure the 10th's right flank. Counterattacks, featuring heavy shelling, ensued and again the 10th and the Brazilian forces sustained many casualties. But the successful conclusion of the mission was in sight. By the end of the day on February 25th, the battles for control of Mt. Belvedere-Mt. della Torraccia Ridge was accomplished.

That evening, after a somewhat larger meal of soup, not just broth this time, a soft roll, and a slightly larger glass of wine, Henry had questions for Daisy.

"Antonio and Isabella are going to Florence tomorrow?"

"Yes."

"How far are we from Florence and does Antonio think the authorities will let me remain in his care?" Henry did not say, 'with you,' but surprising even himself, that is what he wanted to say.

"We are about 65 kilometers from Florence."

"Don't make me do the conversion. Miles, please."

"Roughly 40 miles," she smiled at him. "Not too far. There and back in one day, now that the war is over. I think we will still need passes, but the dottore has always had one."

"Tell me about that. When did the war end? I feel like I must be the only person on earth who doesn't know that. It makes me feel foolish and somewhat useless."

"You are not foolish, nor useless. Henry, you have been unconscious, which Dottore Antonio says is a good thing because it let your brain and your body heal. He did not rush to wake you."

"I know, but I'm not sure I like that," he said somewhat sullenly.

"Be quiet, cara. You won the war."

"Not me."

"Yes, you and every other Allied warrior, including all your families and loved ones. Now, let's talk about your family. I have decided that I need to go to Florence with Zia Isabella and Dottore and see if I can get a call across to your mum. Don't you think she is worried out of her mind?"

"I know she is, but can calls go through? The war must have been over a long time if lines are up and transatlantic calls can be made. I am so confused about everything."

"Okay. Let's take one thing at a time. Your family. If you give me a number, I will move the heavens to try and reach them. If you don't remember a number, I can get her address from your dog tags. If I cannot get a call through, I will send a telegram. I know the Army will send one, but I want them to know from someone who has seen you that you are healing."

"Yes. They need that. Thank you. Tell them I am alright."

"I will tell them as much as possible in our short time. Then I will promise to write to them and I will give them an address where they can write to you. Will that work?"

"Yes. Yes," he remarked smiling at her.

"Finally, just in case your mum and sis think I am playing a cruel hoax, I guess you need to give me a word that would be a signal to let them know I have seen you and am speaking on your behalf. If they question me, what can I say?"

"Wow, Daisy. You think of everything. They will believe you because they want to believe you, but just in case tell them I want to know if someone is exercising Steki.

"Who or what is Steki?"

"My faithful horse, and she does need exercise."

"Good," she said, "Now back to your concern for your unit. As Dottore said, your mates, and others too, can't let you guys have all the credit, chased the Germans North to Lake Gardo. There the Germans surrendered. Dottore learned that they would only surrender to your General or someone from your division, because they said the 10ᵗʰ Division was full of mighty warriors."

"That's true," said Henry, "except for me."

"Henry, you said you could accept things that you cannot change. So accept this. You were severely wounded, almost mortally. You suffered from battle wounds and from a direct gunshot to the head. That you lived is a miracle from God. Think of those who did not live but who were on that mountain with you. Yes, there were many. Does their death make them less of a hero? No, I thought not. Neither do your wounds. Now, stop belittling yourself and listen quietly. There is more."

She looked him directly in the eyes and said, "Your president is dead."

A startled Henry looked at her. "What? President Roosevelt is dead? How? When? Was he murdered by some sniveling coward?"

"No, sweetheart. He was sitting quietly, posing for a portrait I believe, and he died of natural causes. I believe it was a cerebral hemorrhage. They are nasty things. Nothing could be done for him."

"Oh, my," said Henry softly. He was quiet for a moment as was Daisy. Finally he said, "So that makes, who, ah…, Harry Truman our president."

"Yes, I think that is who Dottore said."

"This is all too much to understand. I feel like Rip Van Winkle."

"Who?"

Shaking his head Henry replied. "Never mind. He wasn't real. I take it this is all real."

"Very real, but there is one more thing."

"I don't know if I want to hear it," Henry replied.

"Yes, I think you might. Hitler is dead. He killed himself."

Henry let out a breath but said nothing for a moment. Then he looked at Daisy and asked, "What about the Emperor of Japan?"

"Ah, Japan," Daisy sighed. "Japan still fights. The war is over in Europe, but not in Japan. It should end soon. Everyone is expecting them to surrender, but they have not done so yet."

Daisy and Henry were quiet for a long time. She saw that he was processing all this new information, and she did not interrupt his thoughts. A little while later Esther arrived providing just the distraction that Henry needed. She walked in carrying a tray, beautifully set for two. She set it on a nearby table and walked over to Henry.

"Buona sera, Henry. Good evening, sir. Your dinner is almost ready, cooked I hope to your liking. Ah, I see that your lovely mate is with you. Would you care for some wine?" she said with a big smile on her beautiful face and a wicked twinkle in her eye.

"Please, I would love some wine if it is more than a thimble full. I don't know about my 'mate'. Is she old enough to drink wine?"

"Ah, foreigners," sighed the lovely Italian. "In Italy, one is never too young for wine, but if you like I can water hers down with acqua. Shall I?"

"Not bloody likely, Esterina. Now pour, more than a thimble full, but not too much and pour some for yourself and then join us and let my best friend and my amore get to know each other."

Soon they were all sipping the house wine and talking like old friends. Henry learned that the wine was actually made right there at

Villa Coppo. He learned that Esther, that is Esterina, and Daisy had been friends since they were infants. Their mothers were best friends, having gone through medical school together in England. They both became doctors, married fellow medical students who went on to become well respected doctors. Upon completion of her medical training, Isabella and Antonio left England to take their medical skills back home to Italy while Daisy's parents remained near London. The two doctors and their husbands formed a foursome that loved and supported each other through the years.

As the two younger girls grew up, they spent half of each summer in each other's country. Thus they were both fluent in English and Italian and both felt right at home in the other's country. When Germany began the intense bombing of England, Daisy's mother tried to send her away, but she would not leave her parents who were going to stay and care for the victims of the bombing. One night, late in 1941, they were trapped in the rubble of a school where they had taken shelter as the German planes made a pass over London dropping their first load of bombs. Shortly afterward a second raid rained down more of the destructive missiles and both of Daisy's parents were killed.

Alone, in shock, and devastated, Daisy called Isabella and Esther. "No," she told them through her tears, "I just needed to hear your voices. Don't come. It is too dangerous." Four days later, Dottore Antonio was there taking charge. Daisy was in no mood to argue with him, so she let him rescue her from the fate that still awaited so many of her fellow Londoners.

They took Daisy's parents back to their hometown of Godalming, only 35 miles west of London, for burial. The familiar small streets and quaint buildings of her hometown embraced Daisy as nothing in London could.

Daisy knew, however, that for a short time at least, she needed family and the Coppos were the only family she had left, so she went to Villa Coppo to grieve for her family. Isabella and Antonio held a small ceremony celebrating the lives of their dear friends and mourning their loss. Isabella had a colorful flower garden planted and a lovely memorial table placed in the new garden in their memory. Daisy was told that Villa Coppo was her home.

"It's what your Mum would want. She did, after all, make me your godmother, so I am making this decision for you. You will stay here. You will grieve and begin to heal. You will work with the three of us as we take care of the wounded in our country. You will know that your parents loved you beyond measure as do we."

"I have often felt guilty," Daisy told Henry, "for not being in England to nurse the wounded, but soon there were more wounded here than we could care for, so I wasn't wasting my talent. Then you came, and now I know why I was meant to be here."

"Okay, getting pretty deep mates," interrupted Esther in her best English accent. The combination of her lovely Italian and exaggerated English made Henry laugh. Laughing felt good he realized.

Shortly thereafter, Esther served dinner, refusing to join them because, as she said, "I will have Henry to myself all day tomorrow while you take care of things in Florence, Daisy."

She bent over Henry and whispered, "Sleep well, Henry. Tomorrow we begin your physical therapy. My specialty, you know. Trust me, you will need your strength." She kissed him on both cheeks, said a cheery "Buona Notte," and left them alone.

Chapter 20

Henry slept late the following morning awaking, for the first time, to an empty room. It gave him an uneasy feeling. He had to admit to himself that Daisy had become important to his outlook each day. He reminded himself that she and the dottore and dottoressa would be back later that afternoon, or early evening at the latest.

Relaxing, he raised himself slightly, adjusted his pillows, and looked around carefully inspecting his surroundings for the first time. The room was some type of clinic room. His was the only bed occupied but there were two others flush against the window wall. As he looked toward the open double doors he could see a short hallway with several rooms opening onto it. His bed was across the room from a large double window and through it he could see the greenery of trees. It was through this window that he always heard the singing of birds. They never slept, those birds. The walls of the room were of stone, weathered with time, while the floor was a different stone.

There were the usual medical supplies over in the far corner, and as always, a slightly antiseptic smell. He didn't remember ever seeing anyone cleaning the room, but it was always clean. *Too much sleep*, he thought. *I've had too much sleep. No more.*

Through the large wooden doors, Esther looking fresh and full of energy, entered the room with a tray containing his breakfast.

"Ah, buon giorno, Henry," she said in her lovely Italian voice while placing his breakfast tray by his side, "I see you are awake and waiting for me. That is good. We must get busy."

"Buon giorno, Esterina. I am awake, but not too bright and bushy just yet."

"'Tis okay. You will be ready to work soon. Have you tried our espresso yet? No? Well, you are in for a treat. Here, have a cup," she said handing him a miniscule cup not even full of coffee.

Henry looked at her questioningly. "This is all I get? After months of coffee deprivation, this is all I get? I've never seen a cup this small."

"Ah, Henry. Just drink it. All at once. It will wake you up completely. Then you can have this lovely cup of caffé con latte, coffee with cream. So, drink."

"Okay, here goes nothing, literally," groused Henry good-naturedly. With that, he made a big show of throwing his head back and downing the small cup of strong hot espresso. Immediately he was coughing and sputtering and tears were seeping from his eyes.

Esther laughed, pointed to the small cup of water on the tray and said, "Drink some acqua."

He did so, and tried to accuse her of scalding him and giving him coffee that was strong and bitter, but she was laughing too hard to pay serious attention to his complaints.

"You will get used to it," she finally said. "You must adopt some Italian ways while you are here. So start with espresso and caffé con latte."

She handed him a larger cup of latte. He blew on it, smelled it, and gingerly took a small swallow. It was perfection. "Heavenly," he said smiling up at her.

As she put a small plate of fruit and an oatmeal type hot cereal in front of him, she took the second cup of latte from the tray and sat beside him.

"Let's get to know each other better, shall we? If you are going to be important in Daisy's life, you will be important in mine."

"Will I? Be important in Daisy's life, that is."

"Oh, Henry, surely you know that you are already the most

important thing in her life."

"Well, I know she acts as if I am and she tells me daily that she loves me. She doesn't think I know what 'ti amo' means, but I do. Those were the first words I heard her say. At first I just thought it was her bedside manner, but she says them with such conviction that I think she means them.

"And she kisses me like no one else ever has. Not that many girls have ever kissed me," he added lamely, thinking, for the first time since he met Daisy of Lilly. He was surprised to find there was no hurt, no feeling of loss. Just a memory of another time. Daisy had done that for him, finally.

"She means them, Henry. She had weeks to study you and in some small way get to know you. She fell in love. You really are very important to her."

"She is important to me, too," he said to Esther. "I am surprised, but I mean it. I do not want to spend many days like today with no Daisy in it. She brightens my life as no one has for a very long time."

"Good, then no one should get hurt. Except she might hurt me if I don't get you started on your physical therapy so that you two can go dancing soon."

So saying, she removed the breakfast dishes and tray and began a morning of torture for Henry. They worked for a couple of exhausting hours.

Following the torturous session, that much to Henry's surprise actually made him feel better, he and Esther share a leisurely lunch, and then she ordered him to rest. To the surprise of neither of them, he fell asleep immediately.

By dinnertime Daisy, Zia Isa, and Dottore Antonio had not returned. Esther brought in a delicious smelling tray full of food.

Henry could see that his proportions were slowly being increased. This pleased him for his appetite was returning and the food was always new and delicious.

"Smells good," he said with familiarity to Esther.

"Tastes even better."

"Is that a larger glass of wine?" he asked with a wicked smile on his face.

"It is, because I understand that no one has offered you enough for a real toast. As your nurse and therapist, I am ordering a toasting portion of wine. You and I will celebrate the end of the war. My fellow Italians have downed many glasses of vino since the war ended. So, tonight, you and I will join them. We will have Vino for Victory as so many Italians have been doing."

She handed Henry a glass of vino rosso scelto di Montepulciano, a full rich red wine made from the local Sangiovese grape. This particular bottle came from their winery just outside Montepulciano. It was a spot dear to Esther's heart. She chose it for that reason and because she felt it was smooth enough to satisfy Henry's palate.

Raising her glass to his, she said simply, "Merci, Henry. Merci. And to your good health."

"Not yet" said Henry prompting her to halt her glass just as it reached her lips. "To good things that have come from the hell of war. To you and your family."

They smiled at each other and silently sipped for a moment. Finally Henry said, "Not complaining, mind you, for this is wonderful. It is like nothing I have ever tasted, but I thought Champagne was the drink of choice used for toasting."

"Ah, you Americans," she laughed. "Si, Champagne for the movie toasts, and for the Frenchy way. For heartfelt toasts here in Italy, go with the russo. At least, that is my philosophy."

"Well, who am I to argue," Henry replied, still sipping. "I never had wine until Daisy gave me a sip. Now, I think I'm becoming a real lover of the grape."

"You do not grow grapes in your Colorado?" she asked.

"Just backyard, personal harvest grapes," he replied. "We grow great fruit, so maybe grapes could be a viable crop."

"When you go home, I will send some seedlings with you. You must give them a try. Perhaps you can have vineyards and open a winery, named for me of course."

"Will do," said Henry still sipping.

The travelers returned around 9:00. Their trip took longer than expected because of the conditions of the roads and the many bridges that had not been repaired since the fighting stopped. Still, they were able to make the journey and it was fruitful.

First, Daisy reported, she had been able to talk with both Henry's mum and his sister. They cried, laughed, prayed, and thanked her many times over. A password was not needed. The news was exactly what they had prayed for, and they were not about to doubt it. Still, she asked about Steki and Ginny laughed and said to tell Henry that 'Ol Stek was not being neglected.

Henry was much relieved and calmed by the thought that Daisy had actually talked with them. "Did you tell them who you are?" asked Henry.

"Well, of course. I identified myself, told them I am a nurse, and told them about Zia Isa, Dottore Antonio, and Esther. I described what had happened to you and how we have treated you. They were amazed that you were comatose for weeks. But none of that mattered now because you are awake and sending them your love. That's what I said," she finished smiling broadly.

"Daisy, what would I do without you?" Henry asked.

"Don't worry, mi amore, you shall never know," she replied playfully.

"How about the authorities?" Henry asked dreading the answer.

"Ah, the authorities. That is another reason we are so late. There were many questions. Finally Dottore Antonio asked for a phone and placed a call to the Italian home office. The head of the agency identified Dottore Antonio and spoke of his ability 'above all others' to bring about a miracle for this soldier if anyone could. After several phone calls among their own agencies and after Dottore signed many documents, he was given permission for you to continue in his care.

"You are to sign certain documents, and as soon as the Dottore says you are well enough, you should report to them. They also said something about points. They said you might have enough points to muster out, or something like that. So you stay, amore mio."

She leaned in and kissed him, giving him her very best kiss. As she pulled away, he pulled her back. "One more," he whispered.

They talked long into the night. After she described the rough trip and the official visits, he told her about his day with Esther.

"She is a wonder," he said. "It was almost like talking to Ginny, and she introduced me to some marvelous red wine. We toasted...Vino for Victory, you know."

Laughing, Daisy rose to go. "That's our Esther," she said. When she reached the door she turned back to him. "Oh, by the by, I told your mum and sister that I love you and that I intend to marry you."

With that, she was gone.

Chapter 21

<u>Western Union</u>

hs   44   govt   wux   Washington D.C. May 1, 1945
To: Mrs. Irene Townsend
Townsend Farms, Grand Junction, CO

AM PLEASED TO INFORM YOU REPORT NOW RECEIVED STATES YOUR SON PFC. HENRY TOWNSEND LOCATED. WOUNDED. IN CARE OF LOCALS. WILL PROCEED TO INVESTIGATE AND WHEN FURTHER DETAILS OR OTHER INFORMATION RECEIVED YOU WILL BE PROMPTLY NOTIFIED.

May 1, 1945

Dear Son,

You know I can't sing, but today my heart sings; your delivery has done that for me.

I never once thought you would not come back to us. I repeated my silent prayers daily, 'send him home, send him home, please Dear God, send him home.' And I repeated my belief daily, 'he will come back to us, he will come back to us.'

Then early one morning a very British female voice brought the news. Oh, how I love the British and their wonderful voices. Your Daisy brought the news and I am overjoyed.

I have laughed and cried with tears of happiness since that joyous phone call. I have hugged everyone in town, even total strangers, and told them my son is coming home soon.

Take whatever time you need to heal. Do what is best for you, and then return to us. We will be waiting. You are, always have been, and always will be, my heart of hearts, my special angel.

Mom

P.S.: From Ginny: We are thrilled. You cannot know the joy we feel. Keeping letters short because Mom insists they be mailed airmail and that costs more. But the love is still large. Stay well. Loved talking to your Daisy. Must meet her.

P.P.S: From Walt: Get yourself well, and then come home buddy. We all miss you and will count the days.

Lilly

Chapter 22

The Community in Colorado
1945

It was Mid-August of 1945 when Lilly's world changed once again. The little community decided to send someone out, to the small community of Wayside, to see what was happening and to try and buy some needed supplies. The community was now three years old. The elders wanted to know what was going on in the outside world. Was it safe for them to return home?

Frank was chosen to go. He took the horse and traveled to Wayside. He was allowed to buy some supplies at the isolated general store they had passed on their way in. The older woman who helped him was not friendly and really did not want to sell to him, but a younger man told her to sell to the Jap if he had real American money. Frank showed them his money.

As he was leaving, the man taunted him with the information that America had bombed Japanese cities and killed thousands of "'Japs'".

"You'd better be careful, Jap," the man shouted at Frank. "You're next!"

When Frank returned with that news everyone was upset. The leaders of the community were more convinced than ever that they must remain, and that they had made the right decision three years ago. They all agreed that it would be a long time before they were safe. No one visited the outside world for several years after that.

Several days after Frank's return, Lilly looked at her husband across the breakfast table. She knew that he wanted more from her than she was giving him. She knew she should be giving more, but how could she. Even though all thoughts of flight had fled, she still felt anchored to her past life.

I must let go. For both of our sakes. For the sake of our world, I must let go. So finally, months into her marriage, she took the first step in building a new life. She reached across the table and took her husband's hand.

"Tonight," she said, "if you still want to, I think we should begin our life as man and wife."

Henry

Chapter 23

Villa Coppo, Italy
1945

Several weeks after the trip into Florence, a representative of the U.S. Army suddenly appeared at the villa. He came because American eyes needed to see Henry's condition as well as the condition of the facilities where he was receiving treatment. Although the Italian government, and therefore the American government, trusted the 'good doctor', the Army just needed a complete evaluation of the situation for the present circumstances and solution suggested were unusual.

Henry was surprised by the fact that he was glad to see the representative. He was in the therapy room, one set up recently by Esther so that his living quarters were not so cramped with her equipment. It was adjacent to the room in the ambulatory where Dottore Antonio had performed surgery on Henry. Henry was amazed that this annex the family called an 'ambulatory' was so well equipped.

"We are the only medical service for miles," Esther had explained when he told her of his astonishment.

Recently there had been talk of moving him to the family's living quarters in the villa as soon as possible but Henry was glad he was still in the ambulatory when the visitor arrived. Esther welcomed the visitor with ease and explained what therapy practices she had used with Henry. Then she outlined her upcoming sessions as she steadily increased his involvement. She continued with Henry's session as she talked to the visitor. She later told Henry that she did not stop what they were doing and leave until the session time was over because she thought that doing so would make the therapy session seem inconsequential. She did not want to devalue their importance to Henry's progress.

The visitor mentioned that Henry would be eligible for several medals. When Henry heard this, he was emphatic. "Absolutely not. No. I will not accept them."

"Perhaps they should send them to your Mum," said Nurse Daisy who had quietly slipped into the room.

"I would prefer that she never see them. If they must be sent, I must tell her that I never want to see them. Never!"

Henry and the visitor then had a long session with Dottore Antonio and Dottoresse Isabella. As they were carefully explaining Henry's wounds to yet another American official, Henry fell asleep. They explained to the official that sleep and only limited or supervised movements were essential to the complete healing of his wounds, both those of the body, those of the brain, and those of the soul.

The American left assuring everyone that he agreed with the doctors and their treatment. He said more forms would be coming for Henry and he, like his unit, would probably soon be on their way home.

Making his goodbyes and leaving assurances that Henry's treatment would not be interrupted by the American government, the representative prepared to leave. Antonio walked him out and was surprised when the man congratulated him on Henry's recovery saying he could see how badly wounded he had been. He also gave Antonio a summary of the 10th Mountain's actions in Italy. "Give them to PFC. Townsend when you think he is ready."

Henry's treatment took longer than anyone expected. He had suffered from multiple shrapnel wounds, several bullet wounds, broken bones all over his body, and, of course, the gunshot to the head. The gunshot, that should have been fatal, caused hemorrhaging of the brain and residual traumatic brain injury.

A few weeks after the official's visit, Henry was awakened from his mid-day nap by a loud commotion in the courtyard separating the villa and the ambulatory. There was much talking, all in Italian, some singing, and banging on anything to make a noise. Henry smelled food and heard laughter. Daisy and Esther arrived in his ambulatory room breathless and smiling broadly.

"Hurry Henry, we have a surprise for you," said Esther.

"What is all that racket?" Henry asked.

"Your surprise," answered Daisy. "Delivered to you, along with a festa celebration by the people of the village."

"What?" Henry asked thinking maybe he was still dreaming.

"Wait here," Esther said, rushing out.

"I'll try," responded Henry wryly for he never moved without his therapist or nurse supporting him. "I'll try."

With Daisy still beaming and looking like a proud mother, Esther rolled an ambulatory chair into the room. "Look." She exclaimed. "The Army has sent this for you and the villagers wanted to bring it to you personally. The entire village is outside. They have scoured the countryside and their store rooms and put together a festa, a party, to celebrate your recovery."

"What?" a very slow thinking Henry asked again. "Why does it matter to them that the Army has sent me a wheel chair?"

"Henry, don't forget. You are one of their heroes and this chair says to them that you are improving."

"You know how I feel about that 'hero' label."

"We know," responded Esther, "but Henry, they light candles for you and pray for you daily. They bring what food they can. Did you think Daisy and I had been preparing all those delicious soups and breads for you? And all that wonderfully soft homemade pasta? No, they bring you food whenever possible.

"Don't spoil this occasion for them. Let them celebrate your recovery with you. They will be celebrating you, your entire division, indeed the entire Allied Army and the victory they brought. The women want to give you kisses and the men want to have Vino for Victory glasses with you. Let them have this victory festa with you."

Knowing he was beaten, Henry gave a quick nod of assent. He motioned for the water pitcher from which he threw water on his face, and after straightening his clothing, smiled up at the two women.

"Okay, put me in my chariot, and let's get this party started."

The wheel chair promised more mobility and freedom for Henry. In fact, it made it possible for Henry to move from the ambulatory into the villa and become a member of the family. So, on the morning following the impromptu party celebrating the arrival of the chair, Isabella strolled across the courtyard to the ambulatory.

"I asked to be your guide for your great move," she told Henry. "I want to be sure that you understand that you have the full run of the downstairs. You'll have the upstairs at your disposal when you can manage that impossibly long stairway."

"Now, Zia, I don't want to be any trouble," Henry started.

"Hush, Henry. Our home is your home. You are to feel free to come and go anywhere on the property that you or you and a companion can manage," she said with a knowing smile.

"Thank you, Zia, but again, I don't want to be any more of an imposition than I am already. I will stay out of your way as much as possible."

"No, Henry. You're not listening to me. Stop protesting. You must move about, exercise, and build your physical strength. You must also adjust to being again in society. Now do you see why I am here for you? To countermand your stubborn streak and emphasize your need to use the entire villa, it's rooms, courtyards, and people to get yourself well. Do not be shy while here. Do not be stubborn. I want your promise."

Henry looked at her and laughed. "Scouts, honor," he said.

They were almost across the east side courtyard when Isabella finished her impassioned plea to Henry. For a moment they were quiet and Henry gazed around the yard and smiled. Comfy looking chairs beckoned to him. A large rectangular fountain, now empty and not spilling its water from shelf to shelf fronted one wall. Huge urns, the largest Henry had ever seen, chipped and in varying shades of ocher and sienna stood to each side of the motionless fountain. Smaller pots, some bursting with color, others obviously still struggling to regain life were scattered about. All were sitting on large irregularly cut stones held steady by rivers of grout. Floating about it all was a mixture of smells, some floral, and some like soft fruits just ripening. Henry inhaled and smiled.

Isabella saw Henry's gaze take it all in and heard his sigh and said lightly, "Someday it will all be whole and beautiful again. You must promise to return then."

"It is beautiful now, but I promise to return. I also promise to spend a lot of time out here for I find that I have missed the sunshine and being outdoors. Being housebound, even in your lovely ambulatory, does not suit me."

"Si. I could tell that about you, Henry. Even in your unconsciousness you had the look of an outdoorsman. Then when you woke, your eyes were constantly going to the window. Today, I want to give you part of your world back. I'm glad you like the courtyard, but now we are entering your new home through this side door for it has only a small bump as a threshold. You must feel free to come and go through here anytime you feel like it. Capisci?"

"Si, I capisci." Henry laughed. "It's a good thing Daisy is teaching me elementary Italian for I now understand it a little."

"Si, good thing." His guide laughed.

As they rolled into the wide hallway, the air cooled quickly and the stonework under the wheels of Henry's chair smoothed out completely. Several long stone tables sat in various spots along the two walls. There were few decorative items, but the hallway still felt welcoming, not austere in the least.

Isabella turned Henry's chair into the first room on the right. "The library," she said. Opposite the large doorway and across an open expanse of large patterned stone floor was a wall of tall windows, unobstructed by drapes. The morning sunlight flowed into the room giving a warm glow to the entire space. The courtyard they had just traversed beckoned from the other side of the windows.

Henry turned to his left. Before him, on the far end wall, a massive stone fireplace, with library shelves of dark wood hugging its sides, extended half way too the lofty ceiling far over his head. Above the shelves were shadows marking the spots where large decorative items had been removed. Henry considered asking the whereabouts of those missing pieces, but decided to wait until later.

"I will spend a lot of time in here. I can promise you that, Zia Isabella. It feels so inviting, and with the courtyard outside, who could ever leave it?"

"Bene, good. You love this library as we do, especially on rainy afternoons. Antonio hid most of his books early in the occupation, and he insisted they be recovered and returned to their rightful place on those shelves as soon as the Germans were pushed out. They are his treasures." she laughed. "Please enjoy them."

Soon they were back in the hallway. Isabella pointed out the salon, the informal but enormous dining room and the smaller, more intimate garden room at the back of the house.

"The kitchen," she explained "is on the far side of the garden room. It is a warm and inviting place. Please feel free to go there whenever you are hungry between meals. Cook will welcome you."

As they came back to the side door, Isabella pushed open a doorway directly opposite the library door.

"And here, Henry, are your quarters."

Henry was rolled into a large, light-filled room that housed not only an enormous comfortable looking bed but also a sitting area surrounded by another small library. Again, a massive fireplace filled part of a wall. Large oversized windows did little to fill the massive wall space opposite the doorway. The windows surrounded double doors that led to a private patio, completely furnished and waiting to offer solitude or private conversation space. Off the back wall of the room he could see two closed doors, presumably leading to a closet and dressing room.

Henry turned to Isabella. "Who gave up these quarters for me? I will not put anyone out of their rooms. I will go back to the ambulatory first."

"Calm down, Henry. No one gave up these quarters."

Henry interrupted her. "First floor, no stairs to climb, complete privacy most of the time, and beautifully furnished. These are Nonno Luciano's quarters, aren't they?"

"No, Henry. You are right that they would be perfect for Nonno. In fact, he has his own, an exact replica more or less, at the opposite end of this hallway. He chose that space many years ago because it looks toward his vineyard and is quite close to his beloved wine cellar and tasting room. No, Henry, you have put no one out. This area is one of the guest areas. Now, no more talk of going back to the ambulatory except for therapy and checkups. Capisci?" she asked again.

"Yes," he assured Isabella, he understood. He was grateful and would do all in his power to be deserving of the generosity and care they always extended to him. With a shake of her head and a smile on her face she recommended that he rest before lunch which would be served in the courtyard behind the library.

As the days rolled by, Henry worked hard and continued to improve. His upper body strength improved quickly and he was able to get around parts of the villa by himself. The floors were smooth enough that he could navigate the large living area known to the family as the salon, the dining room, and the library. He could get himself onto the side courtyard, but the front and back courtyards had steps and were still obstacles for him. Nevertheless, he loved the freedom the wheelchair gave him.

What he couldn't navigate for himself, Daisy did for him. They were able to be out on much of the villa grounds, to eat outside, and to simply enjoy being together. During those weeks he learned to love the villa, Italy, and Daisy.

One day, after a lovely picnic on the far edge of the back courtyard, he worked up his courage and began a topic of conversation that he had avoided for a few weeks. It was, however, a conversation that he knew he must have with Daisy if there was ever to be anything serious between them and to his great astonishment he wanted a serious commitment from Daisy.

He finished his lunch, pushed the plate aside and said, "We need to talk."

She leaned over, kissed him and said, "So talk, amore mio."

"I need to tell you about someone. Then you can tell me if there is someone you need to tell me about."

"Nope, no one," she responded smiling. "Only you in my

whole life. Only you."

"I like that, but it makes what I have to say harder."

"Henry, just say it. Nothing will change how I feel about you. Do you think I am so shallow or egotistical that I think you have looked at no other woman but me?"

"Her name was..., is, Lilly," Henry began.

"That's a lovely name"

"Daisy, please don't interrupt me. Just let me do this."

Daisy nodded and gave the universal sign of zipped lips. Henry wasn't sure she would be able to keep her lips zipped, but he began his story.

He left out nothing. He was honest about his feelings. He was honest about Lilly's feelings. As he described their history, he was shocked to find that there was no hurt, no lingering love, just pleasant memories of love and laughter and a lighter time in life.

When he finished they sat quietly, both lost in their own thoughts. Soon, Daisy surprised him by saying, "I like her."

"What?"

"I think Lilly and I would have been friends. I like the girl, the woman, you have described." She looked at him and added, "Never be afraid to speak of Lilly. If something reminds you of her and you want to tell me, then tell me. I am not jealous. I am grateful to her. I believe that we are the sum of our experiences. I am who and what I am today because of what life handed me in my past, and you are who and what you are today because of what life handed you in your past. That includes the people you knew and loved along the way. They were all preparing you for me. I owe them my thanks for helping you to grow into the loving and caring man you are today. I know that Lilly was a big part of that; I owe her."

"Daisy, my love, you never cease to amaze me."

"Henry, my love, I have loved you since you were brought in by

Dottore and Nonno Luciano, head wrapped in bandages with more bandages covering most of your body. You were unconscious but somehow through the mummy wrapping, you stole my heart the minute I saw you. I will never stop loving you."

And so, with no obstacles between them, they began their love affair in earnest. Knowing that their love had blossomed so quickly never gave them reason to doubt it. It felt so right, so safe, and so secure. It was natural to love and be loved by each other.

Later that night, as they lay together on Henry's bed in his downstairs room, Henry brought up something that Daisy had said in passing.

"Dais," he said using the diminutive form of her name that he was slowly adopting, "You said that Dottore and Nonno Luciano brought me in. Where did they find me? I don't think I've been told."

"You were in a deep ravine, apparently thrown, based upon your recollection, by those Germans. Nonno Luciano was in The Great War, the First World War. He thinks that the German soldiers initially intended to take you as a prisoner, but your state of unconsciousness and probably the ongoing battle nearby must have changed their minds. So they ditched you, literally. At the bottom of the ravine is a river. It was still frozen in late February. If your descent had not been slowed by grasping brambles and numerous tree snags, you probably would have landed on the ice, broken through and drown a horrible freezing death.

"When they found you and determined that you were still alive, they managed to get you back up the ravine and using Dottore's coat made a makeshift sling. Thus, they brought you home, to me. Dottore Antonio stayed with you around the clock for the first few days when they finally arrived back at the ambulatory with you. I stayed with him. He thought you were going to die. I knew you would not."

"I owe them my life," Henry whispered.

"We owe them our life together. I will always cherish them for this precious gift they have given me."

"Given us." Henry sighed, shifted his weight, and soon fell into a deep untroubled sleep.

Chapter 24

In mid-June Henry was able to leave the wheel chair behind and progress to crutches. At first he could only manage them on the flattest of surfaces, but soon he could range farther and wider afield. He and Daisy could picnic away from the villa, away from the eyes of anyone who cared to watch them. The feeling of freedom was exhilarating.

Soon he felt comfortable enough with his own mobility and with the immediate surrounding property to go out and about on his own. Thus it was that early one morning in late June, Henry sat alone on a cliff overlooking the greening fields below and watched the sunrise. In the distance he could see a lovely hill town glistening in the early morning sun, sitting wounded but proud on her hilltop.

Tucked away as Villa Coppo was, the damage here was minimal compared to much of Tuscany and the Val d'Orcia. Henry now knew that many villas and surrounding hill towns were destroyed. He learned that the destruction came from both the Axis and the Allies, but that the targeted cruelty came mainly from the Germans. Just how much damage had been inflicted upon Italy, and other European countries, was unimaginable for Henry.

So on this glorious morning, viewing the sky awash with the pinks and golds of sunrise, Henry found the courage to take the neatly folded paper from his pocket. It was information the official had left behind with Antonio for Henry's eyes when he was strong enough. Antonio had given it to Henry last week, but Henry had yet to read it even though it was always in his pocket.

Today, Henry would read it. Before opening it he said a silent prayer that his fellow soldiers of the 10th were all somewhere enjoying a beautiful sunrise. With trembling fingers he opened the short summary.

"The Riva Ridge Operation, 18-19 Feb 1945:
76 total casualties: 21 KIA, 52 WIA, 3 POW.

The Mt. Belvedere-Mt. Della Torraccia Operation, 19-25 Feb 1945: 923 total casualties: 192 KIA, 730 WIA, 1 POW"

Stunned, Henry stopped reading as tears streamed down his face. Facing that glorious sunrise, he reeled with the reality of war. *Slaughter, slaughter,* his mind kept repeating.

Then the celebrations of the local villagers intruded into his thoughts. Henry asked himself, *should they have been left to the hands of the enemy?*

"No," he said aloud. "That is unthinkable."

But why, oh why, was war the only answer. Why did so many men of his own and thousands of other divisions have to suffer and die to stop monsters from taking over the world?

He gazed straight ahead, but saw nothing. Not the pinks, and yellows, not the hills and valleys, he was numb with grief, and he knew that he had not read the entire list of casualties for it went on telling of the 10th Division's movements through March and April. *How many more?* He had the answer in his hand, but he could not look. Not now.

There was another major question looming. How many of those casualties were from his regiment? How many were lost, not lost like him, but truly and forever lost? How many?

No, I will not let them be lost. They will forever be with me. I will carry them in my heart and honor them for all my days. How many, dear God? How many? Not now, but someday, I will look. I must know.

With the help of his crutches, he pushed himself up, looked back out over that peaceful valley, then slumped back to the ground.

Shaking with sobs, he opened the crumpled paper and looked at the bottom line. He had to know.

10th Division: Total casualties in 3 months operations in Italy: 4,866. KIA 975, WIA 3,871, POW 21.

86th Regiment: 3,015 men who shipped over together. 1,770 replacements added. Total casualties: 1,380. KIA or DOW 246. WIA 1,128. POW 6.

Henry's reaction to the devastating news left behind by the visitor, slowed his progress. For days he could not concentrate on his therapy. He would not walk and look at the beauty around him. He wanted to know more. He wanted to know less. He wanted to reach out and learn about specific men in his unit. He wanted to reach out to each family touched by these losses. He could do nothing.

One morning after breakfast, he refused to do any therapy. Since reading the devastating numbers, he had worked at it only because Esther forced him. Today she could not cajole or guilt him into doing anything. She went to Daisy with the news. Daisy approached Henry and suggested they walk to a beautiful spot she enjoyed.

Henry looked at her with dead eyes and shook his head.

"Go away, Daisy. I will not walk with you to a beautiful spot. I will not enjoy today or any other day with you. Go away."

"Henry," she whispered. "You don't mean that. What's going on?"

Again those hard cold eyes bore into hers. "They died. I let them die. They cannot walk with you or anyone else to a beautiful spot. And neither will I. Go away."

"No, Henry."

"Go away, Daisy. I don't want to walk with you. Ever again. I can't."

"Henry, you don't mean that. You are just upset. It is a natural reaction to the news you've recently learned."

Henry turned and stood directly in front of Daisy. "I don't want to hurt you Dais, but I mean it. Go away. How can I carry on with life, a life with you, when their lives ended there on that mountain and mine did not? You don't understand how I feel. You can't understand. If you don't leave me alone, if you don't let someone else care for me, then I will leave Villa Coppo whether Antonio thinks I am ready or not. So just go!" By the time he finished his thoughts, he was almost shouting at her.

A visibly angry Daisy spat words at him. "So I don't know how you feel? The guilt you now carry? Is that what you're saying?"

"Yes. There is no way you could know."

"Did you forget I lost my parents, both of them? Do you think I haven't questioned why I was not killed along with them?"

"I'm sure you did for a while feel guilt, but Daisy, pardon me, I don't think this is the same thing. Your parents were older; they had lived a full and satisfying life if I understand correctly. The men with me were young. They were innocents slaughtered before they had a chance to live life, full and satisfying or not. You can't understand."

"You wretched creature," Daisy shouted at him. "Don't talk to me about loss. Don't tell me I don't understand. I've lost more than you know. I lost the other half of myself, and he was young, but still he was slaughtered and lost. Shot out of the sky over the sea. While I..," she seemed to choke on the words and the emotion, "I remained at home, untouched, alive to go on without him. Do you understand, I lost myself, my soul. My other half. Just two weeks before I lost my parents, I lost the man closest to me in the entire world."

Startled by her outburst and the story she was telling, Henry replied, "But, Daisy, you said there was no one before me. You said there had been no other loves."

Daisy looked at him in such a way that he knew she was lost to him.

"You, bastard. You insufferable bastard!"

She turned and quickly walked away. At the door to the villa, she turned and screamed at him, "He was my twin brother."

By noon the following day, Daisy was gone.

With Daisy's disappearance, complete inactivity seized him. Sleep eluded him. Without knowing it he went through the stages of mourning and of survivors guilt as he thought of Daisy and the men the 10th had lost. He asked himself again and again, *'Why didn't I die?' 'How did I manage to survive?' 'Could I have done something differently that might have made a difference.'*

At first, Esther did not offer therapy. She gave him time and space for several days. Then one morning after she completed her breakfast, she remained in the breakfast room and waited for him. She knew that he was eating very little because he was looking thin and gaunt. When he arrived she jumped up, grabbed a plate, and said, "Here, let me get you some breakfast."

Before Henry could retreat or reply, she was loading the plate with more than she knew he would eat, but still, she must try.

"Sit, Henry. We need to talk. No, I need to talk and you need to listen," she said as she placed the plate in front of him.

"She never told me," Henry interrupted. "She never told me. I said some awful things to her."

"Yes, you probably did, but I know you well enough to know that you would not have been intentionally cruel."

"But, I was. I wanted her to go away. I did not deserve the happiness she was offering me."

"Well, you succeeded nicely didn't you. You destroyed your happiness, and you destroyed Daisy's happiness."

"I didn't mean to. Well, I did mean to drive her away, but I didn't mean to upset or destroy her. I just wanted her to know that I could not live up to her expectations," he said softly as he looked near to tears.

"I know, Henry. I know."

"I love her. I thought we knew everything about each other. Why did she not tell me about her brother. Her twin brother, for God's sake. Aren't they supposed to have some extra bond between them? Why didn't she mention him? I don't even know his name."

"His name was Jeffery."

"Tell me about him."

"No, that is Daisy's story to tell. When, if, she is ever ready. Right now, I want us to get back on track with your therapy."

"No."

"What?"

"No. I won't. I can't. I know you mean well, but, please, Esther, leave me alone."

Finally, a few days later, Dottore Antonio and Nonno Luciano conspired to be alone with Henry on the smaller back courtyard which he could navigate with ease. This was a more intimate setting than the larger courtyards on the front and sides of the villa. An outside stairway led to a private apartment. Cascading down the steps were pots of brilliant red geraniums. Yellow roses supported by trellises clung to the side of the stairway. Large arched window doors ran along the back and the second side of the space. The sun was warm and the setting inviting. With chairs pulled up close on either side of him, and a bottle of vino russo set before them, the two older men started talking.

Dottore Antonio explained to Henry that he must make the effort to come back to his own healing process explaining that depriving himself of future gains in his recovery would help no one. He poured a round of vino for the three of them.

Nonno Luciano spoke of his days in the Great War, of the things he had seen and of the friends he had lost. "I could not understand how God made his decisions," he said. "Was I better than those men? Absolutely not! Never for a second, so why did God allow me to live and so many of them to die?" He paused to sip his wine.

Henry, hunched over with his elbows on his knees, and without looking up, asked, "Did you ever come up with a satisfactory answer?"

"Never," replied Nonno Luciano emphatically. "Never," he said more gently. "Now I know that I never will have a satisfactory answer, but I do now know that there was nothing I could have done to prevent those deaths and those lasting wounds. I was not to blame. Henry, as you are not to blame. You must, however, honor those men and their sacrifices by moving forward and savoring your own life. You have a life. They do not. Now live yours in their honor. Do not pile tragedy upon tragedy. Honor them by living.

"As for Daisy, we shall have to wait and see. We can only hope that she will heal and return to us."

The three men were quiet. More wine was consumed. The two older men saw the tears slowly slide down Henry's cheek, and honored the reason for those tears by saying nothing. After a while the two older men stood and returned without comment to the villa. They left the remainder of the bottle of their smoothest vintage for Henry and his sorrow.

Chapter 25

Dottore had said on that afternoon of bonding that Henry must live again, that he must let his life be full again, and that he must not sacrifice his future. To do so, he had emphasized, would be to belittle the sacrifice that all the fallen and the wounded had made. Henry had a future; many did not.

Slowly, Henry began to understand Dottore's words and slowly, as if he were an old man walking through molasses, Henry began to live again.

His journey was not made alone. Esther saw to that. As she took Daisy's place and nursed his now quickly healing body, she continued and increased his therapy. At the same time, she was always aware of his mental and emotional needs. She nursed those as well.

Weeks earlier, she and Daisy had persuaded him to exercise his brain by learning some Italian. He had smiled and said that he had studied Latin for two years in high school, so why did he need Italian. In her soft persuasive way, Daisy convinced him that his brain needed to be active and she assured him that she would make the lessons enjoyable.

Now, Esther wanted him to keep up those lessons. Henry was not interested. Esther was insistent. Finally, Henry relented. To help her in this, she had several vineyard owners come in and talk with him about the type of grapes he might try growing once he returned to Colorado. She had no idea if the possibility of growing grapes in western Colorado was feasible, but she knew the men and their enthusiasm for their craft would not only keep his mind occupied but would focus some of his attention on the future and his beloved homeland.

In this and in all things, she did not rush him, just as her father had not rushed his physical healing. She sensed when to push and when to back away. She knew when her chatter was welcome and when it was not. She dwelled upon the good and positive things and only went into the negative when he pushed her to do so.

She was glad that they were in Tuscany, the area she loved most in the world. While there was destruction throughout the region, there were also oasis of quiet beauty which the ravages of war and hatred had missed, and there seemed to be a communal spirit of healing which she hoped would be contagious.

Henry, despite the fact that this was the part of the world that had given him his wounds and cast him into his deepest despair, was also glad they were in Tuscany. Just as Esterina hoped, he soon felt that Tuscan spirit of healing all around him.

One of his favorite courtyards was perched just at the crest of a hill. It looked out over hills and valleys of quickly greening trees and of freshly sown wheat fields. Across the lush valley, one could see the local village sitting proudly on its hilltop. This was the village dottore and dottoress called home. Their farms and ambulatories were scattered far and wide throughout Tuscany and even into Reggio Emilia, but still they thought of Tuscany and especially the Val d'Orcia region as home.

Esther was proud of the Tuscan people. She told Henry that much of Tuscany and the Val d' Orcia had sustained damage. Sitting as it did between Rome and Florence, the Val d' Orcia and surrounding areas would have been known to the enemy The entire region was vulnerable from land and air. When their villages and homes were hit the townspeople grew philosophical. She proudly told him of their resolve.

"We are Italy," they said, "When bombs fall in one place, we all hurt. So we share the physical as well as the emotional pain of all of Italy." Now that the war was over, they were slowly trying to put their valleys, their villages, and their lives back together.

It was this spirit of survival that Henry began to feel; this spirit that the war had not destroyed. He came to think of it as the spirit of Tuscany, the spirit of Italy, and he came to love the people and the landscape that offered quiet support and strength. The sunrises still painted the sky with brilliant pinks. The sunsets still encouraged the people to grab a glass of vino and enjoy the evening colors over the vineyards and olive groves. The birds still filled the air with their full throated songs. The people still laughed, and hugged and kissed and loved. These were Italy's healing forces.

These were the healing forces that Henry slowly began to absorb, and without conscious decision he began to increase his therapy beyond Esther's expectations. He was soon encouraging her to give him more, let him do more. He was almost frenetic in his eagerness.

When Esther asked him about the change, his answer was simple. "She will return."

After dinner one evening in late June, one of the older Italian servants approached Henry and quietly whispered, "I just served a late dinner to a lovely, lonely young lady upstairs." She looked up at Henry with a sly smile and hurried back into the villa.

Henry, thanks to Esterina's encouragement and his own hard work over the past weeks, was now walking with only a cane. Upon hearing the news, he grabbed the cane and turned to run up the stairs. Suddenly, he halted in his tracks. *Would she welcome him? Should he barge right in and declare his love?* With the greatest of effort, he walked calmly to a nearby bench to think things through. He wanted no mistakes made when he approached her. He had to convince her of the regret he felt and of his love. *Go slowly,* his mind whispered. *Hurry,* his heart responded.

In the end, he went to his room and waited for the villa to settle down for the night. Finally, after several agonizing hours, he felt the time was right. He made his way up the staircase to the second floor. He went to her room and softly opened the door.

The brilliant moonlight outside was obscured by the heavy curtains on her windows, still he knew that she was in bed. Hating the thump that his cane made, he made his way to the bedside. Just as he arrived at her side a soft voice spoke to him.

"She's in the next room, Henry."

In the next room, Henry repeated his steps and upon reaching the bedside, slid to his knees. "I'm sorry, my love. I'm sorry."

When there was no reply, he bowed his head against the cool sheets on the mattress. "What I said was inexcusable. I never meant to hurt you. I didn't know. Please say you forgive me."

Finally, he felt her hand caress his cheek. For a long time, neither spoke. Then, he heard her softly say, "I'm sorry, Henry. I knew that you did not know about Jeffery, but my mind was reeling from your accusations, so I lashed out with words I regret. Forgive me."

Henry was afraid to move, afraid to break her touch. Instead, he took a chance and asked, "Can you tell me about him?"

Hours later, secure in each other's arms, they slept. She had shared every memory she had with him; the early years when they had no idea what twinship meant, but knew they had a bond and closeness that other siblings in their small town did not have, to the teenage years when she was awkward and he was gorgeous. Then when she found her wings and her self-confidence, he remained by her side as her protector. The arrival of war on their homeland was the only thing that ever separated them. She was proud of him; he was proud of her. While acknowledging the possibility of the unthinkable, neither believed it.

When the news arrived, her world turned black. She ran from the comfort her family and friends tried to extend to her and, alone, made her way to the English seaside. She walked for days, watching the endless stretch that was her brother's final home. One windy, rainy night, she finally acknowledged to herself that he was not going to come out of his cold, watery grave and join her. He was gone, and so was she. She left the coast the following morning and made her way back to London. A week later, she lost her parents.

"I was already dead," she said, "I had no more room for hurt." When she finished talking, Henry felt he knew Jeffery as well as he knew Walt. What he didn't, and couldn't, completely understand was the bond that bound them still.

That bond, she had said, would have made others speak often of their twin. She understood that; but that same bond forced her to never speak of Jeffery. She wanted no one to know him and love him, and miss him as completely as she did. Talking about him, saying his name seemed to divide him and make her share the pieces with others. She still thought of him constantly, talked with him, shared her feelings with him, and called upon him to help her when she had to make difficult decisions.

"He told me to come back to you," she said, pulling Henry closer, "but I had already decided to do that. He just gave me his blessing, more or less. He also told me to let him go. He wants me to let him rest and devote myself to living my life. That is what he wants, he said." She had paused and turned to squarely face Henry. Even in the dark, she wanted to be as close to his eyes as possible when she asked, "Do you think I'm crazy."

"No, my love," Henry replied kissing her on the nose. "I think you love deeply, to the core. I hope you love me that way someday, but I will never intrude upon or impede your love for Jeffery."

Finally, they slept.

A few days later, Daisy packed a picnic basket with local pecorino cheese, fresh bread, prosciutto, olive oil and vino from Villa Coppo. As soon as Henry had completed his morning workout with Esther, he saw Daisy waiting for him.

"My, you look beautiful today. That flowing dress is very Aphrodite-like. And your scarf catches the wind and flows around you. We need a camera."

"I don't need a camera, amore mio. Every adventure with you is imprinted on my heart and in my mind. Shall we picnic away from the villa. I know just the spot and you seem to be ready for any adventure these days."

"I am, my English lass," Henry said giving her a quick kiss on the lips. "You and your picnics do wonders for me, Daisy. Yes, let's picnic away from the villa on this bright, sunny day. There is so much to see. Such beauty. It truly does remind me of home."

"Oh, you have towering Italian Cypress trees in western Colorado?"

"Well, no except for the towering Italian Cypress," he amended.

"Oh, you have olive groves in western Colorado?" she asked.

"Well, no, except for the towering Italian Cypress, the olive groves, and the vineyards, Tuscany reminds me of western Colorado," he finished smugly.

"Good. I think I will like western Colorado."

"Oh? You planning to visit?"

"No, I plan to live there."

"Good, then we can keep seeing each other," he laughed and leaned in for a kiss that he knew she would again quickly and freely give.

They walked for a while past those cypress trees, olive groves and vineyards until they came to a bluff overlooking the valley below. They quickly spread a blanket, looked into each other's eyes and shared their love.

After a long leisurely lunch, Daisy walked to the edge of the cliff. "Don't fall off," Henry admonished.

"Never," was her reply as she twirled in graceful circles and held her gauzy scarf out to flutter in the wind. "Never."

"What ballet is that you are dancing?"

"Oh, Henry. I'm not a dancer. Not a ballet dancer at any rate, but if I were, this twirling that I am doing would be called the 'Ballet of Love.'"

Watching her Henry was filled with love, and then suddenly he was not seeing Daisy, but another love twirling in circles while ice crystals danced around her. Just as suddenly the memory was gone. After its fleeting passing, Henry felt a lightness that he had not felt in a long time. Suddenly he had a freedom, a choice that had been missing.

Daisy whirled her way back to him and sank onto the blanket beside him. She noticed the change in him.

Finally, she asked, "Is something bothering you, Henry?"

"No, why do you ask?"

"You are very quiet. You have a pensive look on your face and you haven't said a word in a while. Are you sure nothing is bothering you."

"Well, actually, I was just thinking that if I'm not careful I might do something crazy like ask you to marry me."

"Why would that be crazy?"

"You mean…, you would…, you will?"

"Henry, I believe that German bullet clipped a part of your

brain. I have been telling you almost daily that I intend to marry you."

"I thought, well, I thought maybe that had changed."

Daisy pushed aside the picnic basket, moved closer to him, and pulled him close. "Yes, amore mio, I will marry you. Yes," and with that she gave him the most special kiss she had ever bestowed upon him.

"Ti amo, Daisy. Ti amo, amore mio."

Later that same afternoon, after a quick letter to his Mom and Ginny, Henry found Nonno Luciano and gave him the news.

Nonno, smiled, nodded his head, and mumbled, "Ah, nozze, nozze."

"Nozze?" Henry asked.

"Wedding, wedding," said Luciano, smiling broadly. "Have you told the others?"

"No, you are the first because I want you to help me plan something for tonight. A surprise announcement to the rest of the family, but I need your help. I need your silence and a couple of bottles of your best toasting wine. I will pay, of course."

With great Italian gusto Luciano started shaking his head. "Non, mi insultare, Henry. Do not insult me, Henry. Sei tu famiglia, ora. You are family now."

Henry knew Luciano well enough by this time to know that he lapsed into Italian when speaking with him only if something was upsetting him. It was clear to see that Luciano would not hear of money passing between them.

Luciano, grabbed both of Henry's shoulders, gave him a traditional kiss on each cheek and said with tears in his eyes, "Il piacero e mio. It is my pleasure. I love Daisy also. We all love our special Daisy."

"Grazie, Luciano, grazie."

When all the family had gathered on the west courtyard, Henry stood, cleared his throat, and asked for everyone's attention. Daisy, beamed up at him, sensing what was coming.

"I have a few things I would like to say," Henry started. "First, I want to thank you for your medical expertise that you so freely bestowed upon me. I thank you, my mother thanks you, my sister thanks you, and my future wife thanks you."

Everyone turned and looked at Daisy. She said nothing, tried to look stoic and unknowing. They turned back to Henry.

"I have asked Nonno Luciano to help me offer a toast or two. Nonno, will you pour, please."

Beaming with pride, Luciano walked to the wall niche hidden by the blooming foliage and retrieved a tray of toasting flutes and a bottle of his special reserve. The family recognized it immediately and turned to Henry for they now knew more had to be coming.

After everyone had their glass filled, Henry continued, "I would like you all to join me in toasting yourselves, your skills, and the fact that you gave me back my life. NO…wait, not just my life, but my happiness. And, please, toast my future wife, Miss Daisy Wentworth." With that he raised his glass with his left hand and his Daisy with his right, and the small gathering laughed, cheered, applauded, and toasted the happy news.

"Oh, brother," said Esther laughing, toasting and talking at the same time. "Such drama for a well-known fact."

"Esterina," admonished her mother.

"But Esther,' teased Henry, "I just asked her today. How did you know?" With that everyone laughed some more, toasted some more, and exchanged many more hugs and kisses.

Over dinner, the conversation became serious when Henry asked dottore what they had to do to marry in Italy. A sharp whistle and a shake of the head told Henry that it would not be an easy task.

"First, if either of you is Catholic, the Pope has to agree."

"Well, good, then scratch that off the list," said Daisy, "for neither of us is Catholic although I go to services here with all of you."

The Dottore smiled at her and further explained what he knew of the many steps a foreigner had to complete to be married in Italy. The fact that Henry was military and that both the bride and groom came from different foreign countries only complicated the process. It would take a while to get all the papers from the two countries and from Italy finalized.

"Okay, scratch the wedding," Daisy announced blithely. All eyes turned to her. Henry raised his eyebrows in question.

"Henry," she asked, "Wouldn't your mother want to be at your wedding? She has suffered a lot during the past few years, and I would hope that she would approve of our love and welcome the chance to share our happiness."

"Well, of course she would, but she isn't within a few thousand miles of here and I thought you would want to share our big day with your Italian family and friends."

"I do and I will. I have been thinking," she turned to Isabella with a gleam in her eyes. After giving Isabella a chance to catch up with her thoughts, Daisy said "Zia?"

"Excellent idea, Daisy. I like it," said Isabella rising and hugging Daisy.

"Like what," asked Henry.

"May I?" Isabella asked Daisy. With a smile and a nod, Daisy gave Isabella the go ahead. Isabella turned to Henry and began.

"We will have a wedding festa here, before the wedding, before you two leave, for I know that will be your next announcement. You can then go home and share the wedding and celebration with your family. I would so love to give you and Daisy a wonderful festa and invite the entire village. They love Daisy, they honor you, and they deserve another reason to celebrate. What do you say?"

Henry wrapped his arms around Daisy and simply said to Isabella, "Si. Grazie, Zia Isabella."

Chapter 26

The day of the wedding festa dawned with a breathtaking sunrise. Pinks, reds and golds splashed over the hillside and onto the side patio. As the sun rose further into the clear blue sky, it traveled around the house and bathed the front courtyard, scene of the coming party, in brilliant sunshine.

Dozens of pots adorned the space with colors of red, blue, purple, and yellow flowers. Off to one side, was a quickly assembled gazebo covered with blossoms in every color. Chairs with colorful pillows were scattered around, but most of the seating was placed at long tables with fresh white tablecloths covered by second smaller cloths of various colors. It was a sea of color and that color extended around the villa to all the courtyards and seating areas. The happy colors even filled the house which would be thrown open to all.

The family and their farm dependents had been planning and preparing for two weeks. The people in the village were doing the same. Isabella was correct when she said everyone would want to honor Daisy and Henry. Henry was not sure the villa and courtyards would hold them all.

Knowing of the destruction and the shortages caused by the war, Henry offered to pay for this party. His offer was soundly rejected. "She is our daughter, now, you know. This is our gift to Daisy."

"Where will you get enough food?" Henry asked concerned.

"Oh, everyone, every farmer, farm wife, village merchant, and village wife will be contributing something. Do not fear, there will be enough to eat. Did you not know that we Italians hid much of our food during the war?"

"Oh, I have heard about burying foodstuffs, but surely, not much could be safely buried."

"You'd be surprised," said Luciano, who had been sitting quietly nearby. "We buried wine, cheese and olives, of course. We also managed to devise ways to protect and bury our prosciuttos, fruits, and spices. We Italians do not give up our stores of food very easily. And in some spots we were able to hide the items and then wall them up. The Germans never knew. Now the people are digging out and digging up, and while the festa may be somewhat smaller than before the war, it will be no less festive. Come let me show you something."

With that, Luciano escorted Henry to an almost invisible door below the first floor of the villa. He pushed it open and stepped aside for Henry to enter.

"Oh, my," was Henry's startled reaction. "No wonder we have been eating so well." As his eyes became accustomed to the filtered light, Henry saw table after table of cheese, wine, olive oils, prosciuttos, and various other fruits and vegetables. Lining the walls were large oak barrels of wine. He led Henry into an adjoining area and glassware, corks, and cutting utensils were lined up, just waiting to be used.

"This is essentially underground," beamed Luciano. "Of course, it might have been found, but it wasn't. The few times the Germans came here they did cursory searches. Because we are so far off the roads, they wanted to get finished with us and get back to their buddies. We always had bottles of wine and a few bottles of olio in the house. They would take that and a few other items and leave. We were lucky, many others were not."

"I am humbled by your outpouring and that of all the farmers and villagers. I will never be able to repay you, or them."

"Non, non…, do not even suggest such a thing. Do not let the others hear you talk of repayment. None is expected, and most certainly none is wanted, by anyone. Keep that in mind, and enjoy our newfound dolce vita" Luciano responded vigorously.

A few hours later, as Henry stood among the crowd on the front steps, he was trying to remember every minute of this for Ginny and his mother. The colors, the flowers, the laughter, and the food and wine. Would he ever be able to paint a picture for his family that would do justice to this wonderful scene, made all the more wonderful because such a short time ago, these same Italians were living in fear, hiding their children and their belongings, and their foodstuffs. *The Italians certainly have a zeal for living and they certainly know how to celebrate*, he thought.

"Buona sera, mia amore. Good evening, my love," Daisy whispered in Henry's ear. "Are you enjoying yourself?"

"Absurdly so," he remarked.

"Well, when the food is presented, don't eat too much antipasta, for the feast to come is something you will want to enjoy to its fullest. But right now, cara, the family is waiting. Are you ready?"

Letting out a deep breath, Henry sighed a big fake sigh, and said, "I suppose so."

"Oh, you," she said laughing and pulling him with her to join Zia Isabella, Dottore Antonio, Nonno Luciano, and Esther by the white flowers at the edge of the cliff. The sun was just beginning to set and the colors emanating from it painted the entire scene as only a true artist could.

When they were all together, Dottore, clapped, and shouted, and called for everyone's attention. Then he spoke to the quieted crowd.

"As you know we are here today to Honor Daisy and Henry and to celebrate this great thing that we now enjoy, freedom. Freedom to again live and laugh and love. Daisy and Henry are just the first of the next generation, I am sure, who have found love amid the chaos and the hatred that brought us so low. Now, we see them as our symbol for the future. They will be married soon, not here, but back in Henry's hometown." There was a good bit of moaning comments from the gathering, for they all would have loved being present at the wedding.

"Knowing that we would all like to be there with them," Dottore said as if reading their thoughts, "they have agreed to take a few minutes today and proclaim their love for each other while you are all present." At this announcement, the gathered Italians did what Italians do so well, they cheered, toasted, clapped vigorously.

"Quite, you rabble," joked Dottore. "We will need quiet for you to hear their declarations of love." He turned to Henry and Daisy who were holding hands in the center of the family gathering. They smiled at each other and Daisy spoke first.

"I Daisy Wentworth proclaim my love for this man. Now and forevermore. From the first moment I saw him," here she turned to the gathering and said, "really, from the very first moment my eyes lighted on him," the crowd laughed, and turning back to Henry she continued, "from that moment, my heart was his. Mi Amore!"

She took a deep breath and continued, "I see no heartbreak in our future. Along with all of you, we have had our heartbreak. There may be times of sadness, but we will not allow heartbreak to cloud our future. We will have happiness, sunshine, and love. This is my pledge to all of my Italian family and friends. This is my pledge to Henry. Come with me, mi amore, and let us begin this journey of love." So saying she reached up and gave him a gentle kiss on the cheek. He looked at her with a question in his eyes. "Later," she whispered.

Now it was Henry's turn. He took a deep breath and turned from her to face those before him. "Before I speak to Daisy of what is in my heart, I would like to say a few words to you, my new friends. Your kindness and generosity have touched my heart. In this time when you need to be concentrating on rebuilding your own lives, you have helped me rebuild mine. I treasure every minute of my time with you. I will always be your friend." Many of the ladies were openly weeping, and more than a few of the men, reached for their handkerchiefs and quietly wiped away stray tears.

"And, now my Daisy," Henry said turning back to a beaming, crying Daisy. "Ah, Dais, don't cry," he said bringing a needed laugh to their audience. "I, Henry Townsend vow before God and all of these good people that I will love Daisy for all of my days. I will strive to keep her happy and to keep heartbreak away. We go now to build a life that others may only dream of, but, thank God, He has given it to us. Ti amo, amore mio." With that he leaned in and gave her a chaste kiss while the audience went wild.

Soon Henry heard a steady tapping with spoons and anything else that would make noise, on glass. Henry looked out at them questioningly. Old Vincenzo, the bookseller from the village stepped forward and said in broken English, "tapping, hitting, our glasses," and here he illustrated, "mean you kiss her good. Not like before."

Suddenly everyone was making noise and Henry grabbed Daisy and bent her backward in a long slow kiss that would be talked about in the community for years to come. Finally, he released her, and the crowd cheered lustily.

After a few moments, the village priest, Father Tucci stepped forward and raised his hand for silence. "Daisy and Henry have agreed that they would like to have me say a prayer for their union. I am honored to do so." Once again the crowd quieted and most of them crossed themselves as the priest began to pray.

"Now," said Isabella as soon as Father Tucci had completed his short prayer, "this festa can really get started. Enjoy yourselves, and would my servers please come with me. Find a seat everyone," she finished.

Even before everyone was seated, someone started clinking his knife or fork against his glass, and others quickly joined in. The bride-to-be looked at the groom-to-be with a smile and a question on her face. Henry knew what was expected of them. Throughout the evening, Daisy and Henry had to satisfy those Italian calls to baciarsi, baciarsi, kiss each other, kiss each other many times over.

Before the servers could begin their duties, Dottore called for everyone's attention and when he had it said to Henry and Daisy, "It is a tradition for the best man to make a pre-dinner toast to the bride and groom of 'per cent'anni,' wishing them 100 years together. Your best man is not here but if everyone will raise their glasses with me we will all wish you 'per cent'anni.'"

"Per cent'anni, per cent'anni," echoed around the group ending with a rousing round of applause.

After that opening toast by Dottore, antipasti trays, prepared by various housewives, were set upon the long tables under the towering cypress trees. Some of the trays were quite sumptuous with greens, salamis, mushrooms, anchovies, and cheeses. Some were more sparse, but all were expertly presented.

After another toast, pastas appeared. Pasta in all shapes and sizes, including the traditional pici, a Tuscan farm tradition. Along with the pastas came the sauces, tomato, alfredo, or pesto, hot and aromatic. Daisy had warned Henry to take a small bit of everything but not a large portion of anything. "If you take too much early in the meal, you will not get through it." She also warned him to only sip at his wine throughout the evening. Henry soon saw the wisdom of her advice on both counts.

After another toast, the hams and sausages, so recently hidden and retrieved, appeared. Along with these came a variety of vegetables. One caught Henry's eye and soon his appreciation. After one bite, Henry was in love with this new food, fried squash blossoms. "You must learn to cook these, Dais," he said.

"I can cook those with my eyes closed," she replied.

"I'm glad I am marrying you," he murmured through a mouthful of squash blossoms.

Soon the tables were laden with food that seemed to glow underneath the many lanterns hung all about. Henry was shocked to see the amount of food presented. Daisy was touched, for it seemed everyone in the village wanted to contribute something.

Just when Henry thought the meal must be over, out came a smorgasbord of cheeses and fruits, artfully displayed and presented. Throughout the meal one could help oneself to homemade breads, wine and olio from any number of farms. Coffee was always available.

No one hurried; people laughed and sang throughout the meal. Some of the long married men would cup the chins of their tired, fading wives and sweetly sing a love song while looking longingly into her eyes. She would listen with tears glistening, and when he finished she would often swat his hand away from her chin. Then laughing she would lean in and kiss him.

Some of the men would stand and start singing and gesturing for everyone to join them. Loud choruses echoed across the valley. Through it all Henry and Daisy laughed and sang along with the others. They often kissed, for the clinking of silver upon glass seemed to ring out between each course or chorus.

"Dessert," said Daisy, "will come later."

"Thank goodness," Henry remarked. "I don't think I can eat another thing. What time is it, anyway?"

"Probably around 10:00 or 11:00."

"Wow. We started before sundown. How long will we party?"

With a careless shrug of her shoulders she answered. "Who knows? Perhaps all night. Now, you must make yourself available to dance with any lady who wishes to dance with you, and from what I've heard, they all do. So wiggle your toes and get ready. But Henry, don't tax yourself. We tend to forget that you are still recovering," Daisy told him.

"Bah Humbug," Henry replied with a wave of his hand as he was quickly claimed by Senora Grande, the mayor's wife, to start the dancing.

Later, while dancing with Esther, Henry said, "You Italians certainly know how to celebrate."

"Yes, we do," she responded. "We've had plenty of practice, even in the hardest of times."

"Was it rough, really rough here during the war?," he asked looking into her eyes?

"Yes, quite rough, but not as rough as many other villages and villas. And even in those times, we celebrated, except when the Germans were actually with us." Seeing Henry look startled. "Oh, yes, they found comfy villas and made themselves right at home. Luckily, the Germans did not often find the food and possessions hidden behind those false walls or deep in wells and caves. Sometimes, all that was left to some families after the war was what had been hidden and not discovered. We were much luckier. They came, plundered a few items, treasures they thought, and went back to the villas more easily reached than ours. We think they thought us too remote for removing large items. Luckily, they didn't know of our hidden canopy lane straight into the village. It really is a nice walk. If they had seen it, perhaps they would have chosen to ravage Villa Coppo and more of our belongings."

"I am so sorry for what you and all these people have been through."

"Grazie, Henry. You are a treasure, now we will stop this conversation and dance, and laugh, and celebrate that we are all here and can share beautiful futures."

"Amen!" Henry said, echoing her sentiment.

As the evening progressed, and the heat of the day subsided, the energy of the crowd seemed to pick up and everyone danced often. Because everyone wanted to dance with the honored couple, their dances together were scarce. Still, they would find each other on the dance floor and smile across the dancers. At one point, the tarantella started and before he knew it, Henry was holding on to Daisy with Isabella behind him, and the entire group was up doing the traditional Italian wedding dance.

Finally, desserts started arriving on a beautifully decorated table. When all was in order, Isabella called Henry and Daisy to the table. Looking at Henry, she explained, "In some parts of Italy traditional wedding cakes are not always served. We decided to leave the traditional cake for your Mom and sister. We do not want to do everything before them, so our dessert table features other Italian wedding desserts."

She paused, smiled at Henry, and pointed to a cake of sorts. "Now, I know this looks like a wedding cake, at least at first glance, but it is a cannoli cake."

"Yum," responded Henry as Daisy laughed.

"Yes, I know you have developed a taste for cannolis. This is simply a multi-tiered serving platform made by Georgio in his forge. Many families contributed some piece of tin to make the platform. If you can figure out how to get it to America, it is a community gift to you and Daisy."

"Oh, we'll find a way, won't we Daisy?" Too moved to speak, she wiped tears from her eyes, nodded in agreement, and raced to kiss an aging man who looked like every children's book illustration of a blacksmith.

When she returned to the dessert table, Isabella continued, "As you can see, the tiers allow the cannolis to be arranged to look like, well…, almost like, a wedding cake. And here," she moved along the table, "we have the traditional wedding cookies from Gabriella's pastry shop."

Not to be outdone by Daisy, Henry, knowing Gabriella very well from his many trips to her shop, rushed through the crowd and gave her a loud, noisy kiss.

When he arrived back at the table, Isabella shook her head and asked him, "How much wine have you had to drink, Henry?" Turning to the crowd, she explained that Henry had never had wine before coming to them. The crowd looked stricken at his loss.

"But I never intend to do without again," Henry quickly assured them. "In fact, I am going to try growing grapes on my land back home."

Suddenly everyone was shouting at him, "Grow giovannesse, Grow moscadello. Grow trebbiano toscano.

"'Scusi," said Isabella over the din. "Henry will be here for a few more days, you may all visit with him and again give him your expert advice on what to grow and how. I'm sure he would appreciate that."

"Si, si," shouted Henry.

Taking up with her plans for the evening, Isabella said to Henry and Daisy. "As you know, the war has left many of us without the benefit of many things and especially money. Every person here wanted to give you a wedding gift, but not all could do so. Finally, a group of housewives came to me and asked if I thought a certain item would be a good gift for you. It was a perfect suggestion and one that everyone could participate in. The mayor's wife will tell you about it."

Short, chubby Senora Grande waddled to stand in front of Daisy and Henry. She was giggling and nodding the entire trip up through the audience, but once she placed herself just where she wanted to be, she proceeded without too many giggles.

"We know," she started, "that 'if you eat well you feel close to God,' 'Chi Mangia Bene Sia Molto Vicino Adio,' and your friends here want you to always 'eat well, and to feel close to your God.'" She paused and looked around. Everyone was looking at her, smiling encouragement, and nodding in agreement. "So we, every family here and everyone not married who wanted to add to it, have made you a cookbook."

She reached forward and took a package from her husband who was now on the front row. She handed Daisy a beautifully wrapped package adorned with flowers and bows. With tears in her eyes, Daisy just looked at it.

The entire group was quiet. Esther leaned in and in a stage whisper said, "I think they want you to open it."

Everyone laughed a short laugh and then became quiet again as Daisy, with Henry at her side, carefully unwrapped this unexpected treasure. It was indeed, a book, not professionally produced in some big city printing office, but assembled, bound and titled by the local librarian.

"'Chi Mangia Bene Sia Molto Vicino Adio.'" Daisy read through her freely flowing tears. Looking at Henry she said, "It means 'those who eat well are closer to God,'" she finished.

Henry wiped her tears with his thumb, leaned in and kissed her gently, and said, "I know love, I know."

Taking the book from her, he opened it with an "oh, my." Before him were pages of hand written recipes, each with the giver's special instructions, name, and address. Many had added little benedictory notes wishing the couple Godspeed or thanking Henry for his efforts on their behalf.

Henry, trying not to be too overcome, pulled Daisy close and turned to the group. "There are not words to express how we are feeling. Just look at my crying bride and I think you will know the depth of both of our feelings. We will miss you and always speak of you with tenderness and love. I came here a broken man. I am going home as whole and complete as a man can be. You have done that for me. We will use this often; even I will learn to cook from it." This brought a note of levity back to the group. "This will be our treasure forever. Thank you, mille grazie."

This speech was followed by a long, loud round of applause. Esther handed Daisy a handkerchief. When she was sufficiently composed, she said "Well, I guess I am practicing letting my husband speak for me, for I could not say anything better than Henry did. Know it comes from the heart. Let me speak for Henry's family in America. Henry and I have both been in touch with them weekly. They have followed his progress and they know of your love for him. His mother and sister want me to tell you that they are here today in spirit and would love to give each of you a hug. They send their heartfelt thanks for all you have done for Henry." She looked around and saw the mothers in the audience nodding fiercely in sympathy for a family so far away. Then she proceeded, "Just let me add that I have known some of you for years. You also took me in when I was broken, and you healed me. Ti amo. Ti amo."

"Well," said Isabella, stepping in to change the tone, "Let me liven this party up again and tell all of you that Daisy explained to Henry the tradition of our fried bowtie dough treats. So, in that tradition, bowties, made, shaped and fried by Daisy and Henry, will be here on the table with the hope from Henry and Daisy that they bring all of you the traditional blessing of good tidings. Also…"

"Also," said Daisy, who had recovered sufficiently to step in "I explained your, our, tradition of presenting each guest with a Bombonieri of five sugared almonds wrapped in tulle inside a small pottery or glass dish. When Henry asked what they symbolized, I explained that they symbolize health, wealth, fertility, happiness and long life, and are meant to represent both the sweet and bitter aspects of life. He said he wanted them to represent only the sweet, for you have too recently had the bitter." Everyone clapped and laughed and loudly agreed with this statement.

"Anyway," Daisy continued, "later tonight, as you are leaving, you must pick up your gift box from us. We hope you enjoy your gift box, folded paper boxes, sorry, no crystal, but these were made by Henry's own hands, and filled with candied almonds made by my own hands. We want to present them to you personally and tell each one of you how much you mean to us.

"But first," interjected Dottore Antonio, "I am ready for dessert and coffee and maybe some grappa and vin santo? The music will play again. Dance, eat, drink, and let's really show Henry how we celebrate amore."

Thunderous applause and loud talking greeted his words and the party was once again in full swing.

It was well after 2 a. m. when the last guest left the villa, and Luciano invited the family to the courtyard to join him in his traditional glass of grappa before bedtime. "We all need to be able to sleep. Grappa will do that for us." So, happy and relaxed, the small group sat together for an hour.

As the others left Henry asked Daisy to stay and watch the sunrise with him. "Even though we are not leaving for a few days, I don't know if we will be awake to greet another Tuscan sunrise. We are here now, still wired in spite of Luciano's grappa, so let's watch the sunrise."

Chapter 27

A week later, Henry and Daisy said a tearful goodbye to Esther and Isabella. There were promises of visits and letters and transatlantic phone calls. After many hugs and kisses Henry pulled Daisy to the waiting truck they were to drive northward. Dottore Antonio and Luciano were driving in front of them in another of the farm trucks.

They knew the journey would take longer than usual since many roads were still in disrepair and some bridges still out. They knew the young couple would see more than they had seen in their protected little area, but it was the best way for them to get to Florence where they would stop for a while and Henry would be examined by an American doctor. Along the way, they would stop at the farms that had sheltered Henry in his first weeks with the Dottore.

At the last farm before arriving in the city of Florence, the foursome had a car waiting for them. Henry ventured the opinion that Dottore did not want to drive into Florence in two worn farm trucks. Whatever the reason, or the method for procuring the auto, it was a welcome relief to Henry that he did not have to drive through the rubble of Florence while trying to keep up with the Dottore.

Henry was expected at the American command center in Florence. The armies had passed through almost two months earlier and the European theater of the war had been over for more than a month, but the Americans still had a small presence in Florence.

It was here that Henry reported. Hours later, after interviews and forms were completed, he was sent to an Army doctor for an exam. Dottore Antonio went with him and waited outside until called. The Army doctor wanted a complete accounting of his initial injuries, treatment, and prognosis. Even though Dottore had given many written accounts of that information, the American doctor wanted to hear it, not just read about it.

At the end of the day, Henry was able to rejoin the other three. Dottore and Luciano were leaving tomorrow to return to their tour of the farms, but the foursome had one final evening of enjoying each other's company. Dottore took them to the restaurant of a friend. Upon opening the door succulent smells greeted the foursome.

Over a long meal Daisy, Dottore, and Luciano heard of the plans the Army suggested to Henry. While at Villa Coppo, many ideas and theories on the best way to get home were tossed about. No idea, no matter how unusual, came close to what Henry heard proposed to him at the end of that day in Florence.

There was, it seemed, a new American university just opened in Florence for American servicemen, both officers and enlisted men, who had fought the Axis powers, and were now awaiting demobilization. The academic terms lasted only one month and the purpose of the curriculum was to prepare the soldiers for a return to civilian life in the states. Two additional campuses were being built, one in France and one in England. The Florence campus had been designated to serve men and women who had served in the Mediterranean Theater of Operations; the local Army commander proposed that Henry remain in Florence, attend this school for the July term, and receive additional medical care from the army doctors in the area.

This was an unexpected and quite novel proposal. It was not an order, Henry assured the other three, but it was highly suggested.

"Where will it be located," asked Dottore Antonio and before Henry could answer he continued, "The Germans occupied Florence for an entire year before the Allies bombed the train station forcing them to retreat. Before leaving, the Nazis burned every bridge over the Arno except for Ponte Vecchio. Much of the city is a rubble."

With a deep sigh, Dottore shook his head and continued. "They destroyed a bridge designed by Michelangelo, and along each side of the Ponte Vecchio. They even destroyed medieval buildings and neighborhoods, things of beauty."

He paused as the waiter brought more wine. Then he returned to his major thought. "Where will this new university be built? There is a lot of work to do before any building can take place."

"Dottore, I didn't mean to cause you pain," replied Henry hastily.

"No, no, it is not you, Henry. It is having almost a full day to see again with my own eyes what I have seen before. To be in the midst of this destruction destroys my spirit. I am glad to be leaving tomorrow, but what about you two, my friends? Will you stay here? Will you go now? How will you go? What does your army say to those questions?" he asked Henry.

"Will we stay? I don't know." Taking Daisy's hand, he continued, "Dais and I have a lot to think about. Major decisions to make. The Army did offer this opportunity as a way for me to stay and get more medical treatment that could lead to my discharge. The officer also pointed out that the army felt responsible for getting me home, but as a civilian or as a member of the military? I don't know.

"This month would give the government time to decide what to do with me and would give them time to make more preparations for getting troops and civilians home. And," he concluded looking around the table, "it does offer me the opportunity to complete my college degree, at the graduate level, no less, in one month. That is unthinkable back home. Still, I don't know what we will do. To stay puts all our plans on hold for another month."

Henry finished speaking and looked at Daisy, who had been

unusually quiet. "Dais?"

"It's your decision, Henry, but I can offer an opinion," she paused, as if waiting for permission to do so.

"And?" asked Henry.

"I think we should talk about it in detail when we get to Dottore's friends' apartment later, but on first hearing, I would say that we have our entire life ahead of us. What is one more month? Perhaps you should take advantage of this offer. Plus, all of Florence is not destroyed, and I can show you Florence, well, parts of Florence, before we cross the ocean."

And so, that easily it was decided. After more tearful goodbyes the following morning, Henry reported to the army while Daisy wrote to his mother and Ginny. They would be upset, she knew, but in little over a month they would all be together, just a few weeks later than planned..

That afternoon Henry took Daisy to the American University campus where the second term was just finishing. The Dottore had been needlessly worried, it seemed, for there was no building to do. They were to occupy a structure that had been untouched by the war. When they arrived at the campus, Daisy was stunned at what they found. Henry had been told the history of the building, but he had not told Daisy. He wanted to surprise her with this discovery because he knew the home of the new university was an impressive piece of architecture.

"It was built in 1938 by Mussolini," Henry said with something of a sneer on his face. "It was a showpiece for the Fascist School of Aeronautics. Since it escaped damage, we, the Americans, simply moved in after the war ended."

With a laugh, he added, "Just think, these buildings once a Fascist school now houses American soldiers. And look," he said with pride, "The buildings' names have been changed and renamed for American colleges. Look at the names on the posters. Here's Princeton. Let's find Harvard, Stanford, and the others."

When his classes started, Henry found there was an acute shortage of classroom materials but there was no shortage of enthusiasm by the soldiers who were there. Their enthusiasm and relief that the war was over and that soon they would all be on their way home helped form an instant bond. They even bonded with the Italian students studying at the University of Florence when that university offered help in the form of books, laboratories and other facilities.

Henry quickly enrolled in the agriculture and forestry classes. He was eager to compare the ideas presented here with those he had been studying at home. He even searched the curriculum for classes on wine fundamentals, but found none.

The liberal arts classes were popular and when classmates gathered in the evenings Daisy would listen intently and bemoan the fact she and other wives or girlfriends could not attend.

Once a week a large group of servicemen would gather to read and discuss the college newspaper produced by the journalism class. Called the US Collegian, it was written completely by students but typeset by Italian typesetters who knew not a word of English. The students found this amusing and always hoped to find an Italian word or two slipped in.

Although there were dormitories for the students, Henry and Daisy chose to live in the apartment belonging to Dottore's friend. After settling in, their apartment, amid the rubble of the great city, became a gathering place for the eager students.

One evening two weeks into the university term, they learned of the destruction of Hiroshima. Both were quiet for a while, but Henry finally declared, 'Now, maybe complete peace."

They waited, as did the world, for Japan to surrender. Japan did not. Three days later, on August 9th Henry and Daisy learned of the second atomic bomb dropped on Japan. Again, they and the world waited for surrender. It did not come until six days later when at noon on August 15th the Emperor finally surrendered.

Henry and Daisy were both quiet and reflective as the news passed through the campus. Finally looking at each other Henry said quietly, "I'm glad it's finally over and laid to rest. Now, my darling, no more heartache. We can go home in peace."

"Home," Daisy repeated and then kissed Henry passionately.

"Home," she repeated more softly.

When the term was over, Henry was given a medical discharge by the army doctors who had cared for him during the last month. Dottore Antonio had provided excellent care but as he himself had pointed out, there were weaknesses in Henry's body that no amount of care could remove. He was, he had told the American medical staff, of the opinion that Henry's days of military service should be terminated. It was an easy opinion for the American staff to agree with, and as Henry had entered the service, 'for the duration,' it seemed that the time had come to send him back to civilian life.

In late August the young couple said goodbye to their newfound friends and to Italy. Their last evening in Florence was bittersweet. Italy had healed them, had given them so much, and had embraced them. Still, they knew their life together was elsewhere. The break had to come and both were glad that they had said their goodbyes to all they loved in Italy a month earlier.

Before leaving Italy, Henry assured Daisy that they could spend time in England before leaving the continent, but she would not consider it.

"No, I have said my goodbyes, Henry. I have visited the places most dear to me. I have made my peace. My loved ones are with me in the only way they can be. We need to move forward."

So, looking to the future, they made their way to Gourock, Scotland, where they boarded a passenger ship for one of her many voyages carrying troops and passengers across the Atlantic.

The five day voyage gave Henry and Daisy more time to plan for their new life and to grow in their love for each other. Debarkation came in New York, NY, and both were spinning in amazement trying to take in every sight, sound, and smell of this great city.

Their stay was short; about 40 hours after arriving they boarded a train for their trip across country. Henry considered flying from New York to Denver, but he desperately wanted Daisy to see cities and towns standing with no wartime destruction. Thus, they left the glamour of New York and Grand Central Station and headed west. Henry was engrossed in giving her history and geography lessons along the way.

Late one night, entwined together in his berth, she had finally told him of the London bombing that killed her parents as they sheltered with others in a school that had been designated as a bomb shelter. She spoke softly of her final days in England. She described the widespread destruction of her native country. She did not speak again of Jeffery, but went on to describe how the destruction she found in her beloved adopted country further bruised her battered heart. She was, she said, eager to see a different landscape.

Henry was eager to give her that different landscape. He wanted her war-torn heart to see the safety that her future was giving her. He felt that she needed to see that there was still calmness and wholeness in the world. On this final leg they felt the world was theirs forever. Daisy's words at the mock wedding ceremony became their battle cry, 'no heartbreak.'

Chapter 28

Their arrival in Grand Junction was all that Henry could have hoped for. He was returning a war hero, whether he liked it or not. He was returning whole and happy. His family and his many friends, who had often wondered if this day would ever come, were overcome with the happiness of his arrival.

His only thought was of Daisy's reception. He knew he loved her deeply. He wanted others to do the same. Soon it was evident that he should have no worries on that account. His Mother and Ginny welcomed her with love overflowing. His friends took one look at her English skin, her lovely blond hair, and the smile she always wore, and welcomed her as if she had always been a part of them.

They finally exchanged their wedding vows in mid-September, 1945. Underneath a late summer sun, high atop a cliff overlooking Henry's beloved Grand Valley, they formally restated their pledge to one another, and had their union blessed by Henry's pastor. Ginny and Walt were by their sides, giving a quick glimpse of the foursome they would become.

As their lives together began nothing but sunshine would Daisy allow into it. That sunshine shone brighter on June 6, 1947, when Daisy gave birth to a baby girl immediately named Belle. The love they felt for each other spilled over to their child, in ways they could never have imagined.

As Belle grew, Daisy cooed to her in not only in English but in Italian. She was determined that Belle would know her namesake and just before Belle started to school, Henry took the entire family to Villa Coppo. For two weeks they were one big happy family reliving old memories and making new ones. Zia Isabella quickly became Nanna Isabella and Doctore became Nonno Antonio. Esther had, from the day of Belle's birth become Zia Esther. The only sadness from the visit came from the emptiness left by Nonno Luciano's passing the year before. He was remembered often and with many toasts.

Back home, Belle learned to ride sitting with Henry on old Steki. She learned to ski, as did her Momma, and to enjoy all things outdoors. She adored her Aunt Ginny and Uncle Walt, and she, alone with Henry and Daisy was devastated when Uncle Walt died suddenly in the late fifties. After an agonizing period of mourning, Ginny moved back to the ranch and soon the household of Grammy T, Aunt G, Momma, Daddy, and Belle were happy again.

In 1960, Henry decided it was time to try his hand at growing wine-variety grapes. If he could sustain a crop, he wanted to make his own wine. Enough, he told Daisy, for at least one bottle for the family. So, together they surveyed the home farm and another Henry had purchased east of town, closer to the small town of Palisade. It was there, they decided, they should try their first crop. It was what Henry had prophesied, just enough for a few bottles of wine for the family. Still, it was a start. It was also a good excuse to return to Italy and confer with the many 'experts' they knew.

After another successful visit, they returned home and began implementing several of the suggestions. Checking the soil and the positions of the sun at different times of the year, they tried another variety of grape and thus began a new venture for Townsend Farms. Within a few years, they produced enough high quality grapes to produce a very limited line of wine. Named, "Ti Amo", the wine was a light white drink, perfect for summertime picnics.

As they were celebrating their small success, Grammy T was stricken with pneumonia and never recovered. A few months into 1966, she left the happy family.

Through all of this Henry and Daisy and Daisy's sunny spirit persevered; she and Ginny became the closest of friends. One day Daisy asked Ginny to tell her about Lilly. Somewhat reluctantly, Ginny did so and soon Daisy was working along with Ginny to keep the little Yamamoto house in good repair,--- 'just in case.'

In early 1967, Belle announced that she was in love. The news was not news to Daisy and Henry, for they had recognized the signs many months prior to Belle's breathless announcement. On August 7, 1967, Belle and Robert Chandler were married in a lovely summer wedding. They moved into an old home in downtown Grand Junction and began a life of loving. In July, 1968, a son, Elliott, was born to the happy couple. Henry and Daisy were grandparents. They couldn't believe it. Two roles they had never contemplated now thrilled them more than any other.

Five months later, in December 1968, Daisy was the first to admit that the despair she had wanted to keep at bay had arrived on their doorstep. Belle and Robert were dead, killed in a highway accident on a small road leading home from a ski retreat where they had spent the weekend. In an instant they were gone. In an instant heartbreak arrived.

After several days, Daisy awoke with just one thought. 'They left us a precious gift. We must fight this despair as we fought to overcome the despair of the war. We must rise and take this gift, our Elliott, and make his life whole and happy.' Elliott was only five months old, but he was the greatest gift their daughter could have left the devastated couple.

Elliott grew up with an irrepressible spirit. He was interested in everything and always lively and laughing for his Grandma made sure his days were sunny and bright. Like her, he talked constantly; he was full of questions and full of answers to others' questions.

Grandmother Daisy and Pops were the mainstays of his life,

and he was their life, totally, until that fateful day in September 1978, when Daisy did not get up. It was an aneurysm, the doctor said. She was buried three days later.

For the first time in 33 years, Henry did not have his Daisy. He was not sure that he could go on. He was not sure he wanted to go on. Nothing had prepared him for this type of loss. Nothing helped heal this kind of hurting. Nothing he had ever experienced prepared him for this kind of pain. It was mental, emotional, and physical. It never left him.

Still, there was Elliott, just ten years old. He was Henry's only link to his Daisy. Henry knew that he must not let Daisy down; he must not neglect the heartache that Elliott was feeling. With the help of Ginny, the three of them began again. It was a lonely, agonizing time. They were all hurting. It took months. There were false starts and setbacks, but finally a new family, a new kind of family, emerged. They learned to rely on each other and to get through the days and nights.

Slowly, life began again for each of them.

Lilly

Chapter 29

Grand Junction, CO
1981

Having reached his sixty-second year, Henry was content. He had lived a good life, loved passionately, and through some miracle of belief, was able to continue to feel the presence of his dead wife. She was always with him; and each evening as he sat in solitude on his front porch overlooking his beloved valley, he communicated with her. She had been gone for three years, but she still guided him. He told her everything, asked her advice, and laughed with her daily.

He was content. She was not. Lately, in these late afternoon sessions she had been urging him to seek more from life. Not to be content. He could hear her clearly telling him that what they had for 33 years was so far above contentment that she did not want him to settle for contentment for the rest of his life.

Just yesterday she had urged him to find something, or someone if that is what it took, to bring passion and excitement back into his life. "Henry," her soft voice whispered to him, "do not merely settle for contentment. Find more, amore mio."

They almost argued. He wanted no passion if not with her. Some excitement, he admitted, might be good for him, but not passion. She urged both.

"If you want me to have passion," he said to her, "you provide it."

Today was a quieter day, and even though she had not spoken, he knew she was with him. Her presence was like a warm blanket on a snowy night. It was a crackling fire and a glass of their favorite vino. He knew she would soon touch him, fully enabling him to enjoy the peace that the quiet evening hours brought him.

Beautiful evenings, such as this one, were the perfect time for reflection. The day's work would have been completed, giving him the time to sit quietly on his long rambling porch and look out over the valley to the mountains on the other side. It was quiet this evening, for Elliott and Ginny seemed far enough away that he could hear no sound coming from within the house. His mind was free to ponder and to wander afield.

He knew that Elliott saw this part of his Pops' day as the time when Pops liked to think whatever thoughts old men thought. Henry smiled, for he knew Elliott would have been surprised, maybe even embarrassed, to know some of the thoughts that filled these quiet moments of reflection, for often they were not the thoughts of an old man, but of a young man so in love, that even in death she was with him.

Until her death, his beloved Daisy would have truly shared this time with him. She would have supper cooked, waiting until the cooler air slid down the mountainside before calling Henry and Elliott to eat. Sometimes they would talk, at other times neither spoke, but they sat side by side in rocking chairs placed close together so that one or the other was always reaching out and rubbing the other's hand or arm. They would turn to each other and smile, and always, just before leaving him to finish the dinner preparations, they would whisper to each other, 'Ti amo'.

When the weather was fine they would eat outside, living la dolce vita, she called it. From their outdoor dining area, they could see across the winding Colorado River, into the valley below, over the hills called the Bookcliffs toward the Rocky Mountains. Often, as the sun went down, it painted the Bookcliffs a glorious shade of pink.

It was a dazzling sight. A sight that made unsuspecting travelers grab cameras and take dozens of pictures. These travelers, if they were still around the following day would learn that this pink wonderland was repeated daily at this time of year. Daisy had laughed at them only because she had also been caught by this unexpected beauty and had taken dozens of photos herself.

Now it was Ginny who would call him to eat. Still, with all they had lost, he and Ginny knew that life had been good to them. They had both loved and been loved. Now they had both lost those loves, but the memories and the love they left behind was irreplaceable.

How can I be so content, Henry often wondered, *when my Daisy is not with me? Because,* he would answer himself, *she was with me. For over 33 blissful years, she was with me. How could I not be happy with those memories to wrap around myself each day?*

On this day, Henry's peace and reverie were suddenly disturbed by his grandson running toward the house from out back and calling his Pops as loudly as possible.

"Pops, Pops, I have found someone," Elliott called loudly. "Or she found me." Pops looked slightly amused as Elliott bounded up the steps.

"Pops, there's a young girl out back. She says she needs help. She says she's walked for two days. She says.... "

"Whoa," Henry interjected, "slow down and start over. Who needs help?"

"This girl. She says her Grandmother fell and is unconscious. The girl, Mara is her name, she has been walking for two days to get help. I don't know if she walked at night. I don't think so because..."

"Elliott," Henry interrupted, "Slow down and make sense. Is there a young girl out back?"

"Yes, Pops, that's what I'm trying to tell you."

"Okay, start over, calmly," Henry replied.

Twelve-year old Elliott thought he was being calm, but evidently Pops didn't think so. He silently counted to five the way

Grandmother Daisy had taught him, took a deep breath and began his story.

"I was in the back corner of the farm, beyond that big boulder near the cottonwood grove, and I thought I was alone. Then I saw some movement out of the corner of my eye. I knew no one was supposed to be there, so I turned quickly to see who or what was nearby.

"Nothing. I saw nothing. I thought maybe it was just a prairie dog, you know how plentiful they are this year. You even commented on it yourself last week. Remember?"

"I remember."

"You know, Pops, if you would let me shoot them like the other boys do, we wouldn't have so many of them."

"Elliott, you will not shoot helpless creatures. Now, stop rambling. What about this girl you claim to have found?"

"Well, for some reason, without thinking I said out loud, 'Well, little prairie dog, you're safe with me.'

"'I'm not a prairie dog,' a strange voice replied.

"I whirled around, and was dumbstruck by the sight of a girl, standing only thirty feet away. Pops, I was speechless."

"I doubt that," said Henry. "Get on with your tale."

"Well I asked who she was.

"'I am Mara, and I need your help,' she finally said.

"Still I just stood there. I know I was gawking, as Aunt Ginny calls it, but I couldn't help it. Then suddenly Rudy, came bounding out of the hills. Only my mind seemed to be working. I wanted to shout at Rudy and asked him where he had been.

"Pops, where could that dumb dog have been? He should have stayed with me rather than running through the hills. Then, when he got close to the girl, you know what he did, Pops? Nothing! He was circling her, kinda smelling her but not going up to her. Then he just sat down. He seemed to like her.

"What if this girl had been dangerous? Rudy is supposed to protect me. You always say you can trust him to take care of me. Well, Pops, he didn't. Not that I needed protection, mind you. But just suppose I had been in danger. What then?"

"And the girl?" asked Henry, ignoring his grandson's ranting.

"Oh, she said, 'I'm sorry if I frightened you. I won't hurt you, but I need to find someone who can help me'" Elliott replied in a girlish sing-song voice.

Realizing that his Pops was not as interested in this adventure as he was, Elliott went back to his story. "I told her she was on our land, and asked her who she was and where she came from. Then I asked why she needed help."

Elliott rolled his eyes, "I think she thought I was dumb because she said 'I told you, my name is Mara and I came from the desert behind the mountains.' She pointed back toward Colorado National Monument or at least in that general direction. I wasn't sure where she was pointing. Then she added 'and my grandmother is injured. We need help.'

"Now, Pops, I know that behind the pinnacles, ridges, and canyons of the monument is a lot of desert, both here in Colorado and over into Utah. Her story was beginning to seem unreal.

"I told her to tell me again why her grandmother needed help and what kind of help she needed.

"She said 'My grandmother fell three days ago. She could not move but was conscious for a short time, then became unconscious. She needs medical help that we cannot give her'.

"Why did you wait three days to come for help? I asked, because now I really was getting a little bit suspicious.

"'I didn't wait three days. A long time ago, Grandmother had explained to me what I needed to do if we ever needed help and she couldn't get it. After she fell, before she lost consciousness, she told me to go to sleep and start out the next morning to get help. When I awoke, she did not. My cousin Cami said she had drifted into unconsciousness during the night. She said I really needed to get started so I started walking immediately. It has taken me two days to get here.'"

Elliott was shaking his head in disbelief. "Pops, she wants us to believe that she has been walking for two days. She doesn't look as bushed as I think I would look if I had been walking for two days." He paused for a second then continued.

"Well, I asked her if she was alone. She said she was. Just think of it. Alone for two days in the desert and mountains. A girl! Wow! Pops, can you imagine?"

When Henry did not respond to Elliott's' question, he plowed ahead with his story.

"'Please, can you help me find someone to help my grandmother?' she asked again. She was almost pleading, 'please, help me.'

"I told her you were a great one for helping others and that you would know what to do."

"Elliott," Henry's voice now stopped Elliott's rambling.

"Oh..., yes, yes. Anyways, she's out on the big boulder, and I told her I'd bring you and some water." Elliott paused, looked at his Pops, who had moved to the edge of his chair preparing to check out the situation.

"Rudy is with her." Elliott continued. "I told her he would protect her, but honestly, Pops, he really didn't protect me from her. She was able to sneak up on me. She was only about 30 feet away when I first saw her. Some protection Rudy was; he was off chasing heaven knows what." This point seemed to be important to Elliott who had always trusted his faithful sidekick.

"Is she Indian?" Henry asked as he rose from the chair.

"Now, that's the really strange part," said Elliott as he followed Henry. "I don't think she is Indian. I think she's Oriental. Japanese, I think. She reminded me of Leni Matsuki, the new Japanese-American girl in my class at school."

Henry stopped dead still for a heartbeat. Then he whirled around. "You get the water, Elliott," he yelled over his shoulder as he raced to the boulder.

Elliott stood dumbstruck for the second time in an afternoon. He looked after his Pops with a puzzled look on his face.

"I'll get the water, " he said to the now empty porch.

Chapter 30

Henry rounded the house and headed for the boulder. Then he saw her. She was sitting on the boulder leaning against the tree with her eyes closed. Looking at her, Henry knew that she was not asleep, only resting.

He walked closer. Rudy lifted his head, looked at Henry, and thwacked his tail against the ground in recognition. The girl heard the movement. She opened her eyes and gazed steadily at the man as he approached her.

Slowly she stood.

Henry stopped walking and looked at her. In return, wide-spaced eyes cast a clear level gaze upon him.

"Hello," he said. "I am Elliott's Grandfather. He said you need help."

"Yes," she said and nodded her head. About that time, Elliott appeared with a glass of water.

"Here," he said to the girl. "Aunt Ginny, she lives with us and takes care of us, said to give you cool water. She says that you probably have a thirst as big as Mesa Lake."

He gave the girl the water and turned to his Pops. "Aunt Ginny said to tell you to bring her to the front porch where she can be more comfortable. She said you should bring her first, ask questions second."

Henry nodded, grateful that his sister was around to think of the girl's needs.

Elliott turned back to the girl. "Aunt Ginny also said that when you finish the water and get comfortable on the front porch, she'll give you a big glass of lemonade."

He smiled at Mara, seeming suddenly to warm to her presence. "You'll like that. Aunt Ginny makes the best lemonade in the valley.

She's real old. She's Pops' sister, and she never uses store bought lemonade. She always makes it fresh. I know you'll like it."

The girl looked puzzled for a moment, then nodded and handed the empty glass to Elliott.

"Well, let's go and get you comfortable, then you can tell us how we can help," Henry said.

Together, the three of them, and Rudy too, walked the last few hundred feet to the house. As they rounded the corner and approached the front porch, Henry saw that Ginny was already there, waiting for them.

"Hello dear," she said as she put her arm around Mara. "Before we settle down and you tell these men your story, would you like to come inside and wash your face and arms with cold water? You must be awfully hot and uncomfortable."

Mara looked at her gratefully and smiled. "Yes," she said as she looked around. "I would like to splash some cold water on my face, but I really must find someone to help my Grandmother. Please," she pleaded.

Elliott saw Aunt Ginny look over the girl's head at his Pops who, now that he thought about it, was being uncommonly quiet and slow. The brother and sister seemed somehow to communicate with that look.

"We'll have you freshened up in less than five minutes. Then you can tell us everything. Will that be alright?" Ginny asked Mara as she guided her into the house.

Henry sat down, took off his glasses, and looked back out over the valley while heaving a heavy sigh. For once Elliott sat quietly, waiting for Mara and Aunt Ginny to return and for Pops to spring into action, racing to help someone as if he were the Lone Ranger and Superman rolled into one. This slowness to action was definitely not like Pops.

Mara and Ginny soon reappeared. Mara looked slightly more alert, and she was smiling more. It wasn't a big smile, but still, there was a smile. Seeing it, Henry smiled back at her.

Ginny poured lemonade for all of them and passed it around. She and Mara sat on the swing, and Henry sat in the high-backed rocker facing them. Elliott left the steps and leaned against the porch post nearest the swing.

"Now," Henry said gently. "Tell me where your Grandmother is and how I can help."

"I can't tell you," Mara replied.

Three startled expressions gazed at her.

"What?" shouted Elliott. "You said..."

His Pops stopped him with a gentle look and shake of the head.

"Why can't you tell us, Mara?" Henry asked.

"Grandmother sent me to this ranch. She drew a map, she seemed to know it was here--in this spot. I don't know how she knew, but she seemed to."

Again, a knowing look passed between the brother and sister. *What do they know that I don't*, Elliott wondered.

"Grandmother once said if we have to go for help, we should ask for the Towsan..., no..., the Townsend family and only talk to them." Mara said.

Elliott leaned in closer, wide-eyed. He opened his mouth to say something, but this time it was Aunt Ginny who stopped him with a gentle hand on his arm and a shake of her head.

Mara continued, "I am to find Mr. Henry Townsend ..."

This time there was no containing Elliott. He bolted upright.

"That's Pops! That's Pops!" He pointed and pranced. "Wow, this must be a miracle! How does your Grandmother know Pops? How did she know he would be here?" he asked Mara, beside himself with amazement.

Mara was not listening to Elliott, although he was hard to ignore. Rudy had heard enough from his young master and taken himself off to a more peaceful place.

Except for Elliott it was now very quiet and very still. Henry looked at Mara in wonder. Mara looked at Henry in wonder. Aunt Ginny looked back and forth between the two.

Finally, wide-eyed with her good fortune, Mara whispered, "You are Mr. Henry Townsend?"

Henry nodded slightly.

Mara closed her eyes and a single tear slide down her cheek.

Again Mara asked, "You are Mr. Henry Townsend?"

This time Henry replied, "Yes. Now tell us where your Grandmother is and how we can help her."

Mara reached into her dress pocket and pulled out a photograph. "Great Grandfather Toru said to give you this." She handed it to Henry. "He said this will tell you who she is."

"Oh, my dear, I don't need the picture to tell me who she is. I only have to look at you," Henry replied.

Mara smiled, really smiled for the first time. She smiled at Henry. Henry smiled at her. For a moment, Aunt Ginny and Elliott were forgotten.

Finally Henry said, "Where is she. What kind of help does she need?"

"She is at home, in the high mountains," Mara explained.

"Why do you live in the high mountains?" Elliott asked.

"Because it is our home," Mara replied, looking puzzled. "Anyway, three days ago Grandmother fell while walking at sunset. We found her at the foot of a ravine. Her leg was badly injured, but we managed to get her back to our house."

Mara paused and took a sip of lemonade. She looked at Elliott and Aunt Ginny and smiled slightly as she explained. "Grandmother likes to walk at sunrise and sunset and then write her poetry. That's why she was out as the light was fading. She says her memory and her words are best then so she had been creating in her head and walked farther than usual. She was hurrying home when she slipped."

"And now she needs to go to the doctor and she wants Pops to give her a ride. Well, why didn't you just say so?" Elliott exclaimed. "Or why didn't you telephone, we do have telephones here in our little corner of the world," Elliott said somewhat sarcastically.

"But we don't," replied Mara

Over the next hour, Henry managed to restrain Elliott enough to learn that Mara and her Grandmother, Lilly, and a few other assorted relatives and friends, did indeed live in what was 40 years ago a deserted mining town.

Three days ago Lilly had fallen, and when she did not wake the following morning everyone knew that it was not a simple fracture of the leg, something Aunt Kiri could have taken care of, if she were still living. This injury was more, and the dwindling community felt helpless, for Lilly had become their leader. They realized that if she did not get help, she might never walk again. They refused to consider the other more frightening thought of a brain injury. She needed help, but help would mean a doctor and, quite possibly, a hospital.

Acknowledging that Lilly needed "outside" help caused a ripple of fear to course through the group. After all this time away from the world, they wondered, was it safe? That question posed two other serious problems. They no longer knew anyone on the "outside" so there was no one to go to for help. Equally important, there was no one to go, at least not until Mara told them of Lilly's prior plan..

Mara continued to explain to Henry and Ginny that the

community had grown increasingly smaller and when Great-Grandfather Toru dies, as he soon would for he was nearing ninety years of age, what would they do? This question had been weighing on Grandmother Lilly's mind for some time, Mara explained. So her Grandmother had secretly conceived of a plan and had shared that plan with Mara. Now it seemed that the time had come, sooner than expected, but it was here.

Mara recalled that entire earlier conversation with her Grandmother.

"We will go to the Townsend ranch and ask for Henry Townsend. He will know if it is safe. If it is, he will help us. If it is not, he will know what to do. I do hope it is safe now. It has been a long time. If Henry Townsend cannot be found, we will ask for any Townsend family member. They are all good people and they will help if possible."

After Mara had explained this to the other members of her community, they agreed that she must be the one to go.

On the evening of that earlier conversation with Mara, Lilly had drawn a map which she said she hoped was accurate. Then she had told her precious granddaughter where the map was hidden. Mara retrieved the map and prepared to go to the outside world and get help.

"Is it safe?" Mara whispered.

"It is safe." Henry gently replied.

After looking over the map Mara had given him, Henry announced, "I cannot drive my truck on the same route that Mara took to get here. Even if it is a four-wheel drive vehicle that can go almost anywhere, it cannot possibly traverse the ravines that Mara crossed."

He looked at Mara and smiled. She looked at Henry with wide, frightened eyes.

Elliott quickly jumped into the quiet moment with, "So, what will you do, Pops?"

"Well," Henry began, "I know most of the country well enough to be able to mark out a trail that was close to hers. The land farther away, the Uncompaghre Range, I am not as familiar with, but it can be charted using the maps I have from the Land Management Office. We'll leave at daybreak tomorrow morning."

"Daybreak," Mara repeated. "But Grandmother needs help now." She looked a bit shy at having to contradict the plans of someone willing to help her. Elliott looked back at Pops, wide-eyed, as if saying 'yeah, shouldn't you hurry.'

"I have to plan our route carefully and get supplies. Mara, you need to rest. We leave at daybreak. We'll be in time," he assured her.

"I'm coming with you," Elliott announced. "What do you want me to do to help get ready?"

"No, Elliott, you're not coming with me. You and Aunt Ginny will wait here, but you can help," Henry told his clearly disappointed grandson.

"After dinner you and Aunt Ginny will go to the grocery store and buy groceries for me to take and leave with the others for I will not be able to bring them all home. Buy a can opener, not electric. Don't buy anything that will perish. Pretend you're shopping for a camping trip." He looked at his sister as he finished speaking. She nodded her understanding.

"Let's feed Mara and then put her to bed," she suggested. "Perhaps over dinner she can tell us more about how many people are in her community and we can get an idea of what they might need." She put her arm around Mara and led them all into the house.

Chapter 31

As Henry and Mara poured over maps in Henry's study, Ginny and Elliott cleaned the kitchen. This was not a chore Elliott usually helped with, but Aunt Ginny had asked for his help, so here he was.

"Aunt Ginny," he began, "do you believe all that Mara told us? I mean, who is she really? Where does she come from, really? Why did she refer to us as the outside? If her Grandmother is old, and she must be nearly as old as you and Pops, why doesn't she know a doctor? Why does she wonder if it is 'safe'? Safe from who or what? And finally, Aunt Ginny, why do you and Pops seem to know more than I do even though I have heard everything that you have heard?"

"Wow. A lot of questions. Let's see if I can answer a few, but I think most will have to wait until Lilly gets back," she answered before pausing and looking through the window into the night sky. "Ok. Yes, your Pops and I know more that you do because we were here when this whole thing, whatever it is, started. Yes, Lilly is my age, but I don't know why she doesn't know a doctor. I don't know where they've been, why we are the outside, or why she needs to know if it is safe. I could theorize, but I won't, because I have to go shopping. Dry your hands and come with me.

After the shopping trip as they were repacking the items for safer travel, Elliott asked Pops if he had ever been shopping with Aunt Ginny.

"No, not recently," was his reply. "Why?"

"Well I go with her a lot, and she is a very calm shopper, but not tonight. She was so funny, Pops, you should have seen her. She bought some strange things. Things that she never uses. Like instant stuff. Instant! Can you imagine Aunt Ginny cooking instant anything?"

"No," his Pops laughed, "I cannot."

"Well, she bought plenty of rice and noodles, packaged noodle dinners. All instant. And she muttered to herself as she shopped. She never mutters when we are shopping. She knows what she wants and just puts it in the basket, but tonight, Pops, you should have heard her. 'Should I send cornmeal?' Mutter -mutter -oven -all these years mutter -mutter. Dry milk? -mutter, cow? -mutter -mutter. Lettuce, fresh vegetables, no, perishable. Mutter-mutter-mmm, just a few, though. Mutter-jello -pudding -mutter, refrigeration, mutter-mutter, better not. .. electricity? Tea, yes tea. Lots of tea. Mutter -mutter -mutter!' Honest, Pops, you should have heard her. She was funny."

"Thanks, Buddy, for that wrap up," laughed Aunt Ginny.

"Then," Elliott continued with glee for he knew he had an appreciative audience, "we reached the rice aisle. Here Aunt Ginny went crazy. White rice, brown rice, instant rice, not-so instant rice. Enriched rice, saffron rice and even rice cereal."

Both Henry and Ginny were now laughing at Elliott for he was mimicking his aunt's movements.

"I suggested some candy and donuts and guess what, Aunt Ginny agreed. So I said how about some soda. She agreed again. Chips? Okay. It seemed that I could ask for anything I wanted, and Aunt Ginny would buy it. But she was buying it for them, whoever they are!"

"Well, I'm tired just hearing about it," replied Henry, "and soon you will have some of the answers to your questions, and you might even understand this strange shopping trip better. Until then, I think we all need to do as Mara seems to be doing and get a good night's sleep."

With an amused smile on his face, Elliott joked, "Yea, we better go to bed before Aunt Ginny gets even more rattled. First, Pops, one final question, please?"

With a sigh Henry nodded his agreement. "Why didn't you

have to look at that photograph that Mara handed you to know who she was? Have you even looked at it yet?"

"She looks like her Grandmother," was Henry's only response as he headed out the back door.

"Where…" Elliot turned to ask Aunt Ginny, but she just shook her head and went to her bedroom.

Just as Elliott thought, Henry had not yet looked at the picture. Wandering through the darkness of the deserted house, he knew what the face in the picture looked like. He had seen it every day for years, and then in his mind's eye he had continued to see it for more years. Even today, forty years later, he could recall every feature.

It was a pleasant memory, but one that led to an unpleasant and still unsolved mystery. For now he knew where she was, but he still did not know why she left. Or more importantly, why she never returned.

By the moonlight softly filtering through the windows Henry inspected the familiar old house. When he reached Lilly's room he gazed around and once again sat on the floor leaning against the wisteria vines for support.

Suddenly he knew he was not alone.

"Hello, amore mio," he said gently.

"Hello, amore mio," she replied.

He felt her presence surround him. He heard her voice, softly entreating him to bring Lilly home.

"Go to her. Help her, and in the end, if she can again bring you happiness, take it.

"Oh, my Dais, I cannot. How can I do that to you, to us?"

"My love, you will be doing nothing to us. We are and will forever be Henry and Daisy, living, loving, and sharing passion most people will never know. Take any happiness she can bring to you. I promise that I will forever be with you."

"Oh, Dais," Henry cried with anguish.

"Live again, Henry. You have a long life ahead, embrace it. Love again, my love."

As Henry sat there, tears again spilled down his cheeks. Softly, like the elusive touch of a mature dandelion's flower, Henry felt his wife caress his cheek, kiss away the tears. He heard her soft whisper.

"Go, mi amore, go to her."

Chapter 32

Henry and Mara left at daybreak the next morning. Elliott was wide-awake, seeing them off. He was also still pleading his case with Henry.

"You might need my help," he repeated several times.

"We'll be fine," replied Henry.

"I could be your navigator," Elliott persisted. "You know I can read a map very well"

"Mara can read the map, I'm, sure. If not, I can do it," Henry replied. "Besides, Aunt Ginny is going to need you here."

"Why?"

"Elliott, please. No more questions. No more pleading. You will stay here. You are needed here," Pops replied more crossly than Elliott had heard him in ages.

"I need to know you are here helping Ginny and waiting for us," he said more softly for he had heard his own harsh reply and had seen the startled expression in Elliott's eyes.

"Okay, but maybe you should take Rudy. You know that the Swiss use St. Bernards for medical emergencies. Well, Rudy isn't a St. Bernard, but she is a Great Pyrenees. That's close isn't it? I bet she'd be lots of help," Elliott suggested.

This suggestion broke the tension that had been building and gave Henry a good laugh.

"No offense, old girl," he said bending and affectionately patting Rudy on the head, "but I think you'd be more trouble than help."

He looked up at his grandson. "No Elliott, I think Rudy should stay here with you and Aunt Ginny. But thank you for the offer."

Now, two hours later Elliott and Aunt Ginny were headed for

the deserted homestead at the edge of the ranch.

"We're going to clean it," she'd replied when she announced that that's where they were headed and Elliott wanted to know why they were going there. "But, why?" he asked again.

"We'll talk while we work," Aunt Ginny said as she loaded a box of cleaning supplies and a picnic lunch into the car. With Rudy in the back seat, they headed south on the small rarely traveled road. It was only a brief ride, walking distance actually.

As they pulled into the never used drive Elliott was surprised that the house and property did not look more run down. No one had lived there for as long as he could remember. He had once asked about it. Pops said the family who owned the place left during the war. Then he had walked away giving Elliott no time to ask another question.

Elliott had been there before, of course. He and Rudy roamed over the entire ranch land, not only that belonging to Pops but the adjoining land as well.

He didn't know who owned it. Whenever he thought about Pops' ranch this seemed to be part of it. Whenever there was a bad winter or a destructive storm, and Pops inspected his ranch, Elliott instinctively knew that he included this section in his inspections, but Elliott had never been here with Pops, or even heard him mention the place.

And still, somehow, even though it was deserted, this homestead never actually felt totally abandoned.

Looking at it now, he could see remnants of what must have once been a well-tended flower garden. Now most of the flowers were wildflowers and those hardy perennials that had clung to life year after year. Even they were sparse and needed attention, but there were enough of them to suggest a better time, both in the past and possibly in the future. There was one long row of bushes, however, that showed care, which pointed to someone giving them attention.

"Aunt Ginny," Elliott asked as they unloaded the car, "why do you always take care of this long row of peonies?" He gestured to the large colorful flowers standing like guards. They were as high as his shoulders. They lined a split-log fence that marked the front edge of the property. "You come here every spring to make sure the bushes are growing, and I know you come several times each summer and weed the beds."

Ginny stopped and looked down the row of picture perfect peonies. She smiled at them as if they were friends.

"That's true, but what else do I do with them?" she asked.

"You make bouquets for the house and the church and for sick friends," Elliott answered.

"Beautiful bouquets," Ginny agreed. "I like vases full of peonies in the house. Your Pops likes vases full of peonies in the house. Your Grandma Daisy liked vases of peonies in the house. She planted them, and she wanted them here. So I look after them each year, and they reward us with their beauty."

"But why did she plant them here and not at our house? Why don't you replant them closer to the house? Then you wouldn't have to walk so far."

"Well, I suppose you're right about that," said Ginny, "but have you seen any prettier peonies in the valley? Think hard now."

Elliott thought about it. Many people had peonies in their yards. One bush on each side of the steps made a welcoming frame for the doorway. Flower beds full of peonies made a colossal splash of color, and rows and rows of peonies edged fences, driveways, and property lines throughout the valley. They grew plentifully and extravagantly. They dwarfed the roses that tried to vie for everyone's attention.

"No," he finally replied. "Of all the peonies in the valley, these are the best." He looked proudly at the long row of flowers, feeling an ownership, as if somehow he was responsible for their being.

"Then that should tell you why I don't move them." She looked suddenly from the peonies to the house.

"This is where they belong," she whispered.

Chapter 33

Ginny took out the keys, unlocked the front door, and stepped inside. "It's not too bad," she said, more to herself than to Elliott.

She turned to him. "Come on, El, while I start sweeping, you run through the house, open all the doors and windows, then run out back to the well and fill all these empty buckets we brought."

Ginny kept him busy for the next two hours. They swept down cobwebs and swept the dust from the ceiling and walls. They washed and scrubbed all the surfaces, walls, doors, windows, and floors. They were too busy to talk.

Finally, she looked at him and smiled. "I don't know about you Mr. Chandler, but I need a rest and something to eat."

Elliott looked at her gratefully and simply nodded. He was too tired to talk.

"Let's go outside under the cottonwoods," Ginny continued. "While we eat the house can be drying, and I'll tell you about this place and the family who owned it."

Until then Elliott had been tempted to say that he would skip lunch and just sleep, but he knew that Mara's coming had everything to do with all this cleaning and he was ready to hear a good story.

"After you, Kemosabe," he said to his aunt with a grin.

"Well, where do I start," she asked after making sandwiches and opening chips and soda.

"Why not start at the beginning," said Elliott.

"Very well, but don't forget now, it was your idea to 'start at the beginning.'"

She warned, "It might turn into a long story."

"I'll remember," he said as he leaned against the tree and shared his lunch with Rudy.

"This homestead was purchased in the late 1800's by Japanese immigrants, Aki and Sumo Yamamoto. There were only a few Japanese in the valley then, but they found the area to their liking and they encouraged others to come here."

"I don't know any Yamamoto's," Elliott replied. "Do they still live nearby?"

"No, but that comes later in the story. Be patient," she smiled at him.

"Okay."

"Grandmother and Grand Pop Yamamoto, as we Townsend children eventually called them, had three children." Elliott looked at Aunt Ginny with wonder.

"Wow," he said, "I didn't know we were Japanese, just think we might..."

"Wait..., wait..., Elliott, hold on. We're not Japanese. They weren't really our grandparents. They were Lilly's grandparents and out of respect...." she tried to continue the story, but again Elliott interrupted her.

"Lilly, the one who's hurt?" Elliott asked.

"Yes, the one who's hurt."

"So you know her." he remarked almost to himself.

"Yes, we know her. Your Pops and I grew up with her. She lived here; this was her home." Ginny finished softly.

Elliott turned to look at the house. He tried to imagine a Japanese family living there. He tried to imagine a young girl who must look something like Mara. Almost, almost he could see the picture, but it was fleeting.

He turned back to his Aunt Ginny who was watching him. "Continue," he said.

"Grandmother and Grand Pop Yamamoto had three boys. They were all born here. They were first generation Japanese-

-American. They still observed many of the customs of the Japanese, but they were proud to be American citizens." She paused, poured some water for Rudy, and when Elliott was quiet, she continued.

"The three boys married three Japanese girls sent here to visit and to be considered as wives for the boys."

"You mean, they ordered wives, like ordering curtains from a Sears catalog? And the girls came on a trial visit?" Elliott asked astounded.

"Well, not quite like that. These young girls and their parents lived in California. There were more Japanese in California than here. Grandmother and Grand Pops Yamamoto knew the parents of the girls and an informal arrangement had been reached by mail, but I don't think it was absolutely binding. I think from what I heard later that the boys or the girls could have refused to marry the other if they wanted to."

"But they didn't want to back out," Elliott interjected, warming to the story.

"There was no backing out, but there were two changes made. It seems that the oldest daughter was meant for Toru, the oldest son. The middle daughter was meant for Sado, the middle son... "

"And the youngest daughter was meant for the youngest Yamamoto son, whatever his name was, Right?" asked Elliott.

"Right," Ginny smiled, "and his name was Akira."

"What changes were made? You said changes were made." insisted Elliott.

"After spending some time together, always with adults nearby, the youngest son and the middle daughter seemed drawn together, and the middle son and the youngest daughter seemed drawn together."

"But the oldest liked the oldest," announced Elliott.

"Yes, Toru and Mariko were well-matched. Eventually, all three couples married and the two youngest couples moved into town, but Toru and Mariko lived here with the parents."

"When did all the marriages take place?" asked Elliott whose genius for math was not his strong suit, but who was trying to work out some kind of time table in his head.

"In 1921," replied Ginny.

"1921, two years after Pops was born." said Elliott.

"Yes, and one year before Lilly was born."

"Lilly, Mara's Grandmother," Elliott clarified.

"Yes, Lilly, Mara's Grandmother."

"Who were her parents, which couple?" Elliott wanted to know.

"Toru and Mariko."

"Ah, the ones who were meant for each other," Elliott teased, remembering the story correctly.

"Yes. And they were a wonderful couple and had a wonderful family.

They were still very Japanese in their customs, but very proud that they and their children were American citizens," explained Ginny.

"And they all lived here," he said again turning toward the house. This time trying to picture the family was easier. He could feel their presence.

"And you and Pops lived on the next ranch," he stated.

"Yes," Ginny replied softly.

"And you were all very good friends?"

"Yes." This time Ginny's reply was even softer.

"Did Lilly have any brothers or sisters?"

"Yes, Franku and Naga, but we called them Frank and Ned," Ginny said with a smile.

"Why?" questioned Elliott, "I like Franku and Naga, that's

different."

"And that's why Frank and Ned wanted to be Frank and Ned. Out of respect for Grandmother and Pop Yamamoto they were given Japanese names, but at school and with their friends they were allowed to be called by the American versions of their names. Thus, the older generations and the younger generations were all happy."

"But what about Grandmother Lilly. Wwhat was her Japanese name?" Elliott asked.

"Ah, Lilly. She was the first girl born and Mariko ..." Ginny began.

"Her mother," Elliott interjected.

"Yes, and her mother, felt that her daughter might have an easier time in life if she had a name that was slightly more American."

"So they choose Lilly?" Elliott asked. "Why not Sally or Sue? They're very American."

"Yes, very. But Lilly could be given a Japanese pronunciation which pleased Grand Pop Yamamoto."

After a pause, through which Elliott was unusually quiet, Ginny looked around again, then proclaimed, "Now, Kemosabe, back to work."

Chapter 34

The first job after their lunch break was to complete the kitchen. It had been scrubbed well in the before lunch cleaning frenzy. Now they lined the shelves with shelf paper and scrubbed the sink one last time. The cleaning was made more difficult because they had to bring water in for soaping and rinsing and then take the dirty water back out.

After that, the front porch and then the back porch were cleaned. Ginny took several hanging baskets of ferns and petunias from her car and hung them at intervals across the front porch. First, however, she had to use the hammer and nails to make a hook on which to hang them.

"Didn't the Yamamoto's like hanging baskets?" asked Elliott.

"Well, they liked flowers, and I'm sure they would have liked hanging baskets, but the flowers were more often in the yard than hanging up back then," Ginny replied through a mouthful of nails.

"Hmm, back then. Exactly when did they move and why?" asked Elliott. "You didn't finish the story, you know."

"Okay, we're about finished, so come sit by me and I'll tell you the rest of the story, at least what's important."

Making herself comfortable, she asked "Where did I leave off?"

"When Lilly was born." Elliott told her. "Did they move soon after that?"

"No. They didn't leave for many years. Lilly was 19 years old when they left. Frank and Ned were just a few years younger. As children, your Pops and I played here, and we ran in and out of this house as if it were our own."

"And did Lilly, Frank and Ned play at our place, your house?"

"Oh yes. We were all very close before they left. Lilly was my very best friend and... " Ginny stopped. She seemed lost in thought.

This gave Elliott the opening he needed. "Aunt Ginny, why do you always say 'they left'? You never use the word 'moved'. For some reason, it sounds different to say they 'left'. Why do you say it that way?"

Ginny rubbed her hand over her eyes, finally raised her head and said "Because it was different. They didn't simply move, like your friends the Chambers did last month. The Yamamoto's left; they disappeared in the middle of the night."

Upon hearing this Elliott sat straight up. His eyes grew wide with wonder. He turned and gazed at the still empty but newly cleaned house. Finally he turned back to Aunt Ginny.

"I don't understand. Why did they just leave in the middle of the night?" He paused, then rushed ahead before she could answer.

"I thought you said you were close, in and out all the time. Didn't you see them packing?"

"No."

"Didn't you see the moving van?"

"Oh Elliott, there was no moving van. There was only dead of the night secrecy."

"But, why?" he asked.

Patiently Aunt Ginny tried to explain the world as it was forty years ago.

She could give him facts; but she couldn't explain her feelings. She thought she could understand, and it had taken years for her to reach that point, but she couldn't explain it fully to this inquisitive great-nephew of hers.

But Elliott, being Elliott, seized upon ideas and quickly interpreted those long ago events in his own way. "They were afraid. I bet they were afraid. Even if they never said so. So, they left. Maybe they went back to Japan."

"No Elliott, they did not go to Japan. There was no going 'back to Japan' as you put it even to consider. Only the old Grandparents..."

"Grandmother and Grand Pop Yamamoto," he interjected.

"Yes, only Grandmother and Grand Pops Yamamoto had ever been to Japan, and they had been away for over forty years. Lilly, her parents, brothers, aunts, uncles, and all the cousins were all born here; they were Americans. Japan was not their country to go back *to.*"

'Oh, well," Elliott said slowly as if thinking of more to say.

"Anyway," continued Ginny, "They would not have been allowed to leave. They would have been detained and eventually placed in one of the relocation centers."

"That's it..., that's it... That's what happened to them." Elliott jumped up and started walking up and down the length of the porch. Rudy, aroused by the excitement of his master, sat up and panted expectantly.

"They were scared, so they tried to run away but they were caught and put in one of those prisons." He seemed pleased that he had figured out the mystery.

He continued, "And now, they're free...,or..., no..., now, they need help, and they don't trust their guards. So, they helped Mara escape and she came here for help."

He plopped down next to Ginny. "Doesn't it make sense?" he asked.

She leaned back against a porch post, closed her eyes and sighed deeply. "No," she answered.

"No? Why not?" Elliott demanded.

"Oh darling," she said as she cupped Elliott's face in her hands, "Don't you think we looked everywhere? Your Pops scoured the countryside, combed the hills, and visited all pockets of civilization he could find. There was no trace of them.

"And not only was your Pops looking, many people were looking for them. Community representatives and many other individuals were trying to find them. Remember, I said all the Japanese families disappeared. They were not to be found.

"And later after we learned where the relocation camps had been established, we wrote letters trying to locate them, but we never heard a word. Now, the camps have been abandoned for almost 40 years."

"So, they all just disappeared?" he asked. "Never to be heard from again, until now?"

"Yes," Ginny said wearily. "Until now."

They sat quietly for a while. Both lost in thought. Finally, Ginny suggested that they pack up and go home. They had done enough for one day.

As they were leaving, Elliott looked back at the house.

"Aunt Ginny, this house has always been empty, never been lived in as far back as I can remember, but it never looked totally abandoned. Why is that?"

She stopped and looked back. After a moment's thought she smiled and said. "Well Elliott, for two reasons. First, your Pops and I, and then your Grandmother Daisy and I when she was alive, have cleaned the place twice a year for all these years, just in case, you know, so that if any of them returned it would be ready or almost ready for them. That's why today's cleaning went so quickly. We weren't removing forty years of dust and grime, just several months' worth. Of course, our twice yearly cleanings were not as complete as you and I gave it today."

"And the other reason? You said there were two reasons," Elliott prompted.

"Love, friendship, and family. The people were gone, but the strength of those feelings, never left." She looked at him and smiled.

"I believe that love and friendship once truly given never dies. It lives on somewhere, on some level. It has lived on here, never abandoning this place."

After leaving Lilly's house, as Elliott now thought of it, Aunt Ginny announced that they had worked enough for one day and that they deserved a good meal cooked by someone else. So, they made a quick detour down the mountainside to pick up a meal. Ginny told Elliott that because he had been so much help today, he could choose a take-out restaurant for their dinner.

He thought about it, playing with menus in his head. Pizza sounded good, but so did tacos and tostados. Maybe a hamburger and fries.

Suddenly, Mara's brief description of her home pushed its way into Elliott's mind. He wondered if she had ever had a Big Mac. Some people thought the valley was in the middle of nowhere, but if she lived two days walk further into the mountains there were probably no fast food places. No McDonalds, no Pizza Hut, Dairy Queen, Arctic Circle, and surely no Der Weinerschniztel, a local favorite. Now that would really be the middle of nowhere. He wished they would return so that he could ask her.

Finally he decided on his favorite Mexican restaurant, Dos Armadillos, the two armadillos. They had good food and he knew that Aunt Ginny liked their Chimichangas better than hamburgers or pizza, and they offered take out.

Now they were back home and it was early evening. "When do you think they will get home?" Elliott asked Ginny.

"Not for a few hours," she said. "if they make it back tonight."

Elliott looked at her startled. "Not tonight?" he asked.

"Maybe not. It was hard to tell just how far their settlement is from here. And Pops may have to go around rather than over more mountains and valleys than he thought. Also, Lilly's condition might make him wait until morning; that is, if they got there today at all." Aunt Ginny answered.

"Or Lilly's condition might make him hurry to get her to a doctor if she's...', Elliott stopped as he saw the anxiety in his aunt's face. He went to her and put his arm around her shoulder. "I'm sorry Aunt Ginny. I didn't mean to upset you," he said softly. She smiled up at him and together they looked out over the darkened valley and waited.

Henry and Mara, after stopping by the hospital with Lilly, returned in midafternoon of the next day. Lilly was not with them; she was to remain in the hospital. Dr. Cochran, a young man himself when the Japanese community had disappeared, was astounded to see Lilly again. He reassured Mara that her grandmother would be well-taken care of while in the care of the doctors and nurses at St. Mary's. Lilly was apprehensive, but allowed Henry and the doctor to make the decision.

Finally, Henry and Lilly persuaded Mara to return to the farm while the hospital started the testing. Henry joined Mara for a quick late lunch and headed back to the hospital, promising to return with more news as soon as possible.

About 9:00 P.M. he returned. "All test results are good so far. She needs vitamins, iron, but nothing major at the moment." He looked at Mara and continued.

"The doctor wants to keep her a few more days. After all those years without proper medical attention, everyone involved wants to be sure that Lilly is okay, and that there are no residual effects of neglected healthcare. So, further tests have been ordered. Everyone is amazed that her health is so good. She pointed out that she was healthy as a youngster and as a teenager, so she never questioned her good fortune.

"The doctors want to keep an eye on that hip for a while. It is deeply bruised and had some swelling, but the swelling is going down. Still, Dr. Cochran wants to be sure that she stays off that leg for a few days, and he seems to think that she will be up and about too quickly if he releases her. He also wants to be sure there are no lingering effects from what was obviously a concussion."

"Speaking of releasing her," Elliott interjected, "where will she go when she is released? Will she come here or go to the little house or back to their village? Don't you think they should stay here for a few more days? I mean…they really shouldn't go back to the village, should they? It's 'safe' on the outside now. Don't you, think… "

"What I think, Elliott," interrupted Henry before Elliott could continue, "is that it's a decision for Lilly to make."

"But what about Mara? Doesn't she have anything to say about it?" he asked. "She should go to school, you know, real school. It's against the law in Colorado not to go to school. She's not old enough to be a dropout. And I know, I just know, that her Grandmother would not ever let her do that. She thinks education is important. I can tell."

His Aunt Ginny laughed. "Oh you can, can you? At least you've been practicing your powers of observation this summer. First your observations about my tending the peonies, then about the little house not truly being abandoned, and now this. Congratulations, Elliott, your teachers would be proud of you. You're actually exercising your brain this summer!"

She walked over and ruffled his hair, but he pulled away, looking embarrassed by both the action and the words. He looked sheepishly at Mara.

"Well, his powers of observation may be working just fine, but I'm not so sure about his power to draw conclusions. He drew one that might be faulty." said Henry.

"What?" asked Elliott defensively.

"You said Colorado law states that you must go to school."

"That's right. That's why our classes at Mesa Valley View Middle School are full. Not because we all are just dying to be there," Elliott replied.

"You've drawn the conclusion that Mara lives in Colorado. I'm not sure that's correct." Henry explained.

Ginny understood and asked, "You mean, it's that far to the village?"

"Yes, and we twisted and turned, and drove on small unmarked roads and trails. A couple of times I had to backtrack. There were no signs that said 'You are now leaving Colorful Colorado', or 'Welcome to Utah, the Beehive State,' but we covered enough ground that we certainly could have been in Utah."

Everyone looked at Mara. With a shake of her head she said. "I don't know, really. We never talked about it."

Chapter 35

Early the next morning, they all went to the hospital. Elliott and Ginny waited in the waiting room while Mara and Henry visited with Lilly. After a while, Henry returned and said to his sister.

"She can't wait another minute to see you, Gin. Go on up. Room 345." Ginny stood and looked back at Elliott, who was looking a little left out.

"It's okay," Pops said. "Elliott will meet her another time. Besides, we have plans to make." He looked at Elliott and smiled.

After Ginny had disappeared into the elevators, Henry looked at Elliott and said, "You were right,"

"Yeah, about what?" Elliott asked.

"You were right, Lilly wants Mara to go to school, real school," Henry said smiling. "They're home to stay!"

After leaving the hospital, Mara was taken to the little house and fell in love with it.

"Even empty it feels like home," she said as she explained which pieces of family furniture she thought Grandmother would consider worth bringing back and using. Some of the original pieces were still in good condition and were, in fact, family heirlooms. She knew they would be used. Other pieces would have to be purchased, but not now. Later, when Lilly could help make the selections.

The next four days were spent in a flurry of activity. On the first day, Henry left early and went back to the village to get Lilly's furniture and to assure those still in the village that she was going to be fine. He also made arrangements for those still there to be picked up and brought back to the valley in two weeks.

Aunt Ginny was busy making curtains and selecting kitchen equipment. That was a must! Kitchens had changed dramatically since 1942. The owner of the appliance store had always been sweet on Ginny, so he promised delivery before Lilly left the hospital.

After the kitchen had been equipped, Mara and Elliott accompanied Ginny to the supermarket. Mara was awestruck with the store. She had never seen a grocery store or so much food in one place. Elliott was a masterful guide. He wanted to buy everything Mara had never had before, but Ginny retained her good sense and only bought half of the items Mara had not had the chance to try.

On the way home from the supermarket, they stopped at the Dairy Queen for Peanut Buster Parfaits. Elliott's 10,000th; Mara's first. She was delighted. He was enthralled.

"I like introducing you to new things," he said to Mara. "It's fun."

On the third morning, after their hospital visit to Grandmother Lilly, the new kitchen appliances were delivered and installed. The furniture retrieved by Henry was unloaded and placed in the little house, and the newly made curtains hung. The house, given one last sweeping and dusting, was ready and waiting for its absent owner.

Grandmother Lilly was being released the next afternoon, along with a walker which did not please her. She did, however, promise everyone to use it for a few days. She would spend the first night with Henry and Ginny. Ginny was planning to watch her like a hawk to be sure that she could handle the walker well enough to be on her own with Mara in their home.

Everyone was looking forward to their one evening together. It would give them time to catch up on all the news.

After lunch the following day Henry asked Elliott if he would go with him to the hospital to pick up Grandmother Lilly.

"Sure, I'd love to," he said, looking at his Pops with surprise.

"You haven't had a chance to meet her, and I thought this

would give you a chance to spend a few minutes with her," Henry explained.

"Also, her room is full of flowers. Your Aunt Ginny told Suzi Anderson that Lilly was back and in the hospital. Evidently Suzi spread the word, for flowers have been coming in from many of Lilly's old friends who are still in the valley." Henry continued.

"So many flowers." Henry replied with a smile. "Everyone was very fond of Lilly. She was a special girl to many. It's really a shame they stayed away so long."

"Why did they?" asked Elliott.

"I still don't know. That's Lilly's story," replied Henry. "Perhaps she will tell us."

She was not as small as Elliott had imagined. She was not as old and wrinkled as he thought she would be, and she smiled a lot, especially when she looked at Elliott.

"Hello, my dear, "she said with enthusiasm when Henry introduced them. "I am so pleased to finally meet you. Your Pops has told me a lot about you."

She smiled at him and continued, "Mara, also, has told me about you. She says that you are taking care of her. Thank you for being so kind."

She was sitting in a wheelchair as she spoke. She reached up and took his hand, not to shake it, but to pat it tenderly and then continued holding it as Henry pushed the wheelchair toward the exit.

Elliott had not said a word and felt that he should. After much thought he asked, "How are you?"

She said she was fine and feeling better with each passing minute. When they got to the car she smiled gently at Henry but firmly insisted that she would sit in the back with Elliott so that they could talk and he could point out areas of interest as they drove passed them.

"I'm sure I won't recognize anything, and Elliott will know what everything is. He will be my guide to the present," she explained.

Elliott was flattered. He thought he was going to like this lady. He took his responsibility seriously. "Well, this is St. Mary's Hospital," he said. "But you know that don't you?"

"Yes, St Mary's was here even when I was young, but it was a very small hospital back then, not the larger medical facility that it is today. If the rest of the town has grown as much, I've got a lot to see and learn about," Lilly replied.

"It's all changed and the growth has been considerable," interjected Henry from the front seat.

Elliott, not to be upstaged by his Pops, pointed out the new high school they were passing. "Oh my," said Lilly. "That is a real change from our high school."

Her astonishment at the size of Food Express, the largest store in the Food Express chain, was wonderful to see. Elliott could hardly wait to take her inside it. They had everything, he told her, from food to drugs to car tires! Boy would she be shocked when she went shopping.

"And here is Robin Hood Park," Elliott pointed out proudly.

"Robin Hood Park," repeated Lilly. "Stop, Henry. I just want to look at it."

Finally she turned to Elliott and explained. "Robin Hood Park was here when we were young. It has not changed much. The playground equipment is new, but the park itself is much as I remember it. It is still beautiful. We used to picnic here." She turned back to gaze at the heavily wooded park.

"Do you know," she asked Elliott turning back to him, "it was named Robin Hood Park because it had more trees in that one area than any other spot in the valley. Someone said it must be like Sherwood Forest, home of Robin Hood. Thus, it became Robin Hood Park."

"Wow. I didn't know that!" exclaimed an excited Elliott.

She took his hand again and smiling said "Thank you for pointing it out to me, Elliott. It brings back happy memories."

As they continued homeward, Elliott pointed out the TV station, and the shopping mall, and the new bridge across the Colorado River. Lilly asked the appropriate questions and expressed just the right amount of excitement.

Elliott thought he was in love. He would have been surprised to know, in fact he would not have believed, that before the evening was over his feelings for this lady would change dramatically.

Chapter 36

That night Lilly was ready to talk. As she settled herself and collected her thoughts, Henry handed her a glass of wine.

"Wine, Henry?" she asked.

"Wine, Lilly. A lot has changed through the years."

The three adults sipped their wine quietly as the two young people sipped their lemonade and, for a short while, no one spoke.

Then Lilly began, and she talked as if she had to talk; as if talking was helping her adjust to the change of the past few days. Her story even abbreviated, was remarkable.

"We left in the middle of the night because the elders knew that some of our friends, like you and your family, Henry, would try to stop us. My grandparents and the elders of the other families truly felt that we had to leave. They thought that while we may be safe for the moment, we would not be safe forever." She paused and shook her head smiling ruefully.

"I think you both," she said nodding toward Henry and Ginny, "should know that neither Ned, Frank, nor I had any idea of what was going on. We did not try to deceive you. We were simply in the dark about it. Ned and Frank learned of it sometime during the day we left. I learned about it much later that same night. I went with my family only because I had been drugged."

"What?" exclaimed Ginny, interrupting her friend's story.

Smiling at Ginny's distress, Lilly quickly continued. "My mom told me later they were afraid I would fight the plans and perhaps run away and make the entire plan known to others. I would have too; she knew me very well."

She paused and looked at Henry, who said nothing.

"It was not a sudden decision, we later learned. The decision had been made that, should the community begin to fear, we would all leave together. The only thing sudden about it was that the established plan was put into action so quickly."

Lilly paused for a sip of wine, then continued, "We left just hours after hearing that the United States was about to begin gathering Japanese aliens and Japanese-Americans together in camps. A letter from relatives in California brought us this news.

"Did they really do that?" she asked looking at Henry.

"Yes, I'm afraid so," He replied, "but I think you would have been safe here."

"You think, but you don't know for certain?"

"No, I cannot say for certain," Henry admitted.

"So maybe they were right? Maybe." Lilly seemed to contemplate this idea for a few seconds before proceeding.

"Anyway, unknown to all the younger people, our parents had been secretly preparing for months. The adults had slowly drawn most of our money from the bank. New cash that Pop and father earned was not deposited, but hoarded, or spent for stocking up on supplies they thought we would need.

"The elders had spent days scouting for places of refuge for small groups of us. Uncle Sado told me later that abandoned mining towns from Durango to Junction and from Utah to Colorado Springs had been visited."

"You mean ghost towns?" Elliott asked wide eyed.

"Yes," Lilly responded laughing slightly. "Ghost towns."

"Cool," said Elliott.

Smiling, Lilly continued, "Eventually a suitable, in the opinion of 'the committee', place was found for both groups. Our buildings had been well built. This pleased the elders who thought this gave us a real chance to survive.

"I felt I was in prison and just wanted to leave. I ran away often in the early days, only to return as night fell, for the darkness in the mountains can be a frightful thing when you are alone.

"At any rate, we left in the middle of the night. My father's new truck was loaded with our family's supplies as was Uncle Nago's and Uncle Akira's trucks. Ned was even allowed to drive father's old truck. He was only 14 or 15 at the time. He must have thought he was starting a grand adventure, but he soon learned differently.

"I now know that we headed southwest. After several hours of winding travel, we switchbacked slowly up a mountain. I learned later that we had passed only one community after leaving the valley. We couldn't see it, of course, because it was dark.

"Later I learned that it was a very small community called Wayside. There was a general store, and one gas pump. Ranchers, farmers and hermits went there for groceries and news. That is the way Frank described it to me years later. Coming back out earlier this week, I think we must have passed it, but I didn't notice."

"I know Wayside," exclaimed Elliott to Lilly. "We've been down there for picnics. It's a long drive, of course, for a picnic and we only go there when we want to get away for a whole day. Aunt Ginny likes to go there because she says the valleys and meadows in that area remind her of the scenery in The Sound of Music." he finished with a broad smile to Aunt Ginny.

"The Sound of Music?" Mara repeated with a question in her voice.

"It's a movie," replied Ginny before Elliott could answer. He would probably launch into a review of the story. "It's a beautiful but isolated area," she continued," but go on with your story Lilly. What kind of supplies did your family take with you? I hope I sent the right kind of stuff back with Henry."

"I'm sure what you sent was perfect, Gin. Don't worry, they are survivors," replied Lilly reaching over to squeeze Ginny's hand before continuing.

"Our families had tried to prepare for a long stay. Not as long as we stayed, of course, but for several years. Thinking back, I am amazed at how well we were prepared.

"As Uncle Sado explained it to me, we had food staples that each family had purchased over the months prior to leaving. For example, each Friday mother bought double the amount of food staples she needed from Alford's grocery. Then she went to Mr. Tidmore's grocery and did the same. Finally, she stopped by Mac's Market and repeated the process.

"Thinking back I wonder how I missed all that, but evidently I was not the only one to miss it. No one suspected that she was buying more than we needed, but if she had bought all of that in one store, someone might have been suspicious. Our elders had thought of everything and wanted to avoid suspicion. At that time I wished someone had become suspicious.

"Anyway, all the Japanese ladies did the same thing. And they bought bolts of fabric to replace our clothing when it wore out or when we outgrew it. We never threw anything away but always passed it on to someone else. Eventually, everyone was wearing hand me downs."

Looking over at Ginny she said, "I even started wearing Ned's trousers and you know how mom felt about women in slacks." Both women laughed remembering Mrs. Yamamoto's reaction the first time she saw a Junction lady wearing men's pants.

"Times were changing for us and eventually many women in the community felt comfortable wearing men's slacks, especially when working in the gardens and during our cold winters. Anyway, once the fabric could no longer be used for clothing we found other uses for it. Nothing was discarded."

"Recycling," muttered Elliott wisely.

Lilly waited for him to explain and when he didn't, she went on. "We had medical supplies, household goods, and hundreds of candles. The planners thought of everything and, surprisingly, we were very well prepared. Too well prepared, I used to think."

Lilly paused and took another sip of wine before looking at Henry and remarking "This is good Henry. I think I like it."

"You'll learn to love it," was Henry's only remark.

Lilly proceeded to describe the abandoned town that had been selected for them. Elliott was enthralled with the idea of the ghost town. Henry and Ginny were dismayed.

"You don't have to tell us this now, or ever, if it is too hard, Lil," said Ginny softly. "Please stop if you want to."

"No, I'm okay. You and Henry deserve to know what happened to us, for I know you were worried." Both Henry and Ginny nodded in agreement, but neither spoke.

Chapter 37

"We settled down to the business of living. I became a teacher, sooner than I expected, but a teacher nonetheless. After I accepted that this was my life, I actually loved those hours in my classroom. They were an escape for me, I believe," Lilly paused and again looked at Henry and Ginny with a doleful smile before continuing.

"As the months rolled into years, we were doing what we would have been doing back here in the valley. Planting crops, preparing for winter, marrying, and having children. We celebrated holidays and birthdays. We buried our dead and mourned. In a word, we survived. Against all odds, we survived and multiplied just as the Bible admonished the early Christians to do. Some hand, if not His hand, must have been protecting us, for we survived for all this time.

"For a while there were many of us but then as the older folks died and fewer babies were born, our numbers dropped. Now, today there are just a handful of us, and because of Mara's bravery, those of us left will continue to survive." She looked at her granddaughter with so much love that the small gathering could almost feel it.

"Throughout all this, the outside world rarely intruded on us, but there was one thing that always broke my heart. Every time I saw them. Airplanes. Of all things to plunge me into despair, it was airplanes.

"There were only a few at first, but in the last few years more planes have flown over. At first they were potbellied, like our stoves, but now they seem to be longer and sleeker looking. They seem to fly higher in the sky and often have a white smoke-like tail following them.

"They look beautiful against our cloudless blue skies but in those early days, when the big round-bellied airplanes droned overhead, we would act like the fugitives we were and hide. We thought they might be looking for us. I secretly hoped they were, but I guess they weren't.

"Seeing those planes always made me wistful. It was then when I felt that life was really passing us by. I always tried to see the plane early on one horizon and watch it slowly make its way to the opposite horizon. Then I felt both in touch with, and apart from, the rest of the world."

"They're really not moving slowly," Elliott interjected. "Those with the white tails are moving very fast. The white tail is called a vapor trail and is caused... "

At this point, before Elliott could get wound up about airplanes, one of his favorite subjects, Henry interrupted him. "Let's save the aviation lesson for later, Elliott," he said.

Turning back to Lilly, he simply said, "Both Salt Lake and Denver now have major airports and your village might have been on one or both of their flight patterns. But that's unimportant; go on with your story. Didn't anyone ever try to return to us? Or to find out what was going on in the outside world?"

Elliott noticed he looked directly in Lilly's eyes and had emphasized the word us. She looked back into his eyes for a long moment and then continued her story.

"We were very interested in what was going on in the outside world. We never meant to stay away for forty years, but after we settled in we felt safe. At least the elders seemed to feel safe. I felt desolate, but my thoughts and feelings changed nothing.

"After several years, we decided to send someone out to that small community to see what was happening. Frank was chosen to go. It was August of 1945. We had been away for three years.

"Frank took the horse and traveled to Wayside. With his photographic mind and memory, he came back and reported all that he had seen and heard, much of it word-for-word, for he knew he was our eyes and ears to the outside. He was allowed to buy some supplies. He said the old lady who helped him was not friendly and really did not want to sell to him. She stomped out of the store saying, 'I ain't going to sell to no dirty Jap.'

"There was a younger man there, and he told Frank he could buy a few things if he had real American money, but he had to be quick about it. Frank showed him his money. As Frank was leaving the man taunted him with the information that America had bombed Japanese cities and killed thousands of 'Japs'.

"'You'd better be careful, Jap,' the man shouted at Frank, 'you're next.'

"You can imagine the turmoil when Frank returned with this news. We were all upset, and the elders decided that it would be a long time before we were safe.

"The news must have been too much for young Ned, for after Frank returned, Ned simply disappeared. Overnight and alone. I was devastated. I thought I had experienced all the heartache a body could hold, but I was to learn that I was wrong."

Ginny let out a soft sob and whispered, "Oh, Lil, I'm so sorry."

"It's okay, Gin. It was a long time ago and we've lost so many since then."

"Still," Ginny persisted, "to just disappear at his young age. I know it still hurts. It hurts me all these years later."

"You still know me so well, Gin. Yes. It does still hurt. It always will. He loved life and was full of spirit. I can only hope he found a way to live a long life and a happy one. After all this time, I doubt that I will ever know."

Lilly stopped speaking and seemed to be collecting her thoughts. Then she said, "Thinking about what the woman told Frank that day in the store, did America really bomb Japanese cities?"

"Yes," replied Henry. "It was the only way to stop the war. It was in August 1945," he said, remembering the day he and Daisy had first heard the news.

"But it did end the war?" Lilly asked hopefully.

"Yes, eventually," said Henry. "I am astounded at what you have missed. I always imagined that you must be somewhere living a life that at least let you know what was going on in the world. Never this."

"Like I said, Henry, we survived. That is the important thing. Anyway, no one visited the outside world for several years after that, but as the years passed we desperately needed supplies, and we desperately wanted news. By then I had married Jock Shimado and had a baby girl named Carole." Lilly stopped speaking and looked at Henry.

"I remember Jock Shimado," he said.

Elliott opened his mouth to say something, but Aunt Ginny put her hand on his arm and gently shook her head 'no'. Mara sat quietly without moving. Lilly continued.

"After several years, Frank was again sent to Wayside. He returned with a similar story. This time, however, it was Korea that was fighting the Americans. But the reaction in Wayside was much the same. Frank said the man said something about 'all Asians being no-good and that as soon as Uncle Sam finished with the Koreans he would get back to those dirty Japanese.'"

Lilly paused and took a deep breath before continuing. "So, once again. we did not feel safe. Again, we went into a renewed period of seclusion. Korea was too close to Japan, and evidently Americans felt Koreans too close to Japanese for us to feel safe."

"Lilly…" Ginny began.

"No, Gin, I am okay. I want to tell this."

Ginny smiled at Lilly and Lilly smiled back. The bond was still there and still strong.

"Life continued as before. I taught, I took care of my precious baby girl, and eventually of my husband. Surprisingly, life was passing. We waited seven years before Frank again made a trip to Wayside."

"Why did Frank always make the trip?" asked Henry.

"We only wanted one of us to be seen, and Frank was healthy and trustworthy. It's strange how well Frank took to that solitary life. He was always quietly happy, content with our lot in life. He never married, worked the gardens and read. Later, I know he started a journal, but I haven't seen it lately. Maybe it will show up. Henry, I think you might enjoy reading Frank's view of our world."

"I would," said Henry. "Even with the slight age difference between us, Frank and I were close and shared many things. I would enjoy hearing from him through a journal. We will look for it when we go back to get the others."

"Good," replied Lilly. "After seven years Frank went back to the little store. This time the people there were very upset, but neither Japan nor other Orientals were the reason. It was the Russians! It seemed that they had sent something into the sky to spy on America. The people at Wayside said they would surely attack from space. This time they encouraged Frank to take extra supplies and to build a 'bomb shelter' like others were doing.

"Frank bought what he could and hurried home. We worried for a long time, but never felt any type of attack. Did the Russians attack the United States?"

"No," replied Henry, stunned by what he was hearing.

Elliott seemed to think Lilly and Mara needed further explanation. "That was just Sputnik," he explained. "It was a satellite. It didn't do anything." Elliott was beginning to sound condescending once again, so Ginny interrupted him.

"Sputnik was a satellite launched by Soviet rockets. It scared us all. Panic took over much of America for many were convinced that the satellite was spying on the U.S. to determine which cities to attack. Many people built and stocked underground bomb shelters for their families to use if we should be attacked."

"They were frightened, just like our people were," said Mara with wonder.

"Yes," replied Ginny.

"But there was no reason to be afraid," Elliott continued. "Russia never attacked us. In fact, we're better in the space game than they are."

"The space game?" Mara asked.

"You know, the space race. We landed on the moon long before they did," Elliott replied.

Mara and Grandmother Lilly looked at each other and then back to Elliott.

"Landed what on the moon?" asked Mara.

"Why men, of course," replied Elliott. "July 21, 1969, Neil Armstrong and Buzz Aldrin landed and walked on the moon. The third astronaut, Michael Collins was... "

"Save it for your aviation lecture later, Elliott," Henry said. "Let's hear the rest of Lilly's story."

Lilly continued, "Again several years passed before Frank visited Wayside. He usually made his trips in late summer or early fall. This year he was a little later leaving. It was late November. When he did not return in the usual number of days we were worried. Finally two days later he arrived home.

"The President has been assassinated," he announced solemnly.

"My first thought, of course, was for President Roosevelt, but then common sense told me that he would no longer be president. I didn't' even know who was President of the United States. That's when I felt totally isolated. That's when my heart wept. Not for a president I didn't know, but for a country I had lost. For a life that had been taken; not the president's life, but mine."

She looked at Henry. "And yours, Henry."

After a moment she continued. "We waited for about three years and sent Frank back to Wayside. He returned with supplies and with news that America was at war again. And again with Asian people who might draw attention to the Japanese.

"This time the war was in Vietnam. I knew where that was, knew that again we would remain in our village for safety.

"For a long time, life did not seem to move forward, but the young have a way of getting on with living. My daughter, Carole, married Peter Maida. Many of the marriages among us happened because the young people liked each other well enough and there was no one else to marry. But Carole and Peter really loved each other. They were very happy and did not seem to care about the outside world.

"Of course, they had never known the outside world, so how could they care about it or miss it. I think that was a blessing to them and their generation. You don't mourn what you don't know. Their happiness was made complete when after two years of marriage, Mara was born. They were all very happy together until Carole and Peter died last year. Mara came to live with me. Now, I think she is happy again.

"After the news of fighting in Vietnam, we waited several years and then sent Frank out again. It was around 1974. He never returned. He was over forty years old at that time. Maybe the trip was too hard on him. Maybe he met with anger and harm from someone on the outside. We do not know. We waited for a long time; then we began to grieve and became more worried for our safety.

Lilly sighed, took another small sip of wine, and continued with her story. "Again, the years went by, and the young people kept us going. They seemed happy. They had no newspaper, no radio, and now after a few days back and in the hospital, I would add that they had no television to tell them what they were missing. They lived a primitive but happy life.

"I think, perhaps, that our lives must have paralleled the lives of the early western settlers. Except that in our case, just a couple hundred miles away civilization seems to have been progressing at levels incomprehensible to us."

Lilly stopped talking and seemed to be gathering her thoughts before she continued.

"Finally it was time to send someone else out to the outside. We sent one of the young men from another family. He was very young and not married. He was gone for several days longer than Frank was usually gone. We were getting worried about him, but finally one day he returned with supplies, but no news.

"Some of our people felt that was good news. Some considered it ominous. The older people wanted to wait and send someone else out in a couple of years. The young man seemed changed by his trip. He became very secretive. One morning we awoke to find him and some of the other young men his age gone. These were the young, unmarried men of the village.

"They left a note saying they could not stay. They understood our fears, but did not share them. They were afraid someone would try to stop them, so they left in the middle of the night. I always thought that it seemed like an appropriate way to leave. Secretly, in the middle of the night.

"At about this same time, somewhere in the late seventies, many of our number became ill. Without apparent cause, they would become very weak and soon die. We could not understand it." Lilly looked toward Henry with a questioning look on her face.

"The deaths might have been the result of some environmental cause," Henry said to fill the quiet void that filled the room when Lilly paused in her story.

"Environment?" she asked.

"Yes, modern scientific and medical research has proven that substances in the environment, in the earth, air, or water, can be harmful. Some of these substances can cause death after long terms of exposure to them," he explained.

"But how were we exposed to anything harmful. We never went anywhere or did anything. We lived quiet, simple lives," responded Lilly.

"You lived your quiet, simple lives in a deserted mining town, quite possibly a uranium mining town, if my guess is correct.

"You and your children and grandchildren lived, played, and ate products of the area. Many believe that mining leaves behind dangerous residues. Perhaps those deaths were the result of the location of your village. It's only a conjecture, and it would take years of research to prove it, and still some would dispute it." Henry concluded.

"But if it is true, we tried to save one generation only to lose a future generation. And it was all unnecessary. We acted from ignorance. Ignorance made us flee, and in our ignorance we ran into a possible breeding place of death."

After a prolonged pause Lilly continued.

"To finish our history, and it is almost over. Since the young men left about four years ago, we haven't sent anyone else out, but about two years ago, many of the young couples who remained left. Again in the middle of the night.

"Those of us remaining behind waited, thinking we would hear from them, that they would send word to us that the world was safe, but we heard nothing. So, again, we didn't know if it was safe or if they had met with misfortune.

"We were simply in a state of waiting when I fell, and the others felt that they must seek help. Mara was the only answer. They could only pray that she would be safe, that she would find you or your children; someone who would help. And she did."

Chapter 38

Everyone was quiet for a moment. Finally Elliott could wait no longer. He had questions that needed to be answered, and he felt that Grandmother Lilly would answer them.

"How did you keep up with time? Not hours and days, but years?"

"We took our 1942 calendars with us. Each new year we made a new calendar using that one as our basis. If you visit our community, you will see a calendar for each year scrawled on the walls of the general store. Some years we had crayons to use, others years just pencils and even porous rocks, and something like coal," she replied. "I know we're okay on the month and years, but I think we're off on the days because of a few leap years we forgot about."

"Did anyone ever come to your village?" Elliott asked

"Occasionally a lone lost man would wander through. Hermits, miners, and prospectors usually avoided us as much as we avoided them. Perhaps they were a hiding also." Lilly replied.

"Ok, next question," said Elliott, leaning in toward Lilly .

"Oh, Elliott, I don't know. Lilly should get her rest," said Ginny.

"Just one more, please," begged Elliott. "It's important."

"One more," said Lilly smiling at him.

Elliott paused, phrasing his question in his mind. If he had only known the answer; if he had known that this one question would change his warm feeling for this lovely lady, he might not have been in such a hurry to ask it.

But he didn't know.

"Earlier you said that you felt like your life had been taken away," he said to Grandmother Lilly. "Then you added that Pops' life had been taken too. Why did you say that? Pops has never been lost except in Italy in the war, and he has never been in hiding. Why did you say his life has been taken away?"

Lilly looked at Henry. Ever so slightly he nodded yes to her. "Well, Elliott, dear," she began and took his hand. "Henry, your Pops, and I were in love. We planned to be married someday."

Elliott looked at her closely. She continued, "When I left and never returned I lost that life, the life I'd always wanted. And Henry lost that life, the life he'd always wanted."

Elliott jerked his hand from her. "No!" he said.

"We loved each other, dear, very much," she continued softly.

He wished she'd stop calling him dear. He was not her dear. He was his Grandmother Daisy's dear, even if she was dead. "No, Pops loved my Grandmother, not you. And he still does. And I loved my Grandmother and not you. And I still do." Elliott was almost shouting.

"He had a life with my Grandmother and with my mother and with me and Aunt Ginny. He didn't need you," This last statement was hurled over his shoulders as he ran from the room.

Elliott ran from the house. Although it was late and very dark on the mountainside, he made his way to the boulder without any difficulty. He looked toward the valley, the lights sparkled like bright diamonds in the night. As his mind raced with thoughts of his Grandmother, the diamonds blurred, and Elliott realized that he was crying.

Elliott did not remember his parents, but he did remember Grandmother Daisy. After the death of his parents he lived with her and Pops on the family ranch. She was the one who took him to his first day of school. She surprised him with a 'big boy's bike' on his birthday. She let friends sleep over. She bought dozens of bars of chocolate when he was trying to be the top seller on his little league team. And she took care of him when he was sick or injured. Even when he was scared.

He remembered the pain of her death. When she died, he felt that life would never be the same. He was sure that he would never be carefree again; never romp with Rudy, never laugh and shout with friends, but somehow he had.

The heart-stopping ache had eased and in its place were wonderful memories. Memories of love. He felt secure in her love for him and his love for her. It had always been freely given and received. So, too, had Pops' love for both of them.

Until tonight.

How could Lilly say that Pops loved her? No, it couldn't be true. Pops loved Grandmother Daisy. He did. He had to.

As anguish tore through Elliott's body, he whispered, "I love you Grandmother. I love you. And I know that Pops loves you, too."

He has to. He always said he loved you, and he loved me.

He did; he does; doesn't he?

Elliott sat for a very long time on the boulder. His mind raced. He relived all his earlier grief, but now there was another element added. He questioned his Pops' love. That hurt. Oh, how that hurt.

Sitting there alone for so long, he was beginning to think that no one cared for him. He was hurting, and in that hurt new doubts and fears came rushing to his mind.

Finally he felt a soft arm around his shoulder. He recognized the feel of Aunt Ginny's body as she held him tight. She said nothing, she only allowed him to cry until he could cry no more.

When all his tears were spent, and the sobs had left his body, he felt worn out, as if he had fought a battle. All he could say was "I love you, Aunt Ginny."

"And I love you too, Elliott. More than you know," she said.

Chapter 39

The following morning Elliott was sitting with Rudy in Rudy's favorite out of the way place underneath a lilac bush. It was private and cool, and under the window of Henry's study.

Henry was there doing some paperwork when Lilly asked if she could come in. Elliott thought about leaving, he knew he should, but he was still too hurt by last night's events to really care whether eaves dropping was right or wrong. He stayed.

"Mara has told me that the house is ready for us. I think we should go there now," Lilly said.

"Are you sure you're strong enough?" Elliott heard his Pops ask in a voice filled with concern.

"I am strong enough. And Mara is strong. You forget what we've been through and how we lived. We're survivors, you know."

"Yes, and I'm sorry." Henry said.

"For what, Henry? I am the one to be sorry. I never meant to hurt or upset Elliott," she said. Elliott crawled closer to the window. Rudy started to get up, but Elliott pushed him down and whispered, "Down, boy." Obediently, Rudy laid down beside his master.

Lilly continued, "If I had had any idea that he would react like that, I would never have told him about us."

"Elliott is imaginative and headstrong. He feels things deeply. He did not stop to remember that you're speaking of the past," Henry replied.

"That's true," Elliott softly mumbled to himself. "But you still should never have loved her."

As if she could hear him Lilly said softly, "That's true, but I'm sure he feels that you never should have loved anyone but his grandmother. She must have been very special. I wish you would tell me about her."

"Boy, could I tell that Lilly about Grandmother," Elliott whispered to Rudy in their hiding place. "She was loving and kind and fun to be with. And I loved her very much." The words silently danced from Elliott's lips.

"She was loving and kind and fun to be with, and I loved her very much," Henry echoed. Elliott sat up straighter, not wanting to miss a word. Now Lilly will hear the truth, he thought. It was quiet in the study. So quiet Elliott could hear his heart beating.

Finally Henry continued. "After you left I searched for you everywhere. I stopped searching only when it was my time to serve in the Army. It seemed that Uncle Sam wanted me. So I went. I told my chaplain that I didn't mind serving my country, but that I wanted to serve on the European front not in the Pacific. I knew that I could fight Hitler. Even after the attack on Pearl Harbor, I knew that fighting the Japanese would be hard." He paused. Again Elliott wished he could see his Pops and Lilly. But he could only listen to Pops' story.

"I rarely came home on leave, even when I was working construction on the base. I finally accepted that you were gone for good. I returned to active service life. I did not want to stay here without you."

Elliott sat back, stunned. Pops had not said he loved Lilly, but he was telling her that he had not wanted to live in the valley without her. Elliott was not sure he should hear more, but then Henry continued.

"In early 1945, shortly before the end of the war, my division was sent to Italy. Soon, I was wounded and left for dead. That changed my life. I was unconscious for weeks. In fact, I did not wake until the war had ended. During that time, I was housed and cared for by an Italian couple, both doctors, and their daughter and her best friend, both nurses. The first person I saw when I regained consciousness was a bright-eyed beauty named Daisy." Knowing the story very well, Elliott was pleased to hear it repeated to Lilly.

"She took my temperature and my heart. The very first words uttered when I opened my eyes were 'Ti amo', I love you." Elliott mouthed the words with Henry for that was how he always started this story. Elliott was not, however, prepared for his next statement; he had never heard it before.

"Until that day my heart had been frozen. I never thought I could love anyone but you. Your laughing eyes and gentle smile haunted me for years. But suddenly here was another pair of eyes and another smile that cut through the frozen tundra of my heart, and at long last, let the warm sunny breezes back in." Henry paused.

Elliott could tell from the direction of his voice that his Pops had moved. Closer to Lilly or away from her he did not know.

"She restored my life, Lilly," Henry said. "She gave me a reason to live. I thought I had lost her once, and again my life was a barren wasteland, but she returned to me. I moved quickly. I didn't want to take the chance of losing her again.

"We had a whirlwind courtship. A few months later we were married. I loved her with all my heart; Elliott was right about that. I still do. And I miss her every day of my life."

Elliott sat back. His world was right again. Pops did love Grandmother. And him, too, he was absolutely sure of it

Henry's next words took Elliott by surprise.

"She knew all about you. She knew and she understood. She even helped look for you whenever a new lead came up. We, the two of us, never stopped looking for you."

Again Elliott was stunned. Grandmother knew about Lilly and didn't care. She still loved Pops. She helped him look for Lilly. Elliott did not understand.

Lilly spoke. "She must have been a wonderful lady. Her love for you was very strong. Strong enough for her to know that your love for her was total. Otherwise, she would not have helped you search for us. I wish I had known her. In my heart she is already special."

Elliott, still under the window and behind the lilac, was trying hard to understand.

Henry continued. "It was her idea to keep the little house ready for you. My family had been paying the yearly taxes so that the property would remain in your family's name. Ginny and I had always made sure that it was in good repair, but it was Daisy's idea to keep the little house always ready, or nearly ready for you. She planted the peonies."

Elliott pictured his Grandmother, kind and loving. He had always known she was those things. He just didn't know how kind and loving she actually had been.

"You were very lucky to have found her," Lilly said. "I am so glad you did."

After a long silence she continued. "And yes, I am strong enough to go to my own home, the home that love kept alive."

As she reached the door she turned to Henry and said, "Someday you should tell Elliott that story. He loves his grandmother very much. I think he deserves to know just how exceptional she was. I think Elliott must be a lot like her."

Outside the window Elliott was confused. After the way he behaved last night how could Lilly think he was anything like the wonderful trusting woman he had just heard his Pops describe.

"He's very much like her," Henry replied.

Chapter 40

Lilly and Mara moved into their own home later that day. Ginny was still anxious about Lilly's health, but Lilly assured her that she and Mara would be fine.

Henry and Ginny went with them to help them 'settle in'. Elliott did not. Since overhearing Henry's conversation with Lilly, he felt better about things, but he still wasn't sure he wanted to be friends with Lilly.

His relationship with Mara had changed also. All morning she had avoided him. Not that he had been looking for her. He had not, for somehow he blamed her for his confusion and hurt. But when they had passed each other in the house, she had thrown back her head and muttered, "Humph."

So she was mad, well, let her be mad. He had more important things on his mind. He knew his Pops would eventually want to talk with him. He knew he would eventually have to face Lilly and even apologize. He wasn't sure he could do it. Not yet. So he stayed out of everyone's way as much as possible.

That was easy for everyone, even Pops, seemed to be giving him time to himself. They weren't avoiding him exactly, but they weren't trying to engage him in conversation either.

Not until late afternoon anyway. Finally, as the sun was going down Henry called Elliott to come join him on the front porch. Elliott knew the time had come.

"This was your Grandmother's favorite time of day," Henry said, surprising Elliott because he was expecting 'you have to apologize to Lilly.'

Elliott looked out over the valley. The wispy white clouds that floated over the valley all day, were turning a pinky-orange as twilight approached. Against the deep blue late afternoon sky they, looked like feathers from some exotic bird.

"I know," replied Elliott. He realized that he was replying as much to what he had expected Pops to say, as to what he actually said. "I know," he said again. He waited for his Pops to speak again.

For a long time, Henry was quiet. Finally he said. "I did love your Grandmother, Elliott. Very much. I still do. I hope you believe that."

"I know," Elliott said again. And he did know, not just because he had heard Pops tell Lilly, but also because the beauty of the sunset seemed to draw him closer to his Grandmother and from somewhere came certain knowledge of love that healed his heart.

"I believe you, Pops, and I'm sorry about how I behaved and what I said last night."

Henry looked at him and smiled. Neither spoke for a while. They just watched the distant mountains turn fiery red in the beautiful sunset.

Finally, Elliott spoke. "I know I owe Lilly an apology. I will apologize to her, sometime," he said.

"That's fine," replied Henry.

Again they sat in silence until Henry continued.

"I did love her, Elliott."

Elliott was about to say 'Yes, I really believe you', when he realized that Pops might not be talking about Grandmother.

Instead, he asked, "Her?"

"Lilly," Henry said softly.

"Oh," Elliott replied.

"And now?" Elliott finally asked.

"Now she is a very dear friend, one I shall always love for the memories of my youth that I share with her."

Elliott swallowed hard and blinked. Before he could say anything Henry continued. "There will always be a spot in my heart where she lives."

Henry turned and looked directly at Elliott, "But, Elliott, there isn't a spot in my heart where your grandmother doesn't live. Do you understand?"

Elliott thought for a minute. "You mean, Lilly has a part of your heart?"

Henry nodded yes.

"But," Elliott continued slowly, "Grandmother has all of your heart, even the part that Lilly has. That part she must share with Grandmother?" Henry nodded yes.

As Elliott looked back to the fading sunset, he felt the warmth of an embrace suddenly surround him. Slowly tears rolled down his cheeks.

"I love you, Pops,"

"I love you too, Elliott."

Chapter 41

Time passed. Henry and Ginny could often be found at the little house. Elliott did not visit at the little house, but when he went by he would wave. No one pressed him to play with Mara or to be close to Lilly.

Others filled their days. After news of their return spread, old friends came to visit Lilly, and through them Mara made friends. From Ginny and Henry's discussions Elliott knew that both Lilly and Mara were adjusting to modern civilization with amazing speed.

Elliott felt a little disappointed about that. He remembered how he had looked forward to bringing Mara up to date on things important to his world. One day, seeing Mara ride past, returning home with a friend's mother, Elliott felt left out. He turned and headed away from the house. He didn't realize where he was headed until he looked up and saw the family cemetery in the distance.

He thought he saw movement. Quickly he stretched to see who or what was in the cemetery. Going closer, he saw that Lilly was placing a vase of peonies on his Grandmother's grave. As she arranged the flowers she seemed to be talking to someone.

Seeing no one else, Elliott crept closer and listened.

"Thank you for being there for him, for knowing and understanding. Thank you for loving him and giving him a lovely family."

She was quiet for a moment. Then she continued. "I hope that knowing that I had been a part of his life, never brought you a moment's pain. Thank you, my sister, for giving him life."

Again she remained quiet for a long time. She seemed content to sit quietly by the grave. Finally, Elliott walked over to her and slipped his arm around her. He gave her a small, timid smile. They stayed that way, remaining quiet for a long time.

When Lilly finally stood and turned to go, Elliott said to her, "I'll walk back with you."

"I'd like that. It's a long way up here, but it is very beautiful. I can see why your Grandmother Daisy wanted to be buried here, rather than in that new cemetery on the highway." She looked around her, and then continued, "With the valley below and the endless sky above, it is a wonderful place to be at peace."

Elliott stopped walking and turned to Lilly.

"Why did you call her your sister?" he asked sheepishly, and then rushed to explain. "I heard you talking to her."

Lilly smiled. "We're all sisters or in your case, brothers. The color of our skin or the slant of our eyes is only exterior trimming. The inner person is what's important. It's what makes us individuals. It's what makes us sisters. The inner beauty of your Grandmother Daisy was great enough to include me. That's makes us sisters. "

After a few steps, Elliott looked up at Lilly. "Lean on me," he said, taking her arm. "Maybe the trip down won't seem so long."

"I'm sure it won't," she replied. "I'm sure it won't."

At the bottom of the hill, Henry and Mara were waiting for them.

"Come with us," Henry said. "Ginny has prepared a wonderful picnic in the peach orchard. Daisy had me build a picnic table out there and it has been our favorite picnicking spot for years. She's waiting."

Lilly looked at Elliott with a question in her eyes. He smiled and ran ahead to catch up with Mara who was not waiting for his permission to join them.

Because they were running ahead, Elliott and Mara did not see Henry and Lilly link pinky fingers and lean in to each other as a sudden breeze softly surrounded all of them.

Epilogue

Grand Junction, Colorado
Years later

We will leave tonight. My beloved and I.
No one will mourn our leaving.

It is not that we have not loved and been loved.
It is not that we have never known the joy of family and friends.
We have known both, to the fullest.
We have loved and been loved by many.
That is all gone now. They are all gone now.
It is just the two of us.

The mind has been stolen
Only the shell remains.
Still, the shell is loved.

Together we pass through this earthly veil.
No one will mourn. We have mourned them all.
I hope they await; all of them.
Such a reunion that will be.
But that is still ahead for we must leave.

Come my beloved; let me climb up beside you.
Let me hold you as we depart this earth.
The doctor has assured me that you will follow shortly.
So one last kiss and one last sleep in your arms, forever.
My Beloved.
Ti amo, amore mio.

Author's Notes

When I started this endeavor, four things were certain: my protagonist was to be from western Colorado, Grand Junction in particular, he was to be a member of a military unit that fought in Italy, Japanese Americans would be part of the story, and the time period was to be WWII.

After a few weeks in Italy, and particularly in the Tuscan area of Val d'Orcia, I knew that I wanted that area to be a major part of my Italian setting. The hills and valleys of western Colorado, and the hills and hill towns of Tuscany, provided colorful comparisons and contrasts to each other.

I knew from living in Grand Junction for many years that the Japanese American community there was an integral part of the wonderful farming community and could provide a layer of characterization that the story would lose without them. Likewise, the colorful Italians in Tuscany could do the same.

Finally, I remembered a middle grades novel that I had written and put away many years ago. The setting was Grand Junction and ghost towns in Colorado. There was the mystery of a missing part of the community, and the eventual solution to that mystery. That story was set in WWII, but the war itself was not a part of the story. That work was told through the eyes of twelve-year-old Elliott and there was no love story involved.

Nevertheless, I pulled that work out, reread it, laughing and crying along the way, and decided that I wanted to rewrite it as an adult historical fiction romance.

Thus, Twilight of Memory was born, but not with that title. Early on I called it Canyons of Memory. Then, Through a Veil (Vale) of Memory, and A Relationship with Memory. I was not happy with those titles. One day I came across Khalil Gibran's "The Farewell."

There I found the phrase, twilight of memory, and knew immediately that I had, at last, found my title.

As mentioned in my disclaimer at the front of this work, this is a novel. Some will call it historical fiction, some historical romance. I call it both.

Fact from fiction: Twilight of Memory and 10th Division History

One of the hardest tasks facing me was deciding which military unit from WWII I wanted for my protagonist. I searched for days, reading countless accounts of brave men fighting in Italy. As my storyline developed, I knew I had a certain timeframe within which I wanted it to happen. Having already declared Henry an outdoor enthusiast, I was thrilled to find the U.S. Army's 10th Alpine/Mountain Division.

As I read and researched this division, I fell in love. Not only was it the right division for Henry, but it was also the right division for me. I knew with a certainty that I had the right division the day I found that they had trained in the newly built Camp Hale high in the Colorado Rocky Mountains. We were meant for each other.

Historically, the need for a division trained in Alpine or mountain warfare became evident when the Soviet Union invaded Finland in November of 1939. The Finnish soldiers on skis destroyed two Russian tank divisions. This provided Charles Minot (Minnie) Dole the opportunity to champion his belief that the U.S Army needed troops trained in winter mountain warfare conditions. After many struggles by Dole, the first mountain unit was born on December 8, 1941 at Fort Lewis, Washington.

The U.S. National Ski Patrol was instrumental in recruiting members. The first recruits included Olympic skiers, Ivy League college skiers, and outdoorsmen familiar with snowy mountain activities. These first recruits trained on Mt. Rainer, Washington.

As World War II intensified in Europe and the Axis Powers were holding strategic mountain locations in the Alps and Apennines, the Army intensified its Alpine training with a new training facility built high in the Colorado Mountain.

Camp Hale, Colorado

Construction of Camp Hale began on April 7, 1942 and the completion date was scheduled for November of that year. The project was massive: an entire base was to be built, but only after a major highway and river were rerouted.

Located in the Pando Valley area near Leadville, Colorado, Camp Hale eventually housed approximately 16,000 soldiers and 3,900 animals, mostly mules. Later German prisoners of war were housed at Hale. Of the total number approximately 14,000 military personnel stationed there were members of the 10th Mountain Division.

The selection of this site for winter/mountainous training was appropriate. The camp lay at 9,000+ feet, and the Weather Bureau estimated that the local annual snowfall average at the time of construction was 163.5 inches. Minimum winter temperatures at construction have been calculated to be as low as approximately -40 degrees Fahrenheit. Over 400 of the camp vehicles had kits installed that would heat the battery and keep the motor warm while the vehicle was turned off overnight. Summer temperatures were approximately 90 degrees.

Camp Hale was placed on the National Register of Historic Places on April 10, 1992. There are interpretive signs at the site of Camp Hale and at the entrance to Ski Cooper. A Colorado highway, U.S. Highway 24, between Leadville and Minturn, has been designated The Tenth Mountain Division Memorial Highway. It is on the National Scenic and Historic Byways.

The 10th Mountain Division

Originally the Division was always referred as the 10th Light Infantry Division (Alpine) or the 10th Light, until it was reorganized at Camp Swift on November 6, 1944 and received the "Mountain Division" designation. Thus, I refer to the Division as the 10th Light Division (Alpine) when discussing the period from July 15, 1943 to November 5, 1944. Prior to July 15, 1943, there was no Division structure. The organization was run under the auspices of the Mountain Training Center at Camp Hale.

For most of 1942, there was only the 87th Mountain Infantry Regiment as a stand-alone unit. This 87th would eventually become part of the 10th Mountain Division along with the 85th and 86th. The 10th Light Division (Alpine) was much smaller; perhaps 10,000 men, and it lacked much in the way of heavy weapons.

On June 22, 1944, the Division was ordered to relocate to Camp Swift, Texas, and the Division was increased to almost 14,000 men and heavy mortars and heavier artillery were added. So, the two configurations were really quite different. On November 6, 1944, the 10th Alpine Division was designated the 10th Mountain Division and the blue and white mountain tab was authorized.

The 85th, 86th, and 87th Regiments departed Fort Patrick Henry, VA for Italy on three ships between Dec. 11, 1944 and Jan. 4, 1945, all arriving in the Bay of Naples and soon departing for the area around Pisa, Italy.

After much study, I placed Henry Townsend in the 86th Regiment. The force guiding my decision was simple; they were in the area I wanted them to be and during the time frame I needed them to be. The 85th and 87th Division were soon nearby, as were other Allied units.

As reported by Henry in a letter home, while still in their staging area at Quercianellla, south of Pisa, the 86th Regiment's Chaplain and four medics were killed and four soldiers wounded by "Bouncing Betty's" even before the regiment was engaged in battle.

On Jan. 8-9, 1945, the 86th Regiment entered the front lines north of Bagni di Lucca, relieving Task Force 45 in the Mt. Belvedere area. The Brazilian 1st Infantry Division protected their right flank. The left flank was open with 25 miles of mountains between the 86th and the next Allied unit. Casualties began to mount.

By Jan. 20th, all three of the 10th's regiments were on or near the front line between the Serchio Valley and Mt. Belvedere. For weeks, reconnaissance and combat patrols, some of them on skis, were used to gather information. At the same time, plans were drawn up for an assault on Riva Ridge and Mt. Belvedere.

Jan. 28-29 troops of the 85th and 87th Regiments relieved the 86th, which moved behind the lines to the Lucca area to prepare for the coming attack on Riva Ridge.

Feb. 18-19 a large contingent of the 86th made a daring night climb and successfully assaulted Riva Ridge, which rises steeply 1700-2000 feet above the rushing Dardagna River. This attack required the element of stealth and surprise. By daybreak, the mountaineers had taken Riva Ridge at the cost of only one casualty, but ferocious enemy counterattacks soon followed. Fighting continued until February 25th when finally the entire Riva Ridge was securely in the hands of the 86th.

Close to midnight on Feb.19, the command to "Move out" was finally heard. Part of the 87th advanced toward Polla and Corona, and on the western slope of Mt. Belvedere along the Valpiana ridge. In the center, part of the 85th headed directly for the summit of Mt. Belvedere, while another part attacked Mt. Belvedere's sister peak, Mt. Gorgolesco. On the right, a battalion of the 86th moved along the side of the ridge toward Mazzancana. Two battalions in reserve waited orders to join the fight.

During this Feb18th-25th time frame, a daring engineering feat was accomplished by the engineers from D Company of the 126th Engineers of the 10th. It was soon discovered that removing wounded or dead men from the high reaches of the mountain was very time consuming and dangerous. Therefore, an aerial tramway was built. It reached to a point near the top of one of Riva's peaks. On the first day of operation, 30 wounded were quickly and safely evacuated and 5 tons of supplies delivered to the summit.

On Feb 24th, part of the 86th renewed their assault on Mr. della Torraccia. It was taken by 3:00 PM. This was the last enemy stronghold in the area.

The figures given to Henry by the Army representative are correct or as close as possible. The Riva Ridge operation had cost the division 76 casualties: 21 KIA, 52 WIA, and 3 POW. The battles for control of the Mt. Belvedere-Mt. della Torraccia Ridge cost the division 923 casualties: 192 KIA, 730 WIA and 1 POW. It was somewhere in these days of fierce fighting that Henry was wounded, taken and discarded by the Germans, shot in the head and left for dead in a ravine above a frozen creek.

On March 3, with Riva Ridge, Mt. Belvedere and Mt. della Torraccia secured, the division began its pursuit of the German Army through the Po Valley. This pursuit was crucial in the final steps to eliminate the threat of the Germans in Italy. Thus, the fighting was not over, and causalities continued to mount for the 10th.

Germany's surrender in Italy finally came on May 2, 1945, at Lake Garda. Nevertheless, fighting in Northern Europe continued until General Dwight Eisenhower accepted Germany's unconditional surrender at Reims, France on May 7, 1945.

In late July the men of the 85th, 86th, and 87th Regiments of the 10th Mountain Division were on their way home. When they arrived at the Statue of Liberty, they were met by tugboats and fireboats and welcomed home as the heroes they were.

For their service during World War II, soldiers of the division were awarded one Medal of Honor, three Distinguished Service Crosses, one Distinguished Service Medal, 449 Silver Star Medals, seven Legion of Merit Medals, 15 Soldier's Medals, and 7,729 Bronze Star Medals.[30] The division itself was awarded two campaign streamers. http://10thmtndivassoc.org/chronology.pdf

In modern history, this division, now stationed at Fort Drum, NY, has seen a different type of service: Desert Shield/Storm, Hurricane Andrew Relief, Somalia, Operation Restore Hope, Operation Continue Hope, 2-14th Infantry Battalion Aids Rangers (Mogadishu), Operation Uphold Democracy (Haiti), Operation Joint Guard – Bosnia, Task Force Eagle (Bosnia and Herzegovina), Operation Enduring Freedom (Afghanistan) and Operation Iraqi Freedom. Even as I was writing this novel, members of today's 10th were killed in action.

For a tribute to the men who made this mighty push through the Apennines and into the Po Valley and on to capture the enemy, please watch this tribute set to music.

http://www.youtube.com/watch%3Fv%3D4tJCjLtlybU

Post WWII: The 10th Division's Legacy to the outdoor life

While the 10th Division's legacy can be felt in many outdoor activities around the world, many of the 10th's ski soldiers returned to Colorado and were instrumental in the development of the Colorado ski industry.

The first major development for these men was the Arapahoe Ski Basin. Aspen, of course, was already a skiing community, but a small one with plenty of room to grow. Just outside Aspen, which is notoriously steep, a gentler area was built, Buttermilk Mountain. Tenth men worked together to establish what has become the largest ski resort in North America, Vail.

Members of the 10th were part of the 1948 Winter Olympics in St. Moritz, both as contestants and as the coach. Others became part of the ski equipment industry, both as manufacturers and distributors. Still others continued to enjoy the ski communities through ski-lift businesses. Others became writers and and editors for outdoor magazines and newspapers.

Their outdoor activities were not limited to Colorado. From university ski teams to the Olympics of 1948, to ski areas in California, Utah, and New Hampshire, the men of the 10th left a peacetime impact.

Not all of the WWII 10th's veterans went into outdoor connected activities. Many are known around the world in various business, educational, scientific, religious, artistic, and humanitarian endeavors. No matter what they did after the war, they all became part of what Tom Brokaw called "the greatest generation," an appropriate name in my opinion.

Grand Junction, Colorado

The City of Grand Junction is the county seat of Mesa County and the largest city in western Colorado. It gets its name from the junction of the Colorado and Grand Rivers which meet there.

Known as the Grand Valley, prehistoric dinosaur bones have been uncovered there. It was once home to the Ute Indians. White settlers arrived in the 1880's.

It is a major fruit-growing region, beginning with apples and expanding to include many tree fruits. In recent years, vineyards have been planted and several wineries now flourish.

The Grand Valley has the monoliths and pinnacles of Colorado National Monument on the West above the Colorado River, the Bookcliffs on the North, Mt. Garfield and the Grand Mesa, the world's largest flattop mountain, on the East, and the valley opens up for miles to the south as one heads to Ouray, Telluride, Durango, and even Gateway, my prototype for Wayside.

Acknowledgements

Even before this project was a thought in my mind or a desire in my heart, I visited Italy and learned from out hostess, Isabella Moricciani at Cretaiole of the great destruction during WWII to the heart of Tuscany. She introduced me to Iris Origo's wonderful journal memoir, War in Val d'Orcia. From that beginning the seed of desire to write about WWII in Tuscany began to grow.

When I first determined that I wanted Henry in the 10th Division, I found Climb to Conquer by Peter Shelton. Reading this book just cemented my desire to write about the 10th. The Last Ridge by McKay Jenkins, and Packs on! by A.B. Feuer were invaluable resources.

I now own a personal library of dozens of books about the 10th Division, have seen countless photographs, read dozens of memoirs and have watched both television and web tributes to these men. I would love to sit down with each and every one of the survivors and have a good conversation and a glass of Vino for Victory.

I have been in touch with the divisions two museums, one in Colorado and one in New York. I have received help and support from the Denver Public Library which houses a wonderful 10th Division Museum and History section. Museums at Fort Drum, NY, Leadville, CO, and the Ski Museum in Vail were most helpful and have wonderful websites.

A recent addition to the websites is Colorado Public Radio's http://www.cpr.org/news/story/audio-photos-tracing-10th-mountain-divisions-long-legacy-colorado.

Too many websites to mention individually added to my knowledge and to my love for this division. One, however, I must mention for keeping the events in correct order was important to me and "The Chronology of the 10th Mountain Division in WWII" (http://10thmtndivassoc.org/chronology.pdf did this for me. Other websites are found in the bibliography.

Special thanks to David Little, a founding member and President of the 10th Mountain Living History Display Group, director of the Board of Directors of the Tenth Mountain Foundation, on the advisory board for the Tenth Mountain Division Resource Center and a former consultant for National Archives and the U.S. Army Museum system for reading the manuscript for historical accuracy. Your suggestions were spot on and your encouragement deeply appreciated, David.

The Museum of Western Colorado in Grand Junction has a wonderful history of Grand Junction and the Grand Valley year-by-year. Their accompanying timeline and photos were most helpful.

To librarians and research assistants at the Denver Public Library a very special thank you. They were always willing to help, "24-7", as they like to say. Special thanks to Lisa Flavin for finding answers to questions that I could not find and for putting me in touch with Mr. Dennis Hagen who was a fount of knowledge regarding the 10th Division. Thank you, Dennis.

To my online support group, the Historical Novel Society, thanks for always being there, no matter the time of day or night. It's nice to have a group struggling with some of the same problems.

Cover design thanks go to Ash Arceneaux, who using a stock photo and a landscape scene from my personal collection gave me what I wanted. Super job, Ash.

Thanks to my blurb and manuscript beta readers Heather Bryant, Jim Rada, Silvia at Silvia's Reading Corner, and editors Debbie Rosier of debbiedits and Jim Smith.

For over a year, at each meal, while riding in the car, and even while trying to read something else, Jim listened to the story in great detail before ever having the privilege of editing it. Thanks, Sweetheart.

To my last defense editors, Lorie Smith, Tricia Knox, and Dr. Paula Chambers, thank you for your perseverance and final input.

Finally, to my family and friends, from Colorado to Florida and all points in-between, this is for you. Thank you for your encouragement.

Especially for SKAJEJL, you know who you are.

References

"10th Mountain Division Descendants, Inc.." *10th Mountain Division Descendants, Inc.*. N.p., n.d. Web. 26 Aug. 2014. <http://10thmtndivdesc.org/>.

"10th Mountain Division History." *10th Mountain Division History*. N.p., n.d. Web. 9 Aug. 2014. <http://www.drum.army.mil/AboutFortDrum/Pages/hist_10thMountainHistory_lv3.aspx>.

"10th Mountain Division Patch | 10th Mtn Div Camp Hale Skis Equipment." *10th Mountain Division Patch | 10th Mtn Div Camp Hale Skis Equipment*. N.p., n.d. Web. 5 July 2014. <http://www.vintageskiworld.com/10th-mountain-division-s/25.htm>.

"10th Mountain Division WWII Oral Histories-YouTube.mov." *YouTube*. YouTube, n.d. Web. 5 July 2014. <https://www.youtube.com/watch?v=oMS_lkM3JDA>.

"10th Mtn Division." *10th Mtn Division*. N.p., n.d. Web. 5 July 2014. <http://www.tenthmtndiv.com/>.

"10th-Mt-Div." *10th-Mt-Div*. N.p., n.d. Web. 5 July 2014. <http://www.collectors-of-schrades-r.us/corners/Albert/pages/10th-Mt-Div.htm>.

"10thMntDiv's channel." *YouTube*. YouTube, n.d. Web. 5 July 2014. <http://www.youtube.com/user/10thMntDiv>.

"1st Brigade Combat Team, 10th Mountain Division (United States)." *Wikipedia*. Wikimedia Foundation, 10 July 2014. Web. 9 Oct. 2014. <http://en.wikipedia.org/wiki/1st_Brigade_Combat_Team,_10th_Mountain_Division_(United_States)>.

"American Anthem." *You Tube*. N.p., n.d. Web. 8 Aug. 2201.
<http://www.youtube.com/watch%3Fv%3D4tJCjLtlybU>.

"Camp Hale." *History*. Metropolitan State University of Denver
, n.d. Web. 10 Oct. 2014.
<https://www.msudenver.edu/camphale/camphalehistory/>.

"Colorado Ski Authority." *Colorado Ski Authority*. N.p., n.d.
Web. 13 Oct. 2014.
<http://www.coloradoskiauthority.com/history/historic-sites/ca
mp-hale/#.VDwgePldWgM>.

"Conquest of the locality Felicari. By Dillon Snell." *Conquest of
the locality Felicari. By Dillon Snell*. N.p., n.d. Web. 9 Oct. 2014.
<http://www.sulleormedeinostripadri.it/en/historical-records/test
imonials-from-books-or-diaries/152-conquest-of-the-locality-felica
ri-by-dillon-snell.html>.

"Daviess County Historical Society : Gallatin Area
Revitalization Alliance." *Daviess County Historical Society : Gallatin Area
Revitalization Alliance*. N.p., n.d. Web. 22 Sept. 2014.
<http://daviesscountyhistoricalsociety.com/modules.php?op=mo
dload&name=News&file=article&sid=460>.

"Italian Campaign." *History.com*. A&E Television Networks,
n.d. Web. 26 Aug. 2014.
<http://www.history.com/topics/world-war-ii/italian-campaign>.

Jenkins, McKay. The last ridge: the epic story of the U.S.
Army's 10th Mountain Division and the assault on Hitler's Europe.
New York: Random House, 2003. Print.

LaSalle, Albert , and Terry LaSalle. *In the Beginning...An Early
History of Public Education in the Grand Valley*. Grand Junction, CO:
LaSalle, 2001. Print.

"Leadville Twin Lakes." *Camp Hale and the 10th Mountain
Division*. N.p., n.d. Web. 10 Aug. 2014.
<http://www.visitleadvilleco.com/camp_hale>.

Monahan, Evelyn, and Rosemary Greenlee. *And if I perish: frontline U.S. Army nurses in World War II.* New York: Knopf, 2003. Print.

"National Association of the 10th Mountain Division, Inc.." *National Association of the 10th Mountain Division, Inc..* N.p., n.d. Web. 5 July 2014. <http://10thmtndivassoc.org/>.

"National Association of the 10th Mountain Division, Inc. Reunion." *National Association of the 10th Mountain Division, Inc. Reunion.* N.p., n.d. Web. 5 July 2014. <http://10thmtndivassoc.org/reunion/>.

Putnam, William Lowell. *Green cognac: the education of a mountain fighter.* New York: AAC Press, 1991. Print.

"Selective Service Acts (United States laws)." *Encyclopedia Britannica Online.* Encyclopedia Britannica, n.d. Web. 24 Sept. 2014. <http://www.britannica.com/EBchecked/topic/1527673/Selective-Service-Acts>.

"Share." *The National Association of the 10th Mountain Division, Inc..* N.p., n.d. Web. 13 July 2014. <http://10thmtndivassoc.org/vides.html>.

Shelton, Peter. Climb to conquer: the untold story of World War II's 10th Mountain Division ski troops. New York: Scribner, 2003. Print.

"Site History." *Camp Hale.* N.p., n.d. Web. 10 Aug. 2014. <http://www.camphale.org/History/History.htm>.

"TENTH MOUNTAIN DIVISION." *TENTH MOUNTAIN DIVISION.* N.p., n.d. Web. 5 July 2014. <http://tenthmountain.org/>.

"Take a closer look at the draft." *The national World War II Museum.* N.p., n.d. Web. 9 Oct. 2014. <http://www.nationalww2museum.org/learn/education/for-students/ww2-history/take-a-closer-loo>.

"US Army Ski troops of 86th Regiment, 10th Mountain Division advance through snow ...HD Stock Footage." *YouTube*. YouTube, n.d. Web. 5 July 2014. <https://www.youtube.com/watch?v=KxvxJt5clAo>.

"WWII World War II Interview 75th Infantry." *YouTube*. YouTube, n.d. Web. 5 July 2014. <https://www.youtube.com/watch?v=H_JYJS9e6-0>.

"Welcome in our father's footsteps." *Welcome in our father's footsteps*. N.p., n.d. Web. 9 Oct. 2014. <http://www.sulleormedeinostripadri.it/en/>.

MLA formatting by BibMe.org.

About the Author

Julia Faye Dockery Smith, is a native of Alabama. She received her undergraduate degree from University of Montevallo and her graduated degree from Colorado State University. She now resides in Tallahassee, FL with her husband of 50 years. She is the proud mother of three and grandmother of five. In her retirement she enjoys reading, reviewing, supporting other authors, and of course, writing. She also enjoys "the art of research and spent many months enthusiastically researching and 'getting to know' the 10th Division. When doing none of the above, she loves to travel.

40502505R00164

Made in the USA
Lexington, KY
08 April 2015